GETTING WET

"Who would have thought it?" Niall said, as he hurried them through the soaking rain. "This just proves that a man's education is never done."

"Nor a woman's," Lona gasped as he hauled her into the forecourt at a brisk trot.

"I thought it was a woman's *chores* that were never done."

"That is also a weary fact."

"That is probably for the best." He pulled her toward the narrow door that led into the kitchen. His hat's bent brim was now holding water like a dish. "As the Puritans know: 'Idle hands are the devil's playground.' Especially women's hands."

"Oh!" The last gasp was of amused outrage. Lona's soft, defensive feathers were ruffling again as she prepared for further verbal battle.

"And as for your earlier observations," he went on, after he had slammed the door behind them, "I have not had much experience with feminine carrying on, but I do not think it engenders in me any desire except to escape it forthwith. Or—since it is you who is carrying on—to kiss you into silence."

"Kiss me?" He couldn't see her face in the gloom, and that was a pity, for he was willing to bet that it had flushed a lovely shade of pink.

"Aye."

IONA

MELANIE JACKSON

LEISURE BOOKS   NEW YORK CITY

In loving memory of James Jackson.

A LEISURE BOOK®

October 1999

Published by

Dorchester Publishing Co., Inc.
276 Fifth Avenue
New York, NY 10001

If you purchased this book without a cover you should be aware that this book is stolen property. It was reported as "unsold and destroyed" to the publisher and neither the author nor the publisher has received any payment for this "stripped book."

Copyright © 1999 by Melanie Jackson

All rights reserved. No part of this book may be reproduced or transmitted in any form or by any electronic or mechanical means, including photocopying, recording or by any information storage and retrieval system, without the written permission of the Publisher, except where permitted by law.

ISBN 0-8439-4614-8

The name "Leisure Books" and the stylized "L" with design are trademarks of Dorchester Publishing Co., Inc.

Printed in the United States of America.

IONA

Prologue

The raven-haired woman stood at a point midway up the scree at the base of the wet cliff that was the summit of Isle Iona and looked down with blurry eyes. The white waves below were pulling the remains of MacKay's body out to sea. The perpendicular slab of rock that rose behind her was the heart of the isle, but it had a ring of teeth at its base that were absent only in the sheltered cove on the opposite side of the bay, and the stone fangs that guarded the island's inhabitants, the MacLean clan, were reluctant to relinquish their prey to the waiting *foaghail*.

In the end, the rising tide and deep currents that bellowed in Beelzebub's cauldron would have their way, and Donnell MacKay would join the other dead raiders at the bottom of the sea. And Lona

MacLean, mistress of the isle of Iona, would again be a widow and safe.

Damp woolen plaid slapped at her legs as the rain-laden wind raced over the western face of the island. An oddly angled peak that thrust overhead shredded the low clouds as they raced for the mainland of Scotland. It was a gray, dreary day but a fitting one to see bloody justice done.

Though news had reached the isle that the wearing of clan tartans had been declared by the English Parliament to be a penal offense, Lona MacLean, the last of Wallace and Lorna MacLean's children, had that morning defiantly donned the plaid dress of her clan before climbing the murderous scree above the dark keep to confront her equally murderous husband.

She had not paused on the trek upward to ask herself how such an event had come to pass; she already had asked herself how and why this thing had happened. Every event had been examined again and again; and again and again the answer was the same.

Fate.

Fate had killed her brother, her father, her mother, her first husband. Fate had arranged the slaughter of April 16, when the death of the Highland Scots at Culloden had put an end to bonny Charles Stuart's bid for the throne of Scotland. Fate had decided that General Leslie would declare soon after that the prince's war was lost and send newly made fugitives to the isle. And fate had sent a deadly treasure her family's way, then decreed that she would marry the murdering MacKay who desired it or perish with her remaining kinsmen.

So marry she had, for the sake of survival for her

Iona

few remaining kin, and for the golden secret fate had left on Iona. Caught in a trap of destiny's grand design, she had done everything needed of her in that black hour, just as fate had decreed on that black Sabbath.

It was begun on the Sunday, two weeks after the news of her brother's death at Culloden. Fate had taken a hand in Iona's destiny, and Lona had been faced with a new threat to her people. Still raw with grief from her many losses, Lona had put off her widow's weeds as commanded by the new principal MacLean of Isle Tiree. She did this because she could see that there was no other choice but marriage to someone in good favor with the English if her people were to live even a few months more. To save them from the Jacobite hunters who roamed the islands hunting for Prince Charles, she had shackled her wild fears and wedded the traitor, Donnell MacKay, and prayed that all would be well.

But Lona had soon found that all was not well. Even the heartfelt wish to reconcile with others of her clan and spare them suffering at the English invaders' hands could not compel her to surrender her family's hard-won independence by remaining in a marriage with a monster—which was what Donnell soon proved to be. For what else was a bridegroom who murdered his bride's young cousin in a drunken rage?

Donnell had gone raving when Simple Robert, a seven-year-old child allowed to run loose on the isle, had come upon him while searching for the treasure in the ancient barrows at the north end of the island.

That was MacKay's first act of butchery on Iona. Lona had been shocked to learn that Donnell knew

Melanie Jackson

of the prince's lost gold and sickened by the attack on the simple-minded boy, but she was not surprised at his act of murder; Donnell was, after all, the same monster who had betrayed the loyal Scots who'd fought on the battlefield of Culloden and caused her own brother's death.

In the days that followed, Lona was wracked with guilt that she had brought the MacKay to her island. With his crimson history, this Judas of the Highlands was a ravening wolf among Iona's old and gentle sheep. She'd known that she must do something to get rid of him, but she could not think what act to carry out that would not worsen the situation her clan found itself in.

On the first dry morn of spring, Robert had been buried under a small cairn of red granite at the edge of the old cemetery where kings Duncan and MacBeth slept; Donnell had refused to send to Tiree for a priest and had not come to the grave.

That had also been the first night that the ghosts of Iona began whispering in Lona's ear. It seemed as if Robert's blood had seeped into the island's stones and woken the old ones in the barrows. They'd begun crying for revenge with a regularity that caused torment in the island's young mistress. Mortal dread had seized her whenever she slept, and for many days she'd seemed to dwell outside herself, watching her own actions with a detached mind and soul.

It had become doubly necessary for her to act in the days that followed Simple Robert's burial, for it grew obvious to Lona that Donnell had turned his search for the Jacobite treasure to the cave crypts below the monks' tombs. It would only be a matter of time before he discovered the old graves and

Iona

began looting them. Once started, he would soon find Hector's false cairn at the back of the barrow and the small cask within it.

For her, personally, the prince's treasure was unimportant. She had privately agreed with their laird when he'd refused to support the Stuart claim, and now she had no heart for her brother Hector's lost cause and the darling prince who had led them all to ruin. She had once naively believed that a union could be achieved with the Sasannach that would be for the good of her clan and Scotland, not just for a bonny prince or the Jacobites, or just Catholics or Presbyterians.

She was naive no more. She did not follow the Stuart prince. Still, honor would not allow her brother's efforts to be made vain by a traitor to their country—especially when Hector's spirit would know that Prince Charles and a few compatriots still lived and had great need of the treasure that Donnell MacKay sought so diligently.

The ghosts had whispered on, and no longer in dread of their voices, Lona had begun to listen to their confused chatter. She'd followed the ancient royals' strategy against the MacKay invaders. She'd made no accusations against her husband while the enemy MacKays remained in numbers in her residence. The murder of Simple Robert was allowed to pass without outcry except by the boy's mother, and she was sent quietly away to Isle Tiree before Donnell could hear her cries of grief and accuse her of treason.

Lona had bided her time and pretended ignorance of the treasure whenever Donnell had asked. Sometimes he'd struck her, but only when drunk and then he was laggard and clumsy, and she was able to escape him. Unfortunately, her refusal to speak of the treasure had never slowed him; he did not grow weary of the task or stop his daily searching.

She'd wanted desperately to act in some manner, but the welfare of her clan, what little remained of it, was too important to risk on a poorly plotted revenge.

Vengeance, whispered the ghosts with unusual clarity, *like the mill of the gods, will be infinitely slow in coming but infinitely fine when it arrives.*

Dinna dry up the burn, her mother had always said, *just because it may wet yer feet.* Or, as her father had put it: *He needs a lang spune that sups wi' the devil.*

Lona MacLean understood. Like all Catholic Highlanders since the rabid John Knox had begun to preach his sermons of Calvanistic damnation from the pulpits of every kirk in the land, she knew a great deal about both patience and the devil. But still, the waiting galled.

Bitterness in those long summer days had been hard to avoid, but life had already taught the young widow about the many futile traps of the spirit, and bitterness was one of the deadliest. Hate would breed hate, and blood would always have more blood as long as the English occupied their lands, but Lona swore to see that the Iona MacLeans did not shed either in any more useless battles. A life-long blood feud with other Scots of the north would not bring her family back and would only weaken them before the enemy that preyed upon all of them.

And in melancholy truth, there were not enough Iona MacLeans left to have a feud with anyone. Unless more bairns were born to the few women

Iona

who remained on the isle, the Iona MacLeans were extinct and the island, so hastily cobbled together out of the ruins a generation ago, would return to the ghosts of its dead kings.

Because she could not risk offending the Mac-Kays who lived in the keep, Lona had sat at the table beside the monster who ruled there, swallowing her bile when she heard his voice toasting the English king, and waited for the right moment to strike at Donnell.

For without a doubt the MacKay had to die. She had finally realized that. It was not enough that Donnell leave the isle, for he would continue to spread his poison and bring death everywhere he went. The ghosts had the right of it. A permanent solution that would not harm her clan had to be found.

An eternity had passed while she'd waited and thought and plotted, a lifetime of uncertainty until a day of vengeance had come at last to the isle.

The MacKays, all but Donnell and a few landless henchmen, had finally climbed into their boats and launched themselves into the turbulent fall sea. Most of the turncoat MacKays had lost interest in the subjugation of destitute Iona and wished to return to their own lands, newly awarded by the Hanoverian, George II, for their timely betrayal of their own blood kin at Pestonpans and Falkirk. And Culloden.

Donnell, though left almost alone in his rule of Iona, had soon been lulled into an inattentive state. Long gone from the Highlands and forgetful of its natives' wiles, he'd accepted deeper drinks from the cook's hand and relaxed his vigil against the simple crofters and weavers. As the Iona MacLeans seemed

Melanie Jackson

to grow subdued to a new master's will, he'd allowed them to return to their appointed tasks at the looms and distillery and crofts, and in his complacency he'd grown careless. More and more often, he'd gone out alone and unarmed to search for the treasure.

Fall had come and Lona had judged it time at long last to strike a blow for her brother, for Simple Robert, for Culloden, and for her clan. She'd known then what she must do, and had resolved that she would be swift and merciless with the murdering MacKay.

Indeed, she'd had no choice. The news from Tiree was grim. Her hands must not shrink from their task, for she could not risk bringing an army of occupation to Iona if she failed and Donnell discovered the treasure. Donnell was not discreet. He would spend the gold carelessly, bragging to all that he had recovered the bonny prince's treasure; and then everyone on Iona, from the old and frail to the youngest born, would be condemned for the treason of harboring the prince's secret.

Nor would her husband lift a finger to save them when the Sasannach came, for he hated them all.

Terrifying visions of mass death had awoken her at night. There were no stout trees on Iona from which to hang her kin; execution would be by musket or beheading. In her visions, the island had run red with MacLean blood, from the granite dome to the stony seashore.

She'd lain upon her pallet, night after interminable night, in a tangle of sweat-dampened sheets, hearing the drunken monster snore in the dark. And she would listen as hard as she could for the spirits' advice.

Iona

If planned right, she'd finally concluded, no one would be able to say murder had been done by a MacLean; and no one else in her family would be tainted by MacKay's death. There would be no guilty knowledge to betray them to the invaders—and no definite proof of murder if no body was ever found.

Poison, she'd thought, but there was none on the isle, and she could not send to British-occupied Tiree with a request for Saint-John's-wort, mandragora or hemlock.

There were no guns. And no strong men who might break his traitorous neck.

She would have to use a knife or some other small weapon that could be used with stealth. That meant getting close to Donnell, perhaps stabbing him in his sleep . . . but then there would be blood everywhere, on the bed linens, in the cracks of the floor. The proof of murder could never be completely concealed.

And what if he awoke and cried out? And his kinsmen came?

Lona shuddered. She'd been realistic enough to know and fear the consequences of what would happen if she blundered in the attempt and Donnell survived to accuse her.

But it had also been the fact that if she failed to hide the evidence that the MacLeans had accepted the prince's treasure, her already decimated clan would be slaughtered for treason. Of the two possibilities, the second was slightly more horrific to imagine and spurred her on to darker thoughts.

If a weapon could not be used, then it would have to be an accident, she'd decided, and most accidents on Iona happened in the sea. Lona had worried at first that she might have to die with her beastly husband in an overturned boat to spare her clan from suspicion of murder. For if Donnell was alone, would they not suspect that the boat was holed?

In her first throes of grief, she might have been prepared to end her life this way, if it meant she would prevail and Hector would have peace. Later, it was harder to contemplate such an act. Harder to contemplate both a cold vengeance and colder death in the ravenous sea.

It had been a late September morn while she was still abed that Lona had awoken from a dream and realized that she was finally done with planning and watching her enemy. The pagan ghosts that came every autumn with the storm winds from the north had whispered in her ear while she slept, telling her of Donnell's weakness.

They had said that when the first of the autumnal lightning storms came to the isle, the dark before the rain would offer her a cloak of concealment under which she could do the bloody deed.

The MacKay does not know how swiftly darkness can fall on the isle, the voices had chorused at her shutters as they'd rattled the old wood bar and scratched at the warped panels with foggy fingers. *All one needs to do is follow Donnell when he goes hunting on the cliffs and take him unaware. The sea is hungry. She will do the rest.*

Still half-asleep, Lona had felt her first moments of peace that dawn. She'd had an answer then. On that pleasing thought, she'd dreamed that it was summer and the heather bloomed. Beside her was a man—perhaps a lover—who had long, dark hair, and by the bed was a cradle.

Later that morning she'd again awoken, this time

Iona

to the whistling north wind that always preceded the isle's worst lightning storms.

"The time has come," she'd said to herself in disbelief, knowing that the thick fog was creeping over the sea's rocks and crawling up the steep cliffs. Soon it would cover the isle in obscuring clouds.

It had been hard to believe that the moment had arrived. It had seemed an eternity while the days had grown shorter and thicker with mist, waiting—always waiting—until the morn when the heather ceased blooming on the open faces of the cliffs and retreated into the crags. By the day of this first storm, the peat had already been harvested against the cold to come. Agaric had been gathered for the Halloween fires.

Still disbelieving, Lona arose from her bed and opened her window to the chill wind from the north, watching as the curlew, golden plover, wood rush, lark and linnet fled from Iona on silvered wings. She thought that perhaps they sensed in their small feathered bodies winter's rapid approach in the wind that ran before the great, black storm front. Perhaps they even kenned that death was coming, too, and were afraid.

She had not dressed, but instead had pulled on a cloak and gone barefoot to the old monastery ruins to say a prayer to Saint Columba, the patron and founder of the isle, and to her restless ancestors who had guided her to this hour. In his devotion Columba had said:

As a lantern raises its light in a dark house, so truth rises in the midst of faith in a person's heart.

17

Melanie Jackson

Her truth was hard, but the wise spirit's lantern had shown her the way. She gave thanks.

Lona had risen from bended knee. Then obeying an ancient instinct, she'd shed all clothing and her trinkets of silver, and went out of the stone shelter to a pagan baptism in the cold drizzle and fog.

After she was cleansed of fearsome thoughts and numbed from head to toe, she'd taken up her cloak and returned to the keep. She'd gone to her brother Hector's chamber and ceremoniously opened Hector's chest of possessions. Uncaring of the English law, Lona put on the MacLean hunting tartan of white and black and grass-green, two arms in width and four in length, and fastened it with the crested badge of an embattled tower.

She had next put on Hector's box-pleat kilt—not his battle dress, since he had been wearing that at Culloden and a battle axe and bayonette had been no kinder to the cloth than to its wearer. No body had come home to the isle, but the reports had said he had been cleaved nave to chops, his clothing shredded.

The grisly thought of her brother laid in a common grave with hundreds of other dead had lent strength to her shaking hands.

Next had come the sporran, the dirk, and even the *sgain-dubh* that her brother had always worn in his right stocking. She'd even donned the proper garters and her brother's boots before entering the monk's old and secret tunnel from the rear of the castle larder. Then she'd climbed half the distance up the gleaming cliffs to confront her murderous husband as he'd stood on Dun I, gloating over stolen MacLean lands.

In the end, a weapon had been unnecessary. So

Iona

confounded had the MacKay been by the sight of her in clan colors, a warrior MacLean with her wild black hair streaming in the wind while wielding an ancient claymore and screaming out the war cry that her brother had called at Culloden—*"Bas no beatha!* Death or life!"—that he stumbled backwards on the slippery shale and had tumbled down Iona's harsh cliff face into the maw of the hungry sea.

The cold sound had sensed his coming and snapped her jaws closed around the MacKay prey so that he was held fast in her stone fangs.

Caught up in her rage and grief, and deafened by the ghostly howling in her ears, Lona had barely stopped her own charge toward the waves, realizing at the last instant that, though prepared, she would not be called to die with the MacKay in Iona's sea.

All had gone well, just as the ghosts had said. No violent marks were upon him; no dirk, no claymore had been used. His dropped mug and the disturbed shale told a clear, if untrue, tale of careless tragedy.

Now Lona stood still, breathing deeply and trying to quiet her heart. By the end of the morning hour that usually saw all the women toiling at their looms, and these screeching oystercatchers well out to sea, the tyrant MacKay was fortuitously dead. Why did she not rejoice?

There were only a few storm birds, the rain, and the ghosts on Dun I to bear witness to Donnell's end; and Lona felt sure that the fierce natives who remained on lonely Iona would never tell the Sasannachs the tale of what she had done.

A great darkness passed overhead and Lona stepped back from both the cliff and her memories, feeling suddenly a dizzying dread as her mind

Melanie Jackson

returned to her body in a rush that bent her in two. She looked up into the sky, superstitiously searching for some light in the heavens; but there was only blackness pressing down on the isle. Twilight had come over them in an instant.

She shuddered. The previous day's sun had set brightly into the copper, bubbling sea. *This noontide*, she thought, *the storm has brought winter's night to the day's dominion*. They would not see the vanquished sun as it set behind the gray ceiling.

Poor Lona MacLean will not find any light in Heaven this day, whispered a new voice. *Or possibly any other day. The Lord's avengers were rewarded with Heaven, but not so the servants of pagan kings*.

Lona shivered as she put a hand to her lips, sealing a cry inside. Her will had remained strong for all this time and her heart resolved on her course of action; why now was she weakening? It was surely God's will that she had been made into a warrior for Clan MacLean; there was no need to repent her deed. No need to fear the darkness which followed her reverent act, for she was already shriven by the ghosts of holy men. She would not sicken and grow pale at this unnerving thought. God had not turned his face from her. It was only a storm.

The wind was icy on Lona's face as it froze the tears she shed unknowingly while she gripped the wet stone beneath her hands, and she stared down at the roiling bay where the mist wove and then parted over their prize. Crimson flowers bloomed on MacKay's body only to be washed away by the milk-white waters that sought to carry him out to sea.

But they could not yet claim their prize as the tide was still at ebb and Iona's fangs would not easily release their catch. There were hours in which Donnell's body could be conveniently discovered by his kin, and no safe way to fetch it from the water's maw when they did. Perhaps, if she was very fortunate, other MacKays might die in the attempt to retrieve Donnell and then all of the invaders would be lost to the same vengeful sea.

Calm again, Lona stepped back from the edge and looked closely at Hector's plaid; there was no bloody clue caught in the weave of the cloth to accuse her later. Not one drop. The unused claymore lay at her feet, forgotten until then, and all around was the exhalation of dead MacLeans' cheers given voice in the startled oystercatchers who screamed like the damned souls of burning witches.

Did they screech at MacKay because he disturbed their autumn feeding grounds? Or was it a pagan paean of triumph over the invader who had come to conquer the ghosts' land?

Perhaps there were still a few muted murmurs of the real ghosts coming through the pale tide of fog that shrouded the keep behind her. Lona did not look over her shoulder, but she would take an oath that they had walked beside her on the scree. It was they who had pulled her back from the cliff's edge and saved her from the sea.

"Fear cile airson Eachainn." Another for Hector, she whispered to them in the old tongue, echoing what the seven brothers had said as they died one by one trying to protect the first of the many martyred Hector MacLeans.

Lona turned her back on the sound of ghostly screaming and closed her burning eyes. She could not afford to lose herself in the voices! She must collect her wits, and soon if she was to have any hope of evading those who would come to seek the truth of Donnell's death.

There would be other MacKays coming to the isle to pick over their kinsman's leavings, she knew, but with God's will, not before the spring. Winter came early to the north and the sea would offer protection from invaders for many months. Plenty of time, surely, for them to better hide any of their portable wealth, or better still, to transport the prince's gold away. Then there would be time for her to grieve in solitude and prepare herself for the next battle for survival—the ugly war of commerce with the English that would commence in the spring.

Lona gradually grew cold, but still she lingered on the scree. Standing again on the cliffs of her homeland after a year's absence, it did not seem odd to think of the English as enemies and invaders, though as a child she had never called them so. Her mother's mother had been English and Episcopalian, and Lona had stayed one summer with her cousins in Bath, and she had enjoyed her time there with her first husband when they traveled in the south.

Now with war come upon them again, the English and the turncoats who supported them were her enemies.

If a Scot takes the king's silver may he spend it in Hell, Hector had once said. *And may the foam of the ocean settle upon him.*

Hector's curse had come true at last. Donnell MacKay, betrayer of the Highlands, was sinking into Iona's frigid sea. And his widow had been granted some time to prepare for the next invasion of King George's buzzards.

Iona

Lona started abruptly away from the tormented waters and the birds' uncanny screaming. The fear of the dark had died in her, but she was cold and wet and it was dangerous to be out in the storm.

When she looked over her shoulder there were no ghosts standing on the hill, just wind and fog and rain. She was all alone with the storm birds.

Lona picked up the fallen claymore and clambered her way with sluggish misery back across the rocks to the underground tunnel that led beneath the south wall. It was time for her to descend from her aerie, change her sodden raiment and dry her hair. Then she would join the other women in the weaving room where they worked diligently over the giant looms, producing cloth from the herders' wool that they would eventually sell on the mainland, along with the fiendish but prized brew of Iona scotch. It would all have to go to the hated but wealthy English.

They had to earn the money to survive somehow, Lona thought bitterly, as she reviewed the year's crops. They could not live on potatoes alone, and that was all that grew on Iona except for a small field of barley, blossoming thrift and bell heather, a coarse bracken, nettles, and a few stands of slender birch and bog myrtle—most of which was inedible to humans, though the few sheep and goats they kept for wool liked the flora well enough to eat it.

It did not help their empty bellies that a profusion of fish thrived in the wicked reefs around the isle, for they had not found many men daft enough to try and fish in them. Of the island's fishermen, those who were able had all gone to Culloden, or died of plague. The few left on the isle who fished from shore dried what little they could catch, but the salt taxes were iniquitous and there was never enough meat to fill all the empty bellies.

Lona pushed the discouraging thoughts away. She had another task to perform before she began worrying about finding meat.

She would have to assume her role as the worried wife of a missing man, Lona reminded herself as she tramped through the thick gorse and sedge that spotted the shale scree. Fortunately for her, no one would expect any real show of grief from the widow when Donnell failed to appear that night; she doubted that she had the will left that day to counterfeit such an emotion for her dead husband.

The deed was truly done, she thought again as she paused at the screen of gorse that ringed the keep and looked about cautiously to see that she was still alone.

Inside she felt as empty as the stones around her. All of the grief and bitterness that had dogged her since Hector's arrest two years before was gone. She no longer mourned for her family's dead; her heart and mind were numb. It was an odd fact, but Donnell's death had freed her in more ways than one. The injustice her family had suffered when she had married the butcher had finally been repaid.

Now all she worried about were starvation and the illness that would come to the old ones with winter.

Lightning filled the sky behind her and rain began to fall in earnest, making the already damp stone underfoot terribly treacherous. Lona felt faint stirrings of satisfaction echoing in her hollow heart as she inhaled the sharp, salty tang of the storm.

The few remaining MacKays on Iona should have no trouble imagining how Donnell had grown con-

Iona

fused while climbing in the thick salt mist, and that when the rain came, the daft man had slipped and fallen to his death in the raging sea. *This was God's judgment against him*—the MacLeans would say to one another—*for carelessly gloating on the cliffs of a stolen home when a fall storm was coming and the ghosts were restless in their graves.*

Chapter One

Niall MacKay watched with interest as the isle of Iona, burial ground of the old kings of Scotland, at last appeared on the southwest horizon. He could not for the life of him imagine why anyone would have chosen to be buried here—let alone live out his entire life in such cold isolation. Perhaps, he thought, the island's aspect had changed over the many centuries since the ecclesiastical MacKinnons had been abbots there.

The head oarsman, Gavin, who had been charged by the new MacLean of Tiree with seeing Niall safely to the small isle had already told him that it was a rare fair day for March and, "We'd best be getting on tae the ghost isle and out of the path of the very nasty rain that was coming from yon clouds in the west."

Niall could see no clouds in the west or anywhere

Iona

else due to the thick mist that lay on the water, but he didn't doubt the old islander's word about the approaching storm. In March a storm was nearly always approaching the western isles, and by all accounts, the ones they had on Iona—unlike nearby Tiree or Mull—were especially fierce. The bald stone at the top of the isle where even hardy bracken refused to grow testified to this fact.

Nor was the sea around them in any way calm on this rare, fair day, he thought, huddling into his cloak with an expressive grimace. As near as he could see, a storm would have been redundant to the danger of the surging tides surrounding the wicked reef that made up the natural breakwater for the small island. He had seen the waters to the east of Iona while on his way to Tiree on a day when a heavy tide was running. The faint ripples eddying just beneath the surface were as black as midnight demons and about as welcoming. And that was on the side of the island that presented the best profile. How unfortunate that there was no place to land there. This approach of the single safe beachhead on the MacLeans' island through waters whipped to hell broth was something he had never imagined braving when making promises to journey to Iona.

It was clear now why the mainlanders had refused him passage beyond Mull and Tiree, and why from Tiree his travels had been delayed two days more; only a master sailor would venture his boat into the dragon's maw lined with these pointed teeth, and only then when the dragon was in the best of moods. He was flattered to think that his health was of such concern to his hosts.

Still, for all their concern Niall's boots were soaked clean through, as was his cloak. And though a veteran sea traveler, his stomach had begun to protest the constant upheaval of bow over stern, followed by the steep drop into the next trough in a counter-wise direction as they rode the watery fulcrum up and down.

Because of running before the as-yet invisible storm, they were approaching Iona from the northwest, or the rough side, and the sea, also on the rough side, was a milk-white torrent of seething currents and fog except for a ridiculously thin cleft in the rocky reef where old Gavin was preparing to steer the suddenly frail-seeming boat. According to the balding elder, it was an easy, slack tide they were riding and it was "showing nae trouble for them in guid order." Niall sincerely hoped that the old man was speaking of the boat and not of anything more final; for instance, a deep desire to meet with God that very afternoon.

Niall could hear around them the muted murmurs of the sea's uneasy breaths as it washed against the rocks in endless tidal rhythms. It looked calm enough between the stones in the narrow channel where Gavin piloted them, and the bit of smooth glass whispered its welcome with the gentlest of sighs. Still, Niall knew that it was a deceptive and dangerous form of respiration for mortal man to follow blindly. The smallest deviation in the curving channel and the rock fangs that lined the watery pass would rip the bottom out of the boat before an unwary could draw breath to cry for aid.

Not that aid would be likely in coming from the tiny hamlet of Iona, made up of a dozen small turf-and-stone cottages cobbled together out of the ruins of Saint Colum's—known to most Lowlanders as Columba—monastery, a modest stone distillery

Iona

located by the lake in the old corrie, and to the north—the oarsman said—a small flensing shed where the oil from the occasional stray shark's liver was extracted for lamps.

Niall had experienced the fearful smell of shark first-hand when just a lad, at the time he'd been sent to live with his mother's family on the Lowland coast. Recalling the vivid and thoroughly unpleasant experience, he was unable to repress a small shudder that set the boat to trembling and tipped more water inside the low-running gunwales. This earned him a baleful stare from the boatman and a nearly silent imprecation.

Niall was not, he assured himself, an overly fastidious man, but he still had no intention of going anywhere near that horror of brine-inspired scents, nor any uncouth person wearing the fearful smell on his clothing—not even to escape drowning in Iona's cold sound or to find a missing treasure.

There was a limit, he decided, on what a sovereign's advisor could ask a man to do. Especially one for whom the cloth of patriotism was running threadbare from overuse. He understood Van de Graaf's reasons for intervention perfectly, but Niall was keenly aware that his list of useful actions was severely limited in this case, and growing more so every day because the hunting hounds were closing in with rapacious intent.

He wondered briefly, as a stray spray of white water washed over the gunwales adding further insult to his soaked apparel, if Hector's sister possessed the wiles to hide the gold in the one place he—or any person with an intact nose—would be loath to search. A rotting shark atop a burial site might explain why Donnell, in the nearly five months he'd had on the island, never discovered the missing portion of Charles' treasury.

Niall shook his head and began to breathe with an open mouth. He would need to think of something less nauseating than rotting shark carcass before he completely disgraced himself by being sick.

The flensing shed dismissed as a source of succor in a time of drowning, Niall's brain was then left with the choice of the old abbey ruins and the reputed ghosts of the monks slaughtered by Norsemen, or the tiny Castle MacLean as sources to consider for potential aid.

Should old Gavin overturn them in the sound, then things were truly bleak for Niall MacKay, he decided. For it was well known that the widow of Donnell MacKay, and mistress of the keep, had no love for her late husband's relations.

Of course, no one could blame her for that, he thought fairly. After all, Donnell had been a hard man to like. Personally, Niall had always detested him for being both a coward and a bully. It was not entirely surprising that the nasty boy Donnell, indulged disgracefully by his widowed mother, had grown into a ravenous, man-sized traitor hungry for wealth of his own. And one none too particular about how he acquired it either, if rumors were to be believed.

And so, given the fact that rescue from the sound was slim, it seemed best not to upset the small boat in any way. This conclusion reached, after another stray wave pushed them dangerously near an upthrust of granite, Niall looked instead at the gray cliffs above them and the rudely constructed toy castle of the Iona MacLeans.

It was only a small keep, hardly the size of a large

Iona

house, short enough to fit in the average keep's hall, and dominated by a crooked, crenelated tower and a ridiculous eighth-century-style corbeled roof. The corrupted dwarf architecture watched over an equally small sound with its tiny, slatted windows and ill-laid chimney stacks squashed together like pairs of praying hands. The abomination was set atop an unstable scree mound and looked dark and unfriendly enough to be mistaken for an abandoned ruin.

All in all, most dangerous surroundings, he decided. Nothing to go to any extreme lengths to possess—unless one suspected what might well be hidden in the maze of caves that honeycombed the north of the island where the holy ruins stood.

It seemed probable to Niall that Donnell had heard the rumors of the prince's treasure and that was why he had pressed so hard for marriage to the last Iona MacLean, rather than risk the greedy MacDonalds accusing her of treason, as they had her brother, and getting a toe-hold on the land. If the rebellion's wealth had survived on Iona, it was reasonable to assume that Hector's sister would know its whereabouts, and Donnell MacKay was not such a loyal servant to his new master, King George II, that he would want to share the bonny prince's gold with the English sovereign if it could be avoided.

"So now, ye've come all the way frae Glasgow. A fine city that is, so they say." The voice of the oarsman was a welcome intrusion on his dark thoughts.

"Aye, so they say. And if a thing's true, then it's nae lie," Niall answered, slipping easily into Lowland speech. He had not actually cared for Glasgow, but there was no accounting for some men's taste.

The unusually chatty boatman pulled hard on the

left oar, checked the running of the tide, and then directed another comment Niall's way. This one contained shades of bitterness. "Ye've had fortune in the weather. Nae like last spring when sae many perished on the way home."

By the burred accent of old Gavin's voice, Niall guessed that the boatman had spent some time in the Lowlands corrupting his Highland drawl. It went without saying that it had probably not been a religious pilgrimage that had drawn him there. The prince's cause had not only pitted Scot against English—again—but also clan against clan, and sometimes brother against brother. Clan MacLean had been divided about the Jacobite cause back to the time of Charles I, and not every MacLean had gathered about the latest charismatic Stuart prince and offered to shed blood. In fact, only the Iona MacLeans had shown in force for the bonny prince at Culloden.

"Aye," Niall answered after a moment, unaccustomed to such loquacity in his fellow countrymen in this age of stern Puritans and not being certain of how to answer a man who, though polite, must surely see him as an enemy scavenger come to feed off the remains of a forced alliance.

It would hardly matter that the clans had fought *'an guailidh a cheile*—shoulder to shoulder—for many princes like Wallace and Bruce; not after Donnell had so blackened the name MacKay by killing a MacLean child.

In recent years, Niall had several times been in difficult situations with people whose many familial, professional and personal loyalties were like strands of hair, and he had needed to think extemporaneously when the loyalties in question had

Iona

grown tangled by the winds of perverse fate; a thing that happened frequently in a nation that was Pict and Gael in the north and west, Anglo and Norse to the south and east, and an uneasy mixture of Catholics and intolerant Puritans in all these places.

With that thought in mind, Niall changed the subject to something less snarled than the final Jacobite battle at Culloden in the spring just past. That name had become a bitter cry of vengeance on the lips of the defeated Scots, and wiser men than he had tried—and failed—to unravel fate's cruel weavings in the Highlands.

Even Van de Graaf, who was the most optimistic of men, felt that the Highland Scots were almost past praying for. And that was before the English reprisals had begun.

"When did the MacLeans return to Iona? I'd no idea that anyone was again living on the isle. I should think that it would be a hard life." Niall swallowed. His stomach was beginning to calm now that the sea had moderated its pitching.

"Oh, aye. But that's a bonny sight is yon piece of stonework built hard by the burn. Nae so great as Duart, mind ye," he said, naming the MacLean family seat, and grossly over-stating the resplendence of the island architecture by mentioning the two abodes in the same breath.

"Aye?"

"Built by Wallace MacLean frae the monk's ruins nae that long past. After the old clan went to Kell that was," old Gavin answered inexactly, gesturing to the keep with a jerk of his head that was bare of all but a bonnet set at a rakish angle over one blue eye.

Niall recalled that Iona's Gaelic residents had gone to Kell at the beginning of the thirteenth century, and there had been any number of Wallace MacLeans since then who might have constructed the modest keep.

Niall suppressed a sigh and reminded himself that he had not had any expectation of receiving any useful information from the cagey old man who owed fealty to the MacLeans. The new Thane of Tiree might disapprove of his own Catholic relations on Iona, but in the end blood was still loyal to blood. And Niall was an invader from a family that had worked diligently for the MacLeans' ruin, and the ruin of Scotland. It was unlikely that the boatman would be overly impressed with Niall's own modest effort to knit up the MacLeans' raveled sleeve.

Getting no enthusiastic response to his polite if uninformative discourse, the boatman's face grew overcast. With the usual lack of Highland subtlety, he changed the subject abruptly back to his former line of questioning by asking straightly: "Ye'll be staying a while then?"

"A while," Niall agreed without inflection. "I've no mind to be at my travels any time soon."

Gavin had no doubt been instructed to question him about his plans, but Niall had no intention of explaining himself to a servant of the new leader of the Tiree MacLeans. The man deserved even less explanation than the MacLeans on Iona who were personally concerned with his mission.

There was also that bit of prejudice of a mainlander that insisted that *cha'n 'eil earbsa sa bith ri'chur anns na h-Eileanaich*—there's no trust be put in islanders. Especially not angry MacLeans.

However, that did not mean that he had to be rigidly silent, and Heaven knew that he had questions of his own about the MacLeans who had pos-

Iona

sessed the nerve to recolonize the abandoned island, and then again tempt stronger raiders by harboring the Jacobite treasure—and that after raising a mailed fist against the House of Hanover! 'Twas an act of defiance that suggested a strain of hereditary madness.

Or great courage; he'd not decided yet which it was. Until he was certain, he would do as he had always done when faced with a puzzle. He would persevere doggedly, politely, and with great caution until all was revealed.

"And so, what do they say on Iona about the fate of Donnell MacKay?" Niall asked with the same lack of subtlety Gavin had shown in quizzing him. Perhaps the boatman subscribed to the sentiment that one should "take one's own tale home," and would respond to brutal candor.

Old Gavin never blinked. "Naebody kens what happened."

"It was an accident then? Not murder?"

"*Murtair! Och—Nay!*" The old man was momentarily startled out of calm and forgot his claim to total ignorance of the event, just as Niall had anticipated. "And we'd thank ye tae nae trouble the puir widowed lassie wi' such thoughts. Nae murthers been done here. The daft crature was oot on Dun I in a storm and fell to his death in the sea. His passing gave puir Lona some more burthen and worry. The ghosts hae him noo—and I say guid riddance tae him!" he added truculently.

"You won't be mourning him them?" Niall asked with a small smile at the flustered boatman. Donnell had obviously managed to annoy MacLeans all the way to Tiree. Not for the first time, Niall wondered if someone hadn't assisted his cousin to his just end.

Melanie Jackson

It could hardly be wondered at if they had; Donnell's list of affronts and crimes was stupendous in one so young and landless.

Blaming a ghost was a new notion though, and not one he planned to pursue, deeming it a fruitless topic to search. Highlanders' superstitious stories about their *ludh an spioraidh*—the way of ghosts—were as notorious as their fairy tales. And mostly as untrue.... Mostly.

Old Gavin snorted at Niall's question but forwent making further comment on Niall's unpopular relation. He had apparently remembered belatedly that he was supposed to know nothing about vengeful ghosts or Donnell's possible fate, and to be very polite to the visiting MacKay.

"And have ye the way of the sea?" the old man asked after the silence had spread out over a long minute, adding a bit of grudging praise. "Ye've done right well on a rough crossing."

"Not of this one," Niall answered as they ran the boat up onto a small patch of sand. He was pleased to find that there was some piece of the unfriendly island that was soft and yielding.

"Thank you for seeing me here safely," he added politely, taking a look at the white surf behind them. "That was quite a feat."

"Nae trouble," old Gavin answered as he stepped from the boat into the frothed waters.

Niall waited a moment, for MacLeans were known for their boasts—*Leathaineach gun dhosd*, such modesty in a boatman being a rarity of note—but the old man said no more on the subject of his seamanship. Perhaps the island MacLeans were different from the mainlanders.

"May I be of some help?" Niall asked.

Iona

"Give me a bit of aid here and I'll see ye tae the castle. The mistress'll offer us a drop of *uisge beatha* before sending me back tae the sea, I warrant," he answered, sounding at once more cheerful.

Niall knew all about Iona's version of *uisge beatha*—the water of life—or whisky, as it was more commonly known. It was Iona's favorite export and they sent out only two score barrels of it a year. Barley malts of the western isles were all exceptionally peaty, and Iona's was admired for both its taste—purest peat-smoked and burning embers, some loyalists swore—and for its potency. Even the smallest cup of Iona's *uisge beatha* could induce unconsciousness in those who were unaccustomed to its strength. He'd been warned on Tiree to be wary of the brew, especially when walking on the cliffs. They certainly didn't want another MacKay to end up in the sea.

"Of course." Niall also stepped from the boat, relieved to again be on solid ground and likewise cheered by the thought of a dram or two. It was, after all, only March in the Highlands, true spring was two months away and he was very wet.

Niall recently had had cause to travel by sea from Scotland to England, then secretly to France and the Netherlands and back again; but the coastal waters and even the channel crossing in December had been nothing like the cauldron of roiling sea around Iona. There was only one other place like it that he'd seen in the North and it was known to the locals as the Mouth of the Grave. The fishermen avoided that sound as if it were infested with the plague, and they spoke of it only in hushed voices.

There were, he noted, no boats around this isle either, and in Niall's opinion Iona deserved an equally hostile title for its portion of sea. The modest Sound of Iona was a great sunken graveyard littered with the bones of Scots and Vikings who rested now—and until the time that the sea rendered up its dead on Judgement Day—in unnatural and surely infuriating proximity beneath its vicious, foaming waves.

If there was anything that would make dead spirits rise up and walk on Iona, it would probably be that.

Niall ceased his musings and grabbed a gunwale. They dragged the boat onto the gray sand above the reach of the tide, and then old Gavin snatched up the smaller valise and headed for the steep trail that snaked out over the shale cliff. Niall picked up the other two bags and followed rather more slowly in Gavin's nimble wake. He didn't trust the loose scree to stay beneath his slippery soles and he had no desire to pitch down the unfastened hill, even if the sand at the base was soft.

"Mistress Lona is expecting me then?" Niall asked of the spry back in front of him. He did not use her married name, suspecting that it would be impolitic to mention Lona MacLean's brief marriage to his unpopular kinsman. Particularly since she barely had been widowed for the first time before being ordered to marry again.

"Oh, aye. Sure enough. Word was sent the day before. Ye'll be expected," the boatman-turned-gillie assured him. "Mind, ye cannae expect tae have much comfort here. Iona is a puir island."

"Hmm," Niall agreed. His time in England, Holland and France had not caused him to forget that the Highland Scots had made a peculiar virtue of

Iona

their austerity. Iona was poor; and Iona was proud of it.

That did not worry him except for the fact that Tiree had not been seated anywhere near the lap of luxury, and for Gavin to speak of Iona as being poor suggested that an uncomfortable—perhaps even dangerous—level of destitution existed on the ghost isle.

On the other hand, Donnell had remained here five months, and he had always had a great liking for his creature comforts. There was a good chance that he hadn't been surviving by the old Highland expedient of drinks from the burn without any bread.

Of course, *he* would be lucky to eat anything except potato soup and nettles for his entire stay on the island. Even if they had more—and he was sure they did—it would not be wasted on another marauding MacKay who had presumedly come West for the purpose of picking over the already stripped bones of the few living Iona MacLeans.

And again he couldn't blame the *puir widowed lassie* for not extending a typical *hieland welcome*. She had her family to feed before strangers and enemies, and the wounds from the defeat at Culloden would have barely skinned over in the eleven months they'd had to heal.

Make that six months, he corrected. There would have been no healing during the time Donnell was master of Iona. The MacKay presence might even have caused bitter feelings to fester.

If his own needs had not been so compelling, Niall never would have given into to his aunt's pleadings to go to Iona and speak to Donnell's widow. His tender

Aunt Elaenor, one of the few MacKays who still received him, was ashamed of her only son's treachery, but she also was praying that a bairn might have survived him. That Donnell's widow could offer her another child to love in her son's place had become her favorite dream.

Niall did not believe that that would happen, even if the widow was with child; most mothers preferred to drown their babes in the sea than to watch them taken to enemy arms. But as he had been sent by Van de Graaf to discover what had become of the prince's lost gold and dispose of it before George's many advisors caught the rumors flying about the Lowlands and urged the monarch to send more troops of occupation, a visit to Iona suited his own needs. Looking for Donnell's possible offspring and offering the widow some support made a good excuse for another seeming turncoat MacKay to be here ahead of the other scavengers.

He had been slightly surprised to find out when he reached Tiree that his cousin's widow had not already sought protection in a new marriage. For however small Iona was, it still offered a roof and land to her master, and there was no means by which a woman alone could long hold the circling vultures at bay.

He had reasoned, upon first hearing the news that MacLeans had remained on Iona without a new protector, that widowed Lona MacLean must either be terrifically ugly or shrewish, or that Iona was carrying a particularly virulent plague that kept potential suitors away. Why else hadn't the MacDonalds descended *en masse* to woo or war upon her?

Now that he had spent a few days on Tiree and seen the lay of the land, he understood Lona's hesi-

Iona

tation to consider a new alliance. If it was true that the gold was here on the bare, hostile island, she could not afford to have strangers about the place even if the sea would let them in.

And yet it was only a stranger, and a strong one—like a MacKay in good standing in London—who could offer any help to the treason-branded MacLeans of Iona when George's troops finally came calling. It left the widow truly stranded between a Sasannach devil and the deep, blue sea around her.

That did not preclude Iona being plague-ridden, Niall thought as he clambered up the steep shale scree. Nor did it rule out the possibility that the widow of the ghost island was both ugly and shrewish.

And it was a ghost isle. No blasted heath or abandoned graveyard could show less life. It was easy to see why the feeble-minded might believe that spirits walked with the living in such a place. The smallest imagination could conjure them! But surely the weak-minded Ionans found it an uneasy alliance and desired to move away as soon as circumstances permitted.

"Guid day to ye, Mistress," he heard Gavin sing out as his head topped the rise. "May God stand between ye and pestilence and give ye the health of a trout."

It amazed and saddened Niall that the old tongue was used so little even among Gael Scots. It was heard—a little—in the western Highlands, but the Lowlands used a bastardized form of middle English and the rest of Scotland spoke some version of the modern Sasannach tongue. Though as a matter of safety he nearly always used English himself, he still felt that it hadn't the music of the lilting Irish—and was an enemy language besides. Scots hated the Sasannachs, yet even in the isolated isles, Gaelic was rarely spoken these days. More than French, English was considered by the Scots to be the grandiloquent tongue and most aspired to it.

"And may I see you grow grayer and your clan sensible," a pleasant voice, shaded with tones of Gaelic music, replied to the greeting. "Good day to you, Gavin. And where is our *guest*? You haven't by chance lost him in the sound, have you?"

Niall heard the irony in her tone and hurried up the last bit of scree to see the pretty-voiced female bold enough to mock the much stronger MacKays.

"Your *guest* is still struggling with the byways of your charming island," he replied, stepping past Gavin to confront the owner of the pleasant voice. He swept off his hat in the grand manner and bowed deeply with a light mockery of his own foppish attire. Not until he reached the depth of his bow and happened to look up under the concealing hood did he get a good view of his hostess, and there, bent in half, he checked himself in sudden surprise.

Lona MacLean was definitely *not* ugly. Niall MacKay realized for the first time in very long while that his blood actually ran as red as any other man's. That same red blood was now busy pounding in his heart and temples—and likely staining his cheeks as well! *By the blood of the martyrs!* She was a stunning sight.

Lona watched with hidden trepidation as the dark auburn-locked head was exposed to the wind that whistled over the craggy rise, waiting for the moment that she would see her enemy's face in the light of the rare sun. The day of reckoning had arrived and she would not get away with pushing this new arrival off the ramparts in the old manner of repelling invaders.

Word had come from Tiree: This Niall MacKay had powerful friends and was not to be repulsed. No other tragic accidents had better occur while he was visiting or it would bring the Sasannach soldiers down on their heads. So her hands were tied and she was back to waiting upon the whims of fate.

The first thing she noticed about her heavily cloaked guest, when his face became visible from under his hat, was that this MacKay possessed a particularly sweet smile, before which, Lona found with some surprise, all expected rancor for the latest invader fled.

A second, and most welcome, surprise was that he favored Donnell not at all. He had no bright Pictish red in his thick hair or brows, and his eyes were pure and fine.

"I am your unwanted guest, Niall MacKay," he said at last, rising from a polished courtier's bow, seeming not one whit discommoded by the two valises clutched in his left hand or the breeze that ruffled his dark lovelock. "Your hill is quite the merry gambol."

"Cloven feet help with the climb, guest Niall MacKay," Lona replied, surprising herself by offering a rare, small smile to the latest enemy to arrive on her island. She approved of his mocking humor and honest grin; Donnell MacKay had had neither. "I see that you've had no great difficulty following our trail. How spry you must be . . . for a mainlander."

One mobile eyebrow flew upward, but the comic

cast of his features did not entirely deceive her; his gaze was too intent for mere comedy, his teasing only a shield to hide his true thoughts.

This one, she had been told by yesterday's messenger, was different. Polite. Clever. Strong without being vicious. And shrewd. A possible ally in the days to come, wrote the nervous MacLean of Tiree, who was fearful of keeping his lands if the English came.

If young Duncan was correct in his reading of this man's character, it made this MacKay more dangerous than Donnell had ever been, especially if this Anglicized Scot had heard about the treasure and come questing on his own.

But another explanation for his presence occurred to her as she studied his angular face, one that agreed with the native truthfulness in the smiling hazel eyes and the easy charm that was an almost-tangible aura about his tall person. Radiant, fiery, this aura was, and kind. It inspired trust.

The possibilities set her heart to racing, for she realized that she had, in fact, seen this man once before. He had been pointed out to her two years ago in London as a messenger who traveled to the exiled prince. She simply hadn't recognized him without his wig, high heels and court finery.

Was it possible that this engaging man of many reputed qualities, including a nimble brain and undoubtedly quick political reflexes, had been sent to render her aid? It would be a rare show of fortune's benevolent hand if Iona's savior had appeared, unsought, and wearing a genuine smiling countenance.

Lona's unexpected moment of cheer grew as she studied the effect of a stray beam of sun glinting on

Iona

her guest's dark hair. There was fire there, buried in the thick curls that reached over his breast and wide shoulders. The warmth she sensed in him drew her like a moth to the flame.

There was danger there, too, she thought, for the foolish moth. But oh how she was tempted to flutter closer to the fire and warm herself for a time!

"Hoots away with ye," Gavin scolded, casting a worried glance Niall's way and trying to see if he had taken the comment the wrong way. Some men would be offended at the suggestion that they carried the devil's mark, and this one looked quite capable of seeking redress for any slight. "Now, lassie, ye mean nothing of the sort."

Lona blinked twice at the admonishment and shook herself from under the MacKay's strange spell. The devil, she knew, would wear a handsome face should it suit his needs. Caution was called for.

Perhaps her careless remark about a cloven hoof had been appropriate after all. She had just remembered another piece of gossip about Niall MacKay; he was thought by some to be a spy for the Dutch.

Another possible MacKay turncoat, she thought sadly, looking away from the smile that warmed her heart for the first time in a twelve-month. She didn't like to believe that it was so, that she could feel such a quick and deep liking for a traitor, but she had her duty and needed to be cautious until certain of his intent. A little distance and a *lang spune* was a good thing to use with any stranger in these dangerous times.

Niall watched and waited as the pleasant voice went mute. She nodded at the old man and when she turned back to Niall the welcoming smile had been replaced with an expressionless mask. Except for the eyes, and those were rather sad.

"But I agree with you, mistress. Alas for my boots, they are but regularly made and lack any useful hoof." Niall finally found his missing tongue, and trying to recapture the friendlier moment, he offered another warm smile that rarely failed to charm. "I might still manage a jig an you wished it."

Lona MacLean was a completely unexpected discovery. He was stunned to find that this somber, gray-eyed waif, with a complexion of sweetest cream and stray strands of gleaming black hair, was patriot Hector MacLean's strong-willed sister and his own vile cousin's widow. He found the latter notion to be an obscene thought.

Seeing her standing in sunshine atop the hill, skirt fluttering around delicate feet, the image of the ugly shrew had died an immediate and welcome death and been buried out of sight. Now, with those misconceptions dead, he was left feeling uncertain of how to proceed with his newfound treasure. For a treasure she was, and he felt that he must count his journey a success even if he failed to help the doomed prince.

The best-laid schemes o'mice and men gang aft a-gly, Grandad had been fond of saying, and he had the right of it, at least this time.

Still, it was damned odd for him to be at such a loss for moving words; usually his tongue was quite facile around a pretty lass, but here he was standing about like one bespelled by fairies.

"Surely God intended Iona for the sheep and goats and water fowl or he'd never have sent the Northmen this way to clear her of good Scotsmen,"

Iona

he heard himself say. "Or had the *Auld Ones* the proper footing for this desolate isle?"

"Who can say? We have few friends here of either cloven hooves or white wings to bear us company in our exile," she answered politely, apparently having no trouble restraining any untoward friendliness now that Gavin had reminded her of her duty to the enemy.

Niall had a sudden impulse to cast the old meddler into the sea. He had quite liked Lona MacLean's first small smiles and audacious teasing. No dour housewife was she.

"Is it exile, mistress?" he asked curiously. "Many would be glad to live among angels."

"Most would call it exile, I think. And you mistake me; we have no angels here, only storm birds and noisy spirits."

Gavin *tsked* at her answer and shuffled his feet.

"Very perishing it is today, Mistress MacLean," Gavin mentioned craftily, cracking the joints in his fingers. "I feel it in me bones, I do."

"Oh, aye?" There was a sudden thickening of the burr in Lona's voice that imitated the boatman at his broad best. Her head again turned in Gavin's direction and Niall watched with fascination as she winked one gray eye. "Then ye'd best see Cook. She'll give ye some soup and nettles. If she cannae warm ye with her pitched tongue speaking of hellfire."

"May Heaven be yer bed, mistress," Gavin answered as he started for the castle. He added over his bony shoulder: "And the Virgin's blessing upon ye. It isn't Gavin MacLean who'll be disagreeing with such sound advice, a wee nasty cook or nae."

The old boatman's usual, glowering expression

was replaced with one of beatific joy as he headed for the kitchen and a foretaste of the Scotsman's paradise. Niall chuckled at the image of a heaven made up of an eternity of distilleries, all well-stocked with Iona's whisky.

"Methinks he's seen Saint Ninian, himself, beckoning in the door. How odd in a Puritan."

Slowly, cautiously, Niall watched as Lona allowed herself to share in his amusement, permitting another reluctant smile to touch her soft lips.

"Gavin is far, far from pure, but he does not usually see Saint Ninian until after he has had two cups full. . . . And you, sir? Are you also desirous of something warming?" she asked. The rough, Lowland burr had disappeared with Gavin.

"Potato, peat, or hellfire?" he retorted, resisting firmly the urge to jest about the Scottish warming pans. He approved of the tradition of sending a housemaid to roll about the blankets and take the chill from the sheets, but he doubted that his hostess would be amused by such ribaldry.

"Either. Cook has all three in the kitchen."

"Well then, perhaps a bit of the first two."

"Very well, then please come with me. We'd best hasten or Gavin will have the lot, and the best seat near the hearth, as well."

"I am yours to command," Niall replied.

Lona's snort was rather more elegant than Gavin's had been, but just as disbelieving.

"I would that it was so," she muttered.

"And you are wondering what-a-plague I want with you and your island," he added cheerfully. Another smile slashed across his face as she sent a long, considering look his way that silently asked his cause for cheer.

Iona

Niall couldn't explain, for he scarce understood it himself, but he believed now that all would be well for them in the end. Fate's hand was clear to be seen in bringing him to Lona's isle.

"And to know for how long you plan to visit us," she agreed, refusing for now to warm herself at his personal fire.

"A while," he answered again, urging himself to patience. Then he added under his breath: "This might be more difficult than I thought."

"What might be more difficult?" Lona asked bluntly, proving that her shell-like ears had hearing that was excellent even in a high wind.

"Saving you and Iona from George's greedy clutches." Niall surprised himself by answering truthfully.

"God keep us," she answered, but did not pause or in any way indicate that she was distressed by his news of impending English arrival, or grateful for his offer of assistance.

Perhaps she did not see any distinction between the MacKays and the British, he thought with a stab of further annoyance at his dead cousin. It was only the filthiest of birds that fouled their own nests, but that apparently hadn't stopped Donnell from soiling this island with his greedy quest.

"And why should you wish or need to save us from the English king?" his reluctant hostess asked, seeming to bear out the truth of his reasoning.

Niall MacKay, sometimes Dutch spy, Jacobite sympathizer, and reluctant guardian of the foolish Bonny Prince's secrets, was dumbfounded by the question. The grievous impossibility of understanding the female of the species had again reared its ugly head and spit in his eye. How could anyone loyal to the Scotland of the Robert Bruce who'd proclaimed: *For so long as one hundred of us remain alive, we shall never accept subjection to the domination of the English*, even consider such a question? Especially with Charles still trapped and hiding out somewhere in the Highlands, and his supporters going under the sword daily as they died martyrs' deaths for their cause.

A less reasonable man, Jacobite or not, would enpurple with rage at the very suggestion that any Englishman would be welcomed on Scotland's soil in preference to another Highlander. Even a MacKay! Niall was not another man and considered himself to be very reasonable. Still, he was a Scotsman when all was said and done.

"Need you ask?" he demanded incredulously.

Lona swung around to face him. Her hood fell back revealing her long, black hair. This time the smile that touched her sweet lips was bitter.

"Look about you, sir!" she commanded, an arm outflung.

Niall did. There was a great deal of rock and water all around them, and away down the hill were some prominent tombstones. The sky above was fast darkening as the wind picked up speed, casting everything in lonely shadow. Suddenly the very stones of the gray isle seemed inhabited with the ghosts of bleak desolation. He could almost hear their dismal murmurings above the whispering waves.

"What could the rich king of the Hanovers possibly want with a pile of rock and a gaggle of Scot women and children—and not so many of the latter anymore!"

Niall realized that she was referring to Donnell's

Iona

murder of her young kinsmen, and again felt shame for the acts of the traitorous cousin who shared his name.

This woman had suffered a great deal in her young life with unflinching fortitude; loss of her mother to fever, widowed to a first husband at nineteen—who also went the way of illness—and then the death of a father and brother at English hands the year just past. And finally marriage to Donnell MacKay, which was a crown of thorns for any brow, let alone a young woman wracked with fresh grief.

Niall had to admire her tenacity of spirit, even as he acknowledged that her strength of character would make his own task more difficult should she refuse to cooperate with him. And not for a single moment did he believe that Lona was ignorant of Hector's doings. There was a fine mind and steel will behind those clear gray eyes; Hector, in his holy zeal, would have made use of her talents, and damn the consequences.

A large cloud appeared in the west and covered up the last of the hazy sunlight in its black fist. The rare, fair day, like their conversation, was suddenly threatening to turn as dark as doom.

"George couldn't care less about your ghostly isle or your women and children," he answered quietly. "But he is displeased with the MacLeans after his loss at Falkirk and looking for ways to offset the cost of this war. You've heard of the clearances? Confiscating Scottish rebels' lands and possessions and parceling them out to the turncoats is one way of doing it."

If he hadn't been watching for it, he would never have seen the slight flinching of her fine smoky eyes as the gloom gathered around them. He wondered again if she knew of the treasure's exact resting place, and if she did, whether she would ever willingly confide in him the whereabouts of the island's less than perfectly kept secret. Her family had made a career of choosing death over what they perceived to be dishonor.

"The costs of this war! Of the thirty thousand of the fighting men who could have come against him only six thousand marched. But does he care? Nay! He'll have his pound of flesh from all of us—"

"And so he shall," Niall interrupted, "If we do nothing to stop him. Not that he'd want Iona for himself, but it would certainly be welcomed by the MacDonalds, think you not? And they have already petitioned the crown for it. . . . They may get it, too, now that Donnell is gone."

He could see that the last threat had struck home. Hereditary enemies of old, the MacDonalds had long felt that they owned much of the MacLeans' lands. They *would* want desolate Iona.

It gave him a little comfort to think that there was one other clan more hated by Iona's mistress than the MacKays.

A fat drop of cold water splattered on Niall's cheek, reminding him sharply of how chilled he was under his dripping cloak.

"But we will discuss this business later," he said with a return to polite placidity, setting his hat back upon his head. "For now, I would be content to have a bit of soup and get out of the rain."

Lona stared at him for a long moment, her mournful gray eyes clearly longing to demand just what he suspected about Iona's treasure. Niall awaited events, but discretion still prevailed with the sad-eyed waif.

Iona

With a quick look around the dark, deserted forecourt, she turned toward the small door on the left, set wide by old Gavin, and pushed her way inside the narrow passage. Niall followed.

The kitchen was a welcome change in temperature even if it was unpleasantly dark and smoky. The only light seemed to come from a lone lantern and a defiant fire of smoldering peat kindled on the giant hearth. He was relieved to note that the unpleasant aroma that hung in the air was that of simple tallow and goat cheese. It was not from shark oil burning in the lamps.

As promised, there was a cauldron of soup hanging from a thick andiron, and as predicted by his hostess, old Gavin was sprawled comfortably in the carve oaken seat at the fire's side. His boots were steaming gently on the hearth as they dried and he was obviously savoring both the whisky in his hand and the warmth of the nearby embers on his damp feet. His gingered mutton-chops had begun to curl, giving him the strange aspect of a contented sheep. A gray moggie sat quietly on the hearth, watching the new arrivals with feline eyes.

"May ye never see or hear what ye hear or see or cut yer throat with yer tongue," he blessed them fulsomely as they drew near the ill-fitted hearth. The cat chuffed once and turned her back.

Niall found the meaning of this phrase to be rather obscure, but offered a polite nod in reply as he set down his bags and stripped off his damp gloves.

"And God save Scotland from all invaders, Episcopals, and Calvinists," bellowed the fat woman in the corner, startling Niall into dropping his leathers. He hadn't seen her sitting in the shadows under her pile of dark shawls.

Melanie Jackson

"Cook is a little deaf on occasion," Lona explained. "Pay her loud quacking no heed."

The stooping bulk cackled, giving lie to the notion that today was one of those times when she was so afflicted in her hearing. Looking at her unfocused gaze, Niall thought at first glance that the crone might also be a bit slack of wit, and drunk in the bargain.

On a second viewing, he was not so sure that she might not be quite sly; the Lowland brogue was overdone. It was the sort of behavior that the English had come to expect from the Scots, and the crafty natives played the role of bovine stupidity to the full measure.

Lona raised her voice, commanding cook in hopeful tones to fetch a trencher of soup for their guest. She then went herself to a shelf to remove a second small tankard before walking over to the large oak barrel standing in the corner. She measured out a modest amount of amber liquid in a large wooden ladle hanging on its side.

"Have you ever sampled our whisky?" Lona asked with a speculative look, filling the mug only part way.

"Only a wee dram tae keep oot the cold," grumbled the cook as she waddled toward the blackened pot, dragging her shawls with her.

Lona rolled her eyes but made no comment to the elderly woman. Cook's wee drams against the cold were apparently nothing new.

"Nay, but I've been warned," he answered with a twinkle in his eye. "That will do nicely, I thank you. I've no desire for my pillow just yet."

"Hmph. Mayhap you'd prefer water." Lona set the

Iona

tankard on the table before him and gestured for Niall to take a seat on the sturdy three-legged stool.

"Nay. That I would not," he answered, reaching for the tankard. "I've seen quite enough of it for one day."

"Water? Aye . . . and may ye live as lang as ye want, and may ye never want for as lang as ye live," Gavin cheerfully saluted Niall. The boatman's usually sharp eyes were bleary above his mug.

Gavin had had only a moment's headstart at sampling the contents of the whisky barrel and he was already wandering in his wits; Niall made a note to drink very slowly until he could accurately guage the effect of the brew. It would not do to grow too garrulous under its mellowing influence.

"You aren't proposing to return to Tiree this day, are you?" Niall inquired, again removing his hat and shrugging out of his sodden cape.

Lona took the cloak from his hand and hung it on a peg near the hearth. Niall made no protest. The fine woolen cloth would smell of peat smoke but would soon dry; that was all that mattered to his chilled bones that felt suddenly naked without its weight about them.

"Och. Aye." Gavin burped softly. "I mon gae."

"Then you'd best hasten," Niall recommended, taking his seat at the rough table. "The rain has already begun to fall and I believe the tide has turned."

"Has it now?" the boatman asked with little interest.

"Gavin, you'll bide with us 'til the storm is passed. I'll not have you sickening on my account as you'd be bound to do did you leave now," Lona said firmly, setting a trencher and spoon before her other guest.

Potato soup, just as he'd expected. But no boiled

nettles, he was much relieved to see. Things were not yet desperate on Iona.

Niall noted that Lona didn't mention drowning as a possible fate for the old boatman, and he wondered if that betokened extreme faith in Gavin's skill. Or perhaps she was simply being tactful with an old man's pride. Iona's young mistress would appear to have a kindly heart to match her bonnie face.

"I've already sent Cook to make up a cot for you," Lona was saying.

Niall assumed that she was still talking to Gavin. Presumedly his own cot had already been prepared. Probably with damp, unaired sheets, since she knew he was another MacKay.

"God keep between ye and all harm, lassie." Gavin smiled gently and settled back into his chair. His eyes closed and he began to snore.

Lona plucked the tankard from his gnarled fingers and set it on the flagstones at his feet. The cat sniffed it once and gave a delicate sneeze.

"I see now why there is so little whisky to export," Niall commented, taking up a spoon. He nodded at the door where Cook had gone and then at Gavin. "A great deal of it seems to be consumed right here on the isle."

"Only a wee dram tae keep oot the cold," Lona answered, mimicking Cook's grumble. "And may the hand of God rest lightly upon you, guest Niall MacKay."

Lona raised a cup of her own and drank deeply, defiantly. Niall hoped that it was water she quaffed, else his hostess would be joining the glassy-eyed Cook and old Gavin in a long, long nap, and he'd be left on his own to find a bed somewhere in the ill-made keep.

Chapter Two

Old Gavin was gone with the dark morning tide taking his fulsome blessings and the nominal spring weather with him. Niall stirred out of a light sleep when he heard the boatman's voice raised in a final salute beyond the bed chamber's lone, shuttered window, and went so far as to slit one eye open far enough to judge the hour as being an uncivilized one.

"From the caves of white death may God keep ye, mistress, and bring ye tae a place of joy," old Gavin sang out into the wind that came tapping at Niall's crude shutters.

"Amen to that," he muttered. Numbed with the "water of life" to a point of near total disinterest, and very aware of the cold and dark beyond the woolen bed curtains, Niall had then rolled himself deeper inside his blanket—which *hadn't* been dampened or in any other way molested—and gone back to sleep.

When he again awoke, the sun, though well-screened with clouds, was considerably past the point when all good Scots were up and toiling at their labors. Niall, who had frequently been told by his aunt that he was no better than he had to be—a sentiment he gladly shared—had no desire to toil at anything on the blasted heath of Iona; but thought being the father of action and necessity its mother—he forced himself to thrust back his bed covers and stir beyond the comfort of his woolen cocoon.

He was not unaccustomed to dressing himself, which was a fortunate circumstance as no one offered any assistance with the adornment of his person. Nor did anyone offer to fetch him any breakfast while he lay abed in comparative warmth and comfort. And once risen, it was cold that compelled him to dress and hurry through the ritual of shaving, for he was not in any haste to consume some of Cook's porridge or, as was more likely, another bowl of her thick potato soup.

Niall wondered, while he laved his face with unpleasantly cold water, if the rebel prince was faring any better than he in his travels in the north. It was possible that he was rethinking his ambition to be king of the Scots. Niall had already reconsidered his desire to see him again. There was something about the cold waters of the north that brought on new clarity of thought.

Rapidly donning his warmest vestments and pulling on his topboots, he reflected on the fact that the Highlands, where the prince was reported to be, still had deep snow on the ground, and that the

Iona

royal blue blood—like his own common red sort—had had many years to grow thin in warmer climates. Praise be that he himself wasn't venturing to any higher latitudes.

Once dressed and shod, Niall pried back the stubborn shutter to have a look at the day. The bar, having been exposed to the sea air for a decade and more, had warped and wedged itself in place inside the small aperture and required great effort to dislodge it from its home. The old brace, defeated at last, was finally thrust aside with a look of loathing, for it was encrusted with a layer of briny dust and cobwebs that clung tenaciously to bare flesh. Obviously this small-windowed chamber was not often used and even less often cleaned.

Niall leaned out over the filthy sill long enough to take a look at the chill morn and then shook his head in disappointment. Winter had returned in the night. It was dark, wet and cold—his three least favorite conditions for exploring abandoned, and probably dangerous caverns. He reflected that it was well that he was mostly impervious to the humors that bad weather caused in more sensitive persons, for the dripping gray prospect seen from his window would blight a more delicate heart.

He took another moment to look beyond the island's gray stone to the dark that was the sea. Waiting there like a pouncing cat was a great, feral fog bank. The unruly mist stalked about the base of the stone breakwater whose long fangs thrust upward like the tall sails of a fleet of black ships permanently besieging small Iona. The vertical stones reminded him of the bars of a cage on a particularly unpleasant island prison, the Chateau d'If, he had briefly visited while in France. In both places there was stone and there was the sea, reaching out like a wild beast at eternal watch in its lair, in case granite walls alone were not a sufficient deterrent to those seeking asylum on, or escape from, the isles.

"'And the children of Israel did evil in the sight of the Lord: and the Lord delivered them into the hands of Midian for seven years,'" he muttered. Then, remembering the next verse and finding it applicable to the rebellious arm of the MacLean clan, he went on: "'And the children of Israel made them the dens which are in the mountains, and caves, and strongholds. . . .' Where—oh, where!—have you been hidden? How far must I seek you if Mistress Lona proves untrusting? And is your discovery the boon Van de Graaf believed it to be?" he asked meditatively of Charles' missing treasure, before a puff of salt wind had him shoving the shutter back into place and shooting the filthy bolt home.

Impervious to the weather's whims he might be, but he did not care for early hours. However, there was every need to dispose of his problem with speed and dispatch, which resolve could hardly be accomplished from the confines of his bed chamber. He must sally forth and face the day, however infelicitous the prospect or the hour.

Still, he waited with one hand on the door's bar as he listened cautiously at the ill-fitting panel. He could hear nothing above the eldritch screaming of the birds trying to escape the next oncoming storm by flying inland. The noise was a lonely one and stirred in him a rare longing—in spite of the season—for his family's snug croft.

Unfortunately, unless he brought Donnell's child

Iona

with him, there would be little welcome for him at his childhood fireside, and perhaps not much of one even then.

And by now his patron's hearth, the only other that he had ever called home, would be cold and swept bare, perhaps even sold to the next man who was to live there, he thought gloomily. Not that Niall would have found comfort there on this dreary morn. With Van de Graaf gone to his grave, that hearth in the Netherlands was just like any other.

Niall shrugged off his exceptional moodiness and turned his mind to the task at hand. He still had an unpleasant chore to do and it would not be aided by a morbid turn of mind.

"I really must bestir myself and see to this pretty coil of Mistress Lona's, for none of us will be safe until you are gone and known to be elsewhere," he concluded with a sigh, and then drew back the bolt on the door. It suggested a distrusting nature to bar his door against his hosts and was even quite rude, but he had been too long among enemies with false faces and falser hearts to abandon the practice. "I wonder if she will be grateful to me for making an end to you? Likely not. I fear that I have been set another thankless task."

Down to the kitchen Niall went, stepping carefully on the treacherous, poorly laid stair. It was shallow of tread and steep of pitch, not unlike the cliff trail he had ascended last afternoon.

So much poor construction did beg the question of whether anyone on Iona knew how to build a stair or hearth, or for that matter, a shutter or door. It was a pity that he could not tactfully inquire of the cause of the poor carpentry from his hostess, for it was a curious feature to have in a home.

At least for this descent he was not burdened with three valises and a wet cloak and hat. Niall sighed. He must be grateful for small favors; in some homes they used ladders to ascend to short lofts. That task would be a dire one after consuming Cook's *wee drams*.

He was relieved to discover that it was Lona MacLean who was gracing the glowing hearth that morning rather than the disrespectful cook. Hers was a pleasant visage to behold even in the early morning hours of a gray day.

"My luck doth hold," he murmured. "At least for this hour."

His hostess looked up from the pot she was stirring with slow deliberation and smiled perfunctorily. He liked this curve of the lips less than some he had enjoyed the day before for it was again a rather wary smile of a type bestowed on someone who was less than an intimate friend. He wondered who had been whispering poison into her comely ears during the hours of rest and repose.

"My brother used to say that when fortune favors, she does it to betray," Lona warned, only half-jesting.

Niall smiled politely in return and said nothing about the possibility that it was Lona, and not fortune, who had turned the cook from her pots. It was his experience that it was women, rather than cats, who were the curious species. They were also every bit as apt to betray one as their male counterparts.

As though hearing a summons, the gray moggie sauntered into the room and took her customary seat at the hearth. She was not an affectionate sort of feline and looked no more inclined than her mis-

Iona

tress to succumb to pretty blandishments.

"Alas! My fate is writ clear," he answered with forced cheer, hoping Lona would smile at his barefaced admission of a disreputable past. "I shall come to a bad end. My aunt has said so from the beginning—and being fate's favorite harbinger of ill-fortune, she should know. However, I don't think that my appointed hour has arrived yet—If, that is, *you* have prepared my morning meal."

"I have. And it would be well if you showed some gratitude," Lona pointed out, but the gray eyes were less than complete in their seriousness. Her manner was reluctantly warming before his good-humored charm. His suspicious mind was glad of the smile. He doubted that she would be so at ease had she actually put something in his food. Forsooth! It took a cold and practiced villain to poison a man and then smile at him while he quaffed from the hemlock cup. He was churlish to even think of such a barbaric contingency at Mistress Lona's small hands.

"Yes?"

"I could just as well have left you to Cook's tender mercies," she told him, turning away.

"I am persuaded that she has none." He studied her profile with a quizzical eye. It was an attractive one, but still a bit tight-lipped and dispirited for one who was still young enough to be gay.

"Very true. Some people curse fate; Cook curses MacKays. Or MacDonalds. It depends on the season." Lona swung the blackened pot off the flames and reached for a trencher. "I wouldn't concern myself too greatly though. Cook is vitriolic but often wanting in foresight, and I know for certain that she does not have sufficient poisons or purges about the place to do you any *real* harm."

Melanie Jackson

"Hmm." *She knew for certain? Why?*

But Niall made no comment on her provocative observation that followed so closely his own line of thought. He had no mind to quarrel with his hostess so he didn't offer the expected censure and admonition for this veiled threat. She had doubtless already received several unnecessary ones from Duncan MacLean; the young man was near desperation now that spring had come to the isles and the English huntsmen with it.

But it was an unnecessary warning only because Niall didn't believe that any sane person would be so stupid as to harm him in any obvious way when clear, outside dangers threatened . . . though there were probably more than a few Ionans who would like to see his body stretched lifeless on the threshold of the kitchen door, innocently felled by Cook's foul-tasting soup or too much whisky.

Of course, there was no saying what she might be driven to if she perceived him as a greater threat than the Sasannach.

Niall peered at his hostess as she tended her pot. Could this bonnie lass do such a vile thing as poison a man? Surely not. But Cook? In Niall's experience, there were two types of old people; the ones like Van de Graaf who gained greater benevolence and wisdom with every passing year, and the ones who didn't. Like Cook.

Once imagined, his demise at Cook's fell hand was a vivid image and an uncomfortably realistic one, so Niall banished the vexing thought from his obedient mind, right along with the tiny but persistent question about whether his cousin might have consumed something that made the *daft creature gae out tae the cliffs* during a bad storm and lose his footing there.

Donnell had been fond of drink, but not entirely lacking in wits; and he hardly would have gone for a walk if Cook had dosed him with a noxious purge or filled him up with the lethal whisky. Nor could he have been drugged and then dragged in full view to the cliff where he fell.

Unless it was done at night?

Niall looked again at the rough table and began to tuck up his ruffles. Iona was harsh with fripperies like lace cuffs, and he had not brought so many garments that he could afford to be wasteful with them.

"I hope you do not suffer from digestive difficulties," she said, apropos to his thought.

"I beg your pardon!" Niall paused until he saw that she was muffling a smile, and relaxed his alert posture. So! She still possessed her humor, at least in private. He wondered how long it would be before she would cease thinking of him as a bullying rascal MacKay and voluntarily bestow another of her gentle smiles upon him.

"I have prepared this morning's meal, but generally I leave this task to Cook, as anyone with nimble fingers and eyes is needed at the looms this time of year. We ship our woolens as soon as the weather permits. This season we shall have sixty ells of cloth to sell or barter," she added proudly.

"All from your island sheep?" he asked, as she laid the trencher and a spoon before him. He had caught a glimpse of the wary beasts the day before. They were strange animals with disheveled pelts bred from indiscriminate stock—part goat, part sheep, part chamois—and with their fat furry sides, they greatly resembled the miniature donkeys of Italy when laden with overflowing baskets of cartage.

"They must be more wool than mutton," he said, while studying the dish before him. "And old enough to be tough on the teeth as well."

"Aye. But as we want them for a purpose other than supper, it does not matter if they fail as meat. We have our barley and potatoes, after all."

Niall again forwent making a comment on a difficult subject. Instead he screwed up his resolution and sampled the porridge.

"And so . . . you see to the weaving as well as the hearth." Niall spoke thickly through a mouth of mushmeal. It had been both salted and sweetened with a bit of honey. Though not fond of pap and treacle Niall had to admit that the food was better than expected. He might have ended up with cold bannocks cakes that were harder than his bones or some of the repellent cheese that hung in the larder. "I suppose that you keep bees for honey and supervise the isle's distilleries as well."

"Aye. And the growing of the barley for our stills, though the crofters do much of the work." Her tone was wry. "As you see, I go from strength to strength . . . farmer, weaver, cook. All things that a *lady* should be—I don't tend the sheep, however. That would offend our loyal Callum's sensibilities— Did I hear you choke, guest Niall MacKay? Shall I fetch you a dram to accompany your repast?"

Niall resisted the urge to demand Callum's last name. It was a small isle and he would probably meet the man soon enough; he'd ask for no irrelevant histories just now. Either this Callum was Hector's *particeps criminis* or he was not. There was

Iona

nothing to be gained by alarming Lona with questions about rebels that she would believe he had no business knowing anything about.

"Thank you, no. I've barely recovered from my last paralysis. Perhaps some water?" He knew better than to ask for tea. Only salt was taxed more highly.

Lona rose and went to a bucket on the far side of the kitchen to fetch a cup. Niall waited until he had swallowed some of the strange, peat-flavored water that was in part responsible for the taste of Iona whisky. He cleared his mouth of all porridge before inaugurating a new topic of conversation, deeming it too important—and filled with gutturals—to speak of through a mouth of pap.

"And so, Mistress Lona, have you sought out some older, wiser council about your dilemma? You must have passed an uncomfortable winter with Charles's firebrand buried in your midst."

Lona's visage remained calm but her breathing grew rapid betraying her agitation to his watchful eye.

"Older council I have, but wiser?" Lona did not pretend to misunderstand the question. Her brow wrinkled slightly as she considered his query. The thought had well-nigh driven her to distraction since the treasure's arrival. She said at last: "And what would it avail me if such council was to be had? Hector took his plans to the grave. Nor do I hate anyone here so much that I would burden them with my brother's responsibilities even should they ask. No, there is no one on Iona who has the knowledge to advise me in this matter."

"No one?" Niall was surprised at both her answer and her lack of dissembling. He had expected some show of ignorance about her brother's activities, but gladly tackled the former question before she reconsidered the wisdom of such a discussion. He asked quietly: "You're certain that your brother confided in no one else? No relative, or perhaps a brother-in-arms?"

"My brother saw no one else before he died," she said rather tartly. "He was imprisoned, if you recall, before the final battle. This made him cautious. I am also by nature very cautious—especially of people named MacKay—who seem relentless in their pursuit or other men's possessions."

"I see. 'Tis understandable, of course." Niall thought for a moment, his hazel eyes staring through the thick stones of the wall as he considered her words. Either this Callum was a different man, or Iona's mistress did not know that he was a companion of her brother's. His tone grew pensive. "This is all for the best, I suppose. There is then no need for anyone here to feign ignorance of the prince's treasure when questions are asked. Innocence can sometimes be a strong shield," he added to himself.

"Hush!" Lona started sharply then whispered reprovingly: "Anyone may be about at this hour."

"Nay. My ears are keen. I would hear any that approached," he answered, impervious to her scolding as well as the weather. Lona hadn't the knack of a true shrew; her natural disposition was too sweet for the occupation. "But why leave the door ajar on such a cold morning? It permits much of the heat to escape."

"The chimney is poorly laid," she admitted, "and I've no desire to be overcome by smoke as happens from time to time in the winter when we must bar the way."

Iona

"I see. Perhaps something may be done in the summer," Niall murmured, then shook his head at the unintentional lie. Iona's keep would probably be gone by summer, razed by angry Sasannachs or MacDonalds.

"I doubt it," came the uncanny reply. Probably she spoke of the possibility of correcting the flawed masonry, but her turn of phrase was too apt for comfort. She added, not quite irrelevantly: "Well-made things will often last longer than the men who build them—and sometimes poorly made things as well, when their maker's life is forshortened as Hector's was."

"You've been most unlucky," was his soft reply. He took another bite of porridge.

"We were helped to our present misfortune." The fey eyes were grave and seemed to peer into his skull as they searched for reassurance of his intentions.

Niall frowned. He was finding that his thoughts were greatly disordered this morning. Perhaps from the whisky he had swallowed the day before. He had never previously believed in anyone having second sight. He should stop thinking on it now as it was a detriment to peace and he had troubles aplenty without hallucinations.

"In any case, we must see about removing this object of the king's temptation and at once," he said, sticking closely to the matter at hand.

"I have seen no treasure to tempt a king."

"Devil a bit! Don't dissemble now."

Her gray eyes stared some more. Then: "And if I say that it is only a wild rumor?"

"That would be an unfortunate happenstance, Mistress," he said without smiling. "The whispers of treasure would be most difficult to disprove and would bring the same carrion crows as any actual gold."

Lona looked away. She stifled a tired sigh. He was tireless, relentless, fit for battle. She was but a woman, and a weary one at that.

She had spent the long night tossing abed. This time, it was not just ghosts that kept her from sleep; it was thoughts of Niall. His presence on her isle left her both disturbed and exhilarated. All through the hours of darkness, she had pursued the answer to her thorny dilemma. Was he offering salvation or destruction? Was he a deadly complication, or the solution to her Gordian knot?

Morning had brought no clear answer, only a loss of appetite, another cold day, and a growing discontent with carrying her burden alone.

She was conscious of a desire to confide in Niall and was vexed with herself for wanting to seek his support and advice. She had managed on her own for years; she could stand alone now.

But how long would she be obliged to stand alone? Forever? 'Til death? And death might be coming very soon, riding the waves even as they spoke.

"I suspect, sir, that you are an artificer."

"Perhaps so." He made a quick nod, not one whit abashed. "Rejoice in the knowledge. It is a talent much envied by the powerful."

Her lips curved scornfully.

"Lady Disdain, my advent is surely your blessing."

"You mock me."

"Nay, that I do not." Her silence continued. "For whose sake do you remain mute, Mistress? Your brother is gone, and your continuing silence does not aid his cause."

Iona

"For whose sake should it be but my own?" she parried, still thinking.

"For any number of people, I should think. But do not let excessive caution make you foolhardy."

"There is no such thing as excessive caution, and you know this."

"Hm. . . . Can you be browbeaten?" he asked whimsically.

She feigned another look of scorn, but hid her hands as they betrayed her with their trembling.

He had the right of it, of course. She could be beaten down. Eventually. But there were other considerations, too. Lona knew that she had reached the end of her wits and nearly the end of her strength. The island that had brought them safety was, thanks to Hector, now a trap. Since escape did not seem possible, the hounds would have to be redirected to some other path.

Somehow, she must rouse herself for a final effort to save her clan. She could no longer cower in her hole, peering out at the world with frightened eyes, and praying that English justice would pass the isle's poor people by. Time had run out and so had her nerves. Whatever Niall was—destruction or salvation—he had to be faced immediately.

Lona drew a deep breath. She decided that she would collaborate with his plans. He seemed to have taken her acquiescence for granted; let him believe in her calm acceptance of fate. It was a useful stratagem to allow one's enemy to underestimate one's strength.

And if he betrayed her, what mattered it? She was lost from the moment Hector had brought the treasure to the isle. If they could not get the cursed thing away, then she would take the treasure out into the ocean. And if she could not escape, then she would martyr herself before the Sasannachs came, joining the other lost MacLeans who slept in Iona's cold sea.

She found, to her surprise, that this decision, grim as it was, still brought her relief.

"Such sad eyes in one so young! You will not trust me, then?" His words interrupted her dark thought. Niall reached across the board and tucked a stray black lock behind her ear. Blood rushed to her temples.

"Sirrah!"

He laughed softly. "Ah! My impertinence has roused you. You look as haughty as a queen, Mistress. Though prettier than any I have ever been privileged to see."

She glared ferociously, hoping to conceal the exhilaration that came with his touch. It would be unwise to let him know that she could be moved in this way.

"Remove it where? Prince Charles is still at large, we think, somewhere in the Highlands. Maybe Skye." Her fists drew up and were planted on her slim hips to give her size and menace as she asked belligerently: "And what is this treasure to you? Why should I give it into *your* keeping?"

"Such a fearsome fire-eater!"

"I'll swear you're not!"

Niall thought Lona looked rather like a fledgling plover, puffing its down in an effort to appear large and fierce. He had to remind himself that it was entirely possible that she was, if not large, at least quite fierce in the defense of her clan; for unless he was mistaken, it was her will and ready wits that

Iona

had saved the other islanders from destruction in the year just past.

Niall stopped his teasing banter and answered her straightly.

"You must surrender it because it is only a matter of time before the English king hears of its existence from the spies sent to find escaped Jacobites, and then his soldiers will arrive post-haste. George—though fairly wise as kings go and not especially sadistic—is not presently over-burdened with the quality of mercy when it comes to the Scots. I do not doubt that he would be willing to put you—and every other person on Iona—to the question, if the need arose. And should that fail to win a response," he added brutally, "George will probably order the island torn down stone by stone until the treasure is discovered."

Niall didn't add that it was entirely possible that the monarch would do this anyway, for it was plain to see even in the dim light from the open door that Lona had grown pale at the thought.

"He would destroy everything? The looms? The distillery? Even if I—someone were to explain that the others knew nothing? That it was only Hector?"

"Mistress, the reprisals have been unspeakably brutal. If the English find the treasure here, you are damned."

" 'Tis worse than I thought. But how could anyone know of this?" she whispered, stricken anew. "It was a secret. Everyone involved swore an oath of silence. Lord Lauderdale . . . Buckingham . . . my brother! They were all sworn. The only other who knew is dead—"

"It would be a wonder only if George *didn't* know of this eventually," Niall replied, steepling his fingers and resting his chin atop as he studied Lona's face. His fierce little bird did not conspire well. He hoped sincerely that no shrewd Sasannach ever had opportunity to question her. " 'The ear of jealousy heareth all things.' And, sweet innocence, there is no such thing as a secret when so many persons need must be employed in the task of shifting the treasure. It must have been a wearisome chore for your brother—if he had no help hiding it on this island," Niall added, thinking still of the sensible Callum and the morsels of gossip he had heard about him.

"It is not so heavy or grand as you may imagine," she answered, shifting painfully on a wooden stool and propping her arms on the table as though she hadn't the strength to remain erect without aid. "The season was a calm one after April. And the cask is but a small one, only part-filled with trinkets and gewgaws. 'Tis a beggarly pittance for a rich king."

"Aye? But then, George does not pursue this treasure for material gain, but rather to see that Charles has no possible backing for a further effort to regain his throne. The size of the catch matters not at all—a great deal may be made of this treasure politically if not monetarily."

"There will be no further effort," Lona said tiredly. "This war was suicide, and everyone knows it."

"You speak as if you were not yourself a Jacobite." Niall's demeanor was stern. "That you do not believe in the cause. And I assure you that every man at Culloden believed that they would triumph."

"Aye. And they are all dead." Lona shrugged and pushed away another strand of black hair that had escaped her braid to lay along her too-pale cheek. Her eyes were as sober as they had ever been as she

Iona

stared at her unwanted guest. "Please understand me. I followed Hector because he was my brother and only living kin. But women—poor ones, in particular—rarely have time for such things as princely uprisings and the king's politics."

"No?"

"No." Her tone was deliberate. "When we are young and heedless we concern ourselves with escaping from the prison that is our family home by marrying some handsome, likely lad; and then when we are older and a bit wiser, our days are by then taken up with the running of the workhouse we have somehow inherited with our wedding vows."

"The workhouse?" Niall asked. The word invoked a strong and unpleasant image. He did not care to think that she viewed marriage as a form of servitude.

"Aye. The workhouse." Lona gestured about her. "Running a home is in large part drudgery. Necessary, of course, and in some ways rewarding. But . . ."

"But still drudgery." Niall looked about the dark, cheerless kitchen that varied only in its shades of gray, and had to agree. He imagined that to a woman who had known a more elegant life this place must seem doubly crude. He asked sympathetically: "Do you see Iona as a prison or a penal colony?"

Lona shook her head and lied. " 'Better a dinner of herbs where love is than a stalled ox with hate therein,' " she quoted, at once straightening her spine. She pointed a finger and charged: "And you have not answered my question, guest Niall MacKay. All that you say may be true, but it is not enough. What is this treasure to you? For whom do you seek it? Whom do you serve?"

Melanie Jackson

"In this, I serve the prince and Scotland," he said sincerely, willing her to a belief in his words. "Charles's claim is just and so he must be given his due; but also must he be first got and then kept from our soil, for he shall be the murder of us all if he remains. The English will not rest until he is found or exiled, and there will be more religious persecutions here—and in England and Holland—if he is not removed from play."

"And you feel it is better for the Scots, good Catholics or no, to wear the English yoke than die in futile struggle against her. . . . Or perhaps you feel that the vanquished should go to the colonies, as so many have done now that they have run out of the desire to fight but have no stomach to repent their politics," Lona said, surprising Niall yet again. Was it possible that she truly had the sight? Or was she perhaps a soulmate at last sent to him by a lately merciful God?

"Men only repent when they are unable to face their sins," he answered quickly. "This revolution was no sin of Scotland's making. After Culloden the will was hardened in any that did not break, but why should they go as sheep to the butcher when there is another, better way? General Leslie—"

"I blame no one for being stomach-turned by Culloden! Or for wanting to escape the Sasannachs. How should I, when this is mine own secret desire?" Lona swallowed and looked away, feeling ashamed of her admission but determined to have her say. "I would not disdain anyone else for feeling the same as I do. I know why they flee. These endless religious quarrels weary the souls of men. I think they must even weary God by their monotony and futile repetition."

Iona

"Mistress Lona—" Her words had struck at his heart, a place he had considered invulnerable to such attacks, and he found himself on the verge of saying something far too personal, far too precipitously.

"No! Cease—please! I spoke out of turn. This is not a *drudgery* but an act of duty freely undertaken. I do not ask for the cup to pass me by. I could not face myself did I avoid this duty. Too many depend upon me here."

Lona made an agitated gesture and Niall subsided. Now was not the best moment for a discussion of this kind. There would be time enough for conversation after Hector's inheritance was sped on its way. Then he could lay his dream before her with a clear conscience and not feel any guilt for luring her away from the dreary isle.

It was a pleasing thought.

"As you wish," he said quietly. "Please believe that I've no wish to distress you, Mistress."

"Then instead expound, dear sir, on your previous words. How are we to remove this blight from my island and restore it to its missing master? You have a plan, I hope, for prayer alone will not suffice. The Lord's ear is weary of Scot petitions. I have already made the attempt to plead for divine intervention; none is presently forthcoming unless it is in the form of your elegant person. Are you Heaven-sent, guest Niall MacKay?"

"Assuredly I have a plan," Niall answered after a long moment, a little shocked at his hostess' irreverence. Said elsewhere in the Highlands, such sentiment would have her hauled before the kirk on a charge of blasphemy. If this was the direction she was leaning it would be best to remove her swiftly to more tolerant climes. "It may tax my ingenuity to the uttermost, but we'll have this cursed treasure off Iona before spring is very far advanced. Once it's safe away, we'll let it be known that your brother arranged to have it taken directly to the Continent. With any luck the rumors about Iona will die a quiet death and everyone shall be spared the English presence.... If we are *very* fortunate, Charles will also turn up on the Continent and that will see an end to so many spies and soldiers in the north."

"It will go to France?"

"Aye. Those loyal to Charles are there." Niall stood. "Now, perhaps you should show me the resting place of the prince's treasury. I can't help but feel that time is fleeing at an indecent pace."

"It is in a barrow," she warned him. "In a grave deep and dank."

"And moldering? And malodorous? You sound as bleak as *De Profundis*." Niall began to smile. "He did not hide it beneath the flensing shed, I trust!"

"Nay! I said it was in a grave! We would not set a shed above a king's grave," she said indignantly. "Though your cousin thought we had."

"Donnell was not a wise man." With that gross understatement, Niall changed the subject to one slightly less inflammatory and much more to purpose. "Well then! If I am not to be bedeviled by my nose—"

"Ha!" Lona snorted contemptuously and did not rise at the hint.

"—then let us be off to our appointed task. A grave, you say? A fitting place for the finances of a lost cause, one supposes. Was it prophesy do you think, that led your brother to hide it there?"

"You are irreverent, sir. I suspect that you did not love the cause as much as you claim." But there was no heat in the accusation. Had she not herself just made mock of the power of prayer? What were the affairs of princes to compare to that?

"I might answer in kind—were I not so well-mannered."

"Upland folk hae muirland manners," she retorted, beginning to smile again.

"Aye. And truth and honesty keep the croon o' the causeway," he answered back. "Not that I would ever suggest that you were less than honest—"

"You just did! And it is obvious to me that you have not seen our causeway for there is no crown upon it, and honesty will not hold a man atop it when the tide is in—even if he speaks truth all day! And since we are speaking of the wet, it is come over rain again," she pointed out, even though she knew that she was fighting a losing battle against superior forces. "You dislike the damp, I observed yesterday. And in any case, I should like to hear a little more about this plan of yours before we spend a morning outside in the cold and wet."

"We will don suitable apparel against the elements," he answered, undeterred by her foot-dragging. "And we may discuss my plans as we walk. Or climb, as the need may be. Is any part of this isle flat?"

"Nay—except the beach. But that is not of import. What is important is the want of wit in this act. This troubles me, not the want of wear. I greatly mistrust turning the riddle—"

"As do I! I do not suggest that magic be involved. Surely a shovel would suffice." A large hand was held out to her. It was polite but demanding.

"We'll need lanterns," she said with a sigh, unable to think of any pressing reason that they should delay, and weary enough to be willing to cast her fate upon the winds of Niall's determined fortune. She allowed him to assist her to her feet with a warm, hard hand.

"Very sensible. But put no shark oil in them, if you please."

She ignored the comment while she retrieved her hand from its warm cocoon. "And we'll need a crowbar for the stones. The cask is not buried under mere earth. . . . Are you sure that you would rather not wait for better weather?"

"When is it likely to stop raining?" he asked, going to the door and staring out at the courtyard. A gust of wind blew back his dark locks and had him retreating into the room with a grimace of distaste.

"July," she said, and then smiled, her sense of the ridiculous coming to her aid and banishing her dark mood.

Her possible rescuer was as fastidious as a cat and had no liking for the damp and cold. If she had wanted to bedevil him, she couldn't have thought up a better method than digging up heavy stones in the rain—unless it was to have requested Hector to bury the cask under the foul flensing shed.

Of course, had it been buried there, she would have missed the pleasure of seeing the cat get his paws wet as he picked his way over the tidal stones, having no desire to visit the foul shed herself.

"Then perhaps we should not delay. I doubt that George's soldiers will be so courteous as to wait for the summer to come calling." Niall reached for two cloaks that hung near the door waiting to be donned.

Neither garment was his or in any way elegant. They were not even very clean, but they had the rec-

Iona

ommendation of being heavy and warm, and made of a skin that would shed water while the two of them performed what promised to be a wearisome chore.

Lona accepted the proffered wrap with reluctance. She did not entirely trust this MacKay, but he was absolutely correct that the treasure must be removed from the island before George's soldiers came to hear of it, and she could not do it alone.

And, now that she recollected, hadn't Hector also chided her for her excessive caution by saying: *If yer hemming and hawing were hams and haggisses, this island would be well-fed.*

She might worry later that she was being too trusting with a man whom she hardly knew. But want of acquaintance or no, that this other MacKay also knew of the treasure's existence supported his claim that the secret was becoming common knowledge.

This occurrence left little time for considered thought, and really the matter was a plain one. Jacobite enthusiast or no, she had a duty to her brother and his prince to see this treasure properly disposed; but above that, she had a duty to keep her people safe from the English, for the welfare of the MacLeans had call on her loyalty before a prince, however bonny. Since it was her flesh and blood that had placed them in jeopardy, it was her lot to turn the peril away if she could manage it.

Another pleasing thought: Even if this inventive MacKay was proved a thief by keeping the gold for his own use, giving him the treasure would still serve the purpose of removing some of the immediate danger from her isle as the hounds would turn the chase after him.

Melanie Jackson

He also was the only hope that the Lord had seen fit to provide her. She would simply have to make do with the tools at hand.

Lona looked steadily into Niall's kindly hazel eyes and felt again the warmth of his nature in their steady regard. Surely that could not be false? She had seen and heard so many lies from Donnell and the rogue MacKays. Only truth and real compassion would warm her frozen soul.

For whatever compelling reason, Niall MacKay was reaching for her with his able mind and iron will, and he would not be turned aside by her misgivings. It would be simplest to acquiesce.

"Very well, Niall MacKay. We shall pay a call on the dead of Iona and you may see this damning treasure with your own eyes."

"I should thank you for this privilege I suppose, but I think that I will confine myself to gratitude for your trust. One does not, after all, usually thank someone for helping place one's neck in a noose." Niall looked wry, but his smile was still as warming as the hearth behind her.

Lona began to relax and returned his smile with one just as wry.

"I'm so glad you understand exactly how I feel on this occasion," she said.

Niall stared at her for a minute and then began to laugh. The cheery sound shook the kitchen and seemed to banish its shadows.

"I hadn't thought of it that way, Mistress. It is a small consolation, but consider: If you hang for this treasure, you shall not hang alone."

Lona did not smile at his jest. "I already knew that, guest Niall MacKay. And it is the image of every MacLean on the isle swinging from the gal-

Iona

lows at Creiff that has moved me this last year and more. I would not rejoice to see you dangling from another gibbet—even should you deserve it."

Niall stopped laughing, but a hard smile remained.

"Be at ease, Mistress. I have other plans for my future and they do not include swinging at the end of a Sasannach rope. Our destinies are elsewhere. We shall survive this mad venture—my word on it!"

Lona looked at the stern face that had peeped out from under the well-mannered mask and believed its vow. Reassured, she offered an equally grim smile and pulled a hood over her head.

"Then follow me, guest Niall MacKay, and I shall take you to your treasure so that you may hurry on to your other destiny."

"*Our* destiny, Mistress." His words were quiet and lost in the wind that suddenly filled the narrow passage. "*Our destiny*, m'dear, and by all means, let us make haste toward it."

Chapter Three

The remote barrow where the treasure lay was filled with damp and cold in abundance in spite of it being located well above the reach of the highest of the isle's tides. A naturally formed cave hollowed out by percolating waters, it had been improved upon by the ancient islanders, chipped and carved to suit the will of the Iona Pict priests. They were the pagan ones who had lived there before Saint Columba of the Gaels brought Christianity and literature to Pictland. It had to have been the Picts who had done this—Picts or their ghosts, Niall thought with a grim smile for his sudden fancies, for he felt certain that no Christian hand had shaped this long barrow.

The ever-present wind followed Niall and Lona into the narrow cleft in the sea wall where the unknown kings'—or queens'—graves were hidden, and there spent much of its effort and time moaning

Iona

and sighing about the graven carvings that adorned the perpetually wet walls and damp, curved ceiling.

If Niall had been a more imaginative man, he would have said that the damnable, persistent breeze that carried the clinging fog after them into the shale cave sounded like the bones of the restless dead rubbing together, or perhaps earth-bound spirits whispering their Pictish chatter with smashed jaws from under their heavy cairns where they twined and twisted in uneasy rest. A superstitious man might even have supposed that he had entered the first of Purgatory's rings, the limbo of the unbaptized dead.

Fortunately, he told himself, he was not a man given to imaginative musings. And he always had been told that hell would be uncomfortably warm and sulphurous—which this cave was most emphatically *not!*

The first cairn they passed in the narrow way was all neatly laid with ordered round stones; and then another grave which was less orderly, some vandal having stolen many of its rocks for a purpose that was easy enough to guess.

Niall paused beside the upset stones, head cocked as he listened for the slightest sound to come from under the looted pile, and all the while berating his sacrilegious imagination for raising gooseflesh on his arms, for it was asking questions like: How much stone was needed to keep the dead safely in their graves? And did enough stone remain behind?

"The nearer the grave, the greedier . . . you're a braver man than I, Hector MacLean." Niall spoke softly, but the cave amplified like the finest theater and Lona heard him.

"He did not loot the grave. This one would hardly

be worth it." Lona insisted, guessing part of Niall's thoughts with the accuracy of a seer. He began to give serious consideration to the idea that she carried some form of the sight as many islanders were said to do. Her guesses were uncanny in their accuracy, if guesses they were. "This is a pagan grave and they were all very poor by our measure of earthly goods, even the kings and priests. All that is here is cast-off bones and furred shrouds."

" 'Build thee more stately mansions, oh my soul!' I never thought Hector had come looting," Niall said, abandoning his listening pose, answering truthfully and without calculated thought. "I was thinking of Donnell. I've rarely met a colder man. This cold tomb would be a just place for him."

"The sea is wetter and colder, still."

Niall paused as a new chill crawled down his arms. He reminded himself that he had gooseflesh because it was cold. There was not a blessed thing stirring in those caves except himself and his reluctant guide. And, as Lona had reminded him, Donnell had most definitely drowned in the sea; he was not lying here among the Pict dead, listening to their words with hostile, frozen ears.

Still, the subject did put him strongly in mind of one of Scotland's larger cultural chasms. In the north, it was considered a sign of respect to add stone to a grave; in the South it was a deadly insult. It made a man wonder how they felt about such things in the isles, and why, on an island with no scavengers, they might have come to believe weighting the dead with stones was a good idea . . . particularly if the dead was the enemy, Donnell MacKay.

"That is not what makes the dead uneasy. Though Donnell would hardly be welcome here for all his

Iona

diluted Pictish blood. Come, we're almost there. Hector did but borrow some rocks from this grave, and I doubt that she minded since they were there in over-abundance . . . so much weight for one small body," Lona added as an afterthought.

"*She?*" The hair on his arms refused to lay flat. Niall looked about in the wavering lantern light, but the tomb was empty of all but wind. He could not even claim to feel observed, but the notion that someone was listening to them was very strong. Even unnerving. The sensation was a plaguing nuisance.

"Aye." Lona paused long enough to direct her own lantern's beam over the partially dismantled cairn, her head also cocked in a listening attitude. "So I believe."

"Indeed? Do you come here often?" he asked curiously, unable to imagine her indulging in such morbid pursuits, but wishing to make certain that she did not often commune among the dead.

"No, not often. . . . There's no need. I can feel the ghosts everywhere on Iona, and it would not be discreet to be seen here regularly."

For a moment it occurred to Niall that his hostess might be attempting to test his nerves in the hope that he would turn back from the prince's treasure, but he dismissed the notion because it made no sense. Any sane person would wish the cursed treasury off the island and with all possible haste.

"You've never *seen* any ghosts have you?" he asked before he could stop himself.

Lona hesitated a moment. Then: "No . . . I never turned to look when the voices called—not knowing for certain just who was behind me, and not wanting to see."

Under other circumstances, Niall would have

found their conversation bizarre; perhaps he would have even wondered if Lona MacLean had gone mad from grief and started communing with imagined spirits because she sought her lost family among the island's dead.

But standing in the cold barrow, he had no difficulty comprehending what she meant. Not that he believed in literal spirits haunting them as they visited the ancient graves! But there was a certain atmosphere of cold habitation about the isle, not unlike what he had felt one autumn sundown when walking alone in Flodden Field—the place where James IV had been hacked to bits along with his eight most trusted earls, thirteen barons, and thousands of common men—and that feeling of being in a place of concentrated death made it possible to believe that the last emanations of the sentient dead dwelt on Iona in abundance.

Nor could he blame his hostess for never turning to look behind her. In all honesty, he could not categorically state that he would have nerve to confront a spirit if he felt it treading on his shadow—conjecturally speaking, of course, since there were no real ghosts, any more than there were boggles or brownies. It was just dripping water and an unfortunate wind that mimicked human sighs and moans inside the old cave that made one think such irrational things.

"Thomas doubted also," he thought he heard Lona say.

"Mistress, you're going to be hanged for witchcraft as well as treason, should you persist in reading men's minds." *Those who sup from a fairy cup had best hide their second sight*, he thought to him-

Iona

self. Then aloud: "You've come to know the ghosts of Iona well, then?"

"Aye, too well. They came nightly when I was in my deepest despondency." Her tone was funereal.

"What have they to say about your present difficulties? Surely there is some wise man among them who might give you advice, if you do not trust Cook," he said lightly, still thinking of dead Scot kings. The ones before Kenneth MacAlpine, first king of both Pict and Scot. "Or can they not speak Gaelic?"

Lona sent him a withering look. "Do you make mock of our illustrious dead, *sirrah*?"

"Nay! Behold me abashed, Mistress."

"I should hope to do so."

"But did they not protest Donnell's presence here?" he persisted, for the first time truly desiring an answer about what befell his greedy cousin. He followed Lona's misty wake as she turned away from him. "Didn't they tell you to be rid of him at any cost? Didn't they order the MacLeans to repulse him? Or was that unnecessary? I imagine that your people hated to have him here," he said to her rapidly retreating silhouette.

"All made cry," she answered in perfect seriousness, quickly disappearing down the dark passage. Her footsteps echoed softly, the crunching shell and shale underfoot muted by the thick mist. "But it was to no purpose."

"I'm certain they did—especially Cook. It must have been hard to see Donnell set in your brother's place—"

"Not the MacLeans," she interrupted. "We were ordered to remain silent on fear of death at Donnell's butchering hands. It was the ghosts who cried out in protest when we were held mute. It was the ghosts that wished him gone."

"Did they? But no MacLeans?" But the skeptical question was too soft to hear above the cave's renewed mutterings, and lacked force, besides. He was not accusing Lona, but asking for another undeserved show of trust.

"Their voices were raised in lamentation the night Simple Robert died. I heard them say plainly that the MacKay would die in the first storm of autumn."

"Perhaps that was just Cook wailing in her whisky," Niall suggested, regretful at the mention of the death of her kinsman. He had not thought to discuss anything other than Donnell's timely demise, and had not meant to carelessly revive her sorrow at her family's many recent, unhappy deaths.

But damage done, it was carrying things too far to suggest that he accept that Donnell's death was caused by the vindictive ghosts of Iona. Better to lay it at fate's door and be done with it. That intention in mind, he said firmly: "It was a fortunate accident that took him—and so I've said to my aunt. I shudder to think of George's wrath did Donnell keep the treasure. It would have been the death of all of you."

"I never heard its like," she went on in a whisper, paying his sensible words no heed, and making Niall more uneasy with each thick, foggy breath he drew into his lungs. "I tried to stop my ears, but the voices persisted. I thought that night that our clan was truly forfeit. I felt at first that I wanted to die, too. Gladly would I have lain down in Robert's grave and joined my family had the voices let me— And such was my intent, but . . ."

Iona

"But," he prompted very softly, wondering if his pretty hostess were mad after all, and remorseful at introducing the sad subject into their conversation if it had led to a lapse of her reason. It was doubly reprehensible to speak of such things while still in the tomb with the dead nearby.

"I had another calling and it gave me purpose." Her voice was suddenly brisk and quite reassuringly sane. "You jest about the spirits, guest Niall MacKay, but there are ghosts on Iona, never doubt. No place so seeped in blood could be otherwise. They're at rest again, now that winter's gone and Donnell—Well, they'll not harm *you*, and that is all that matters."

"No? You relieve my mind," he muttered.

Niall looked at the thick vapor that lay on the floor. It was indeed ghostly in appearance. His boots were obscured at mid-calf and completely invisible from the ankle down. He might have been concerned about being swallowed by the mist, was he possessed of a mind given to fanciful turns. But he was a practical soul and knew well that his feet were still in place under the gray shroud, for they were telling him plainly of the damp and cold that had penetrated his leathers.

He thought that Iona might well have its revenge by giving him the grippe, but that would be the extent of the harm he anticipated from inhuman agents, and that had naught to do with angry spirits.

Still, he understood where the notion of ghosts had been born on this isle and he answered Lona with care.

"I do not mock your ghosts," he said gently, reaching out a hand and putting her flight to a sudden halt. He could feel her pulse racing under his fingers as her heart beat an over-quick tattoo. "Nor would I ever jest about the grief you feel. But can you truly lay Donnell's death at the spirits' door?"

She stared up at him, blinking like one coming out of a cave into bright sunlight. Her expression and over-fast pulse put pay to the notion that she might have been teasing him for some purpose. Her distress was not feigned.

"Certainly I do. Everyone else does." Lona's voice was sharp as she dismissed their disturbing conversation. She pulled out of his loosened grip and resumed her quick pace into the cliff's dark bowel. "Do make haste, sir. It grows cold."

Lona stopped at the third and last pile of stones in the narrow tunnel. It was considerably smaller than the other two cairns and might be mistaken for a child's grave. It was slightly less damp here and Niall also noticed that the noisy wind had most appropriately ceased its murmurings.

The mist, also conversant with dramatic timing, no longer churned about his feet like a hell-pot at boil, and for this reason, the last grave felt more dead than the others they had passed.

Perhaps because it had no dispossessed ghost to mutter over its cold, forgotten bones.

Then, realizing what thought had just passed through his head, Niall snorted at himself with disgust. The chill and damp were affecting his bodily humors. The cave's ancient air was most likely unhealthful as well.

"I hope the wood has not had time to rot," Lona said practically, shining her light on the gleaming stones. He could hear water trickling nearby, but saw no source. "It was wrapped in oiled cloth and set in a sherry cask, so perhaps the chest is still dry."

Iona

"A sherry cask?" he asked, feeling off-balance by the sudden change of tone and subject to pragmatic things. He shook his head to dislodge his uncharacteristic musings about the spirit world, and set aside the matter of Lona's apparent belief in spirits for later contemplation.

When this task was done, Niall vowed silently that he would see to it that both of them stayed far away from insalubrious air. 'Twas no place for a sunny-dispositioned lass.

"Aye. We use them to store our whisky. It gives the barley a grand flavor—much better than new oak."

"I see."

"Hector also thought to remove the treasure with our other stores when we ship them to Tiree and then the mainland. It seemed a reasonable place of concealment for the journey."

"A plan with merit," Niall admitted. "If the chest has not been crushed beneath the weight of these stones. Need he have used so many?"

Lona turned amused eyes his way. Her tone held hints of buried laughter that was completely at odds with their melancholy surroundings.

"You have obviously never laid a proper grave. Now that you see the stones' size and numbers, do you wish to get on with the plundering and exhume the remains? Or shall we leave them at rest with a suitable prayer until other arrangements are made?" she asked. "Do you know any Pictish prayers for the dead? Or one for dismantling cairns? I don't think I have heard any Catholic Mass for such an occasion."

Niall also began to feel amused at their dark endeavor. If one discounted the notion of the listening dead, the situation was indeed rather humorous. No one who had ever known Niall in his alter-identity in Paris and Hague would ever guess that Flambard's carefully cultivated, elegant and indolent personage would be called upon to loot an ancient king's—or queen's, if Lona was to be believed—cast-off grave. Flambard did not indulge in tasteless, impolite acts, so it was indeed a ridiculous picture that he would make should anyone else see him at toil and carry the tale abroad. Even amongst his own kin, such an act would be considered beyond the threshold of his limited sensibilities.

If Van de Graaf's ghost walked the earth, even he would be laughing at his protege's predicament. Niall found the thought of his former employer's amused spirit rocking with laughter to be oddly reassuring. Perhaps that was why the MacLeans had no fear of ghosts; affection robbed the dead of terror.

Of course, not all the dead here were MacLeans. Not even most of them.

Again sobered, Niall took a quick turn about the grave, searching for signs that anyone else had been there before them, but the wet stone told no tales. Irksome and muddy as the task was bound to be, the cask would need to be exhumed before he could be certain that the contents were still secure. He would not risk others' lives in that treacherous sea to rescue a treasure that might not even rest where it should.

Though it would put pay to the disguise of his ineffectual persona, it did not disturb Niall that Lona MacLean would be witness to his work. She might dislike the MacKays but she would think nothing of his turning his hand to physical tasks;

Iona

too much labor did she do herself to sneer at another who used his hands. Also, he suspected that he had not fooled her uncanny eyes with his courtier's act.

Niall glanced Lona's way. She looked serene even in the cold and wet. He was grateful that she was not an hysteric; too many females were prone to useless behavior when confronted with the thought of invaders, ghosts or graves. Many ladies would find the very mention of the barrow enough to curdle their blood. But not Lona MacLean. Her blood was quite well and calm, and would probably remain so even did a Pict ghost appear to protest their doings.

It was, he reflected, very helpful to have a companion who could hold a lantern steady while he wrestled with the cairn. There had been more than one occasion in his recent past when he could have made good use of a second pair of deliberate hands.

"It will be a deal of work to shift the stones," Niall conceded. "But I will feel more at ease once I have seen with mine own eyes that the double-damned treasure is indeed here and intact."

"As you wish." Lona set her lamp on the floor and stepped back a pace to give him room to ply the crowbar. "Have a care that nothing tumbles down upon your feet. Hector was a valiant soldier but he had no particular talent at mending walls, and the cairn is as ill-built as our chimneys back at the keep."

Niall first set the bar aside and removed his cloak. He tucked up his ruffles for a second time. It was not necessary to pry the grave apart. The stones had not been set with mud or lime, nor had time and dripping water had occasion to fuse them together. They were heavy and wet, but still movable.

Melanie Jackson

They would also ruin his gloves, he realized, but he supposed that that was preferable to ruining his hands. Damaged gloves could be hidden from curious eyes that might well ask why he had been toiling in Iona's caves.

"Wait," Lona instructed. She then again surprised him by reading his thoughts. "There should be some other gloves tied inside the left— Yes," she said, as she found the stiffened leathers fastened inside her cloak and pulled them free.

"No need to spoil your fine pair," she pointed out, taking the cloak from his arm and folding it in half. She put out a hand for his own gloves. "A pity that you did not wear a smock. I fear that your shirt shall be quite soiled. But this is what comes of too much impetuosity and too little reflection."

Niall studied her briefly and saw none of the earlier amused malice in her face. She was sincere in both her regret about his shirt and her sentiment on the nature of haste.

The unlooked-for kindness made Niall somewhat hopeful of their future partnership. He did not relish moving the cold, damp cairn stone by heavy stone, but it made him feel almost warm to realize that his cautious hostess was showing possible signs of thawing and trust by first leading him to the treasure, and then by saving his apparel from certain ruin. Surely such a gesture was not caused by mere housewifely thriftiness!

No, either she was blessed with a kind heart that looked favorably upon him . . .

Or, said the sensible part of his mind, *she is insane and planning to pick up the crow and dash my brains out after I have opened a convenient grave—and having an aversion to doing laundry, she doesn't want to*

Iona

ruin either my cape or gloves by getting unnecessary blood upon them.

Niall frowned at the thought and began hoping that it was the former emotion that moved her, since it would make any subsequent dealings difficult if she attempted to murder him here in the barrow. A fey maid with steady nerves was one thing, but marriage to a murdering mad woman was absolutely out of the question. Lona simply could not be so alienated from her senses, or so hostile to the MacKay name. It would ruin everything he had begun to plan for them.

Still, Niall was well versed in matters of violence and deception, and prepared himself for the latter eventuality by facing his hostess at all times, and keeping a weathered eye on her idle, steady hands.

Impetuous he might be, and careless of his clothing, but he was not reckless of his life.

They returned to the warmth of the kitchen two hours later to find that Cook had resumed her accustomed place at the fire and was busy preparing barley cakes.

Niall turned rueful eyes in Lona's direction and she murmured: "Bannocks are better than no bread at all."

"A bannock is a guid beast," said Cook firmly, proving she could hear just fine and her sudden deafness was only brought on by bad manners. "And ye may eat the guts even on Friday."

"We have them on other days as well," Lona said, taking off her damp cloak and hanging it near the fire. "Flesh is scarce here and rarely in the pot. Would you care for a wee dram to warm your cockles, guest Niall MacKay? By now you must be perishing from cold."

97

"Many thanks, mistress. A very small one. Your whisky is near poison to me, I fear. Until yestermorn I had thought myself to have possessed a hard head."

"'A horn spoon holds nae poison.' 'Tis only lairds who worry," Cook commented disrespectfully, but Niall was amused rather than insulted by her sharp tongue. His mood had improved considerably since Lona had made no effort to murder him, but had instead held the lantern and sung gay, silly songs to while away the time during which he labored. It was also fact that the fire, though quite smoky, was very pleasant to his chilled bones.

"Am I so humble then? Very well! A dram and a bite's but small requite for using a horn spoon." He also sometimes practiced the deceptive art of lowland yokeldom.

Lona made a *tsk*ing noise and frowned at Cook in vexation. The old harridan sniffed delicately and turned to the fire, deliberately putting her bulk between them and its warmth. The gray cat was nowhere to be seen. Perhaps it was tending to the chore of catching mice.

"Did yer mither never tell ye tae never speak ill of them whose bread ye eat?" Cook muttered piously. "But 'tis always fiddler's dogs an' fleas that come tae feast uncalled."

Niall opened his mouth to answer back in kind, but Lona overspoke him before he could demand if Cook was calling them uninvited guests or blow-flies.

"'And are ye not a bonny pair?' said devil to his hooves. Shame on both of you," Lona chastised. "Cook, you'll be civil to our guest and offer our hospitality without backtalk. Besides, it's sorrow and ill weather that come uncalled—"

Iona

"Not on Tiree." Cook interjected, returning to one of her favorite complaints. Some days Lona wished that she would make good on her threats and leave Iona.

"In any case, there are no dogs on the island." Lona's frown reproached, but Cook seemed completely unaffected by the stern glance.

"There are blow-flies aplenty, and midges," Niall muttered under his breath. "And you, mistress, already called me a devil, which is worse, I think."

"What blather! Hard words winna make this pot boil," Cook said truculently, proving absolutely that her ears were more than fine. They had to be keen, indeed, to have heard that utterance.

Niall watched as she carefully turned the cakes before they burned. She wouldn't ruin a meal to make a point about greedy layabouts.

"I'd rather be yer Bible than yer tongue, ye old haggis," Niall countered, now thoroughly enjoying himself as they shared some mutual spleen before the fire. There was nothing like a verbal tussle to warm a frozen hide. "Ye greatly overwork the latter by shaking it like a lamb's tail."

"Niall!"

"I crave pardon, Mistress."

"Yer mind's away chasin' mice," she answered, affronted, as if his words were untrue. "Ye've come to fetch fire—frae our puir hearth, more shame to ye and all MacKays."

"*Cuiridh peirceall—*" he began ruthlessly, lapsing into the old tongue, which had more imaginative curses.

"Niall MacKay! Mind your manners. There is no point in asking pardon if you commit the same sin again." Lona's voice was as stern as any mother's at

Melanie Jackson

kirk on the Sabbath. "Give me your cloak and remove your hat. Not another rude word from either of you—or you'll be sent out to tend sheep without any meal at all."

Both Cook and Niall turned to stare at her, and Lona could feel her cheeks grow warm. The rude combatants were working to contain their smiles at her scolding but succeeding poorly which, she supposed, was understandable, both of them being older and larger than she.

"Give a purse to a lass and she gets breeches in the bargain," Cook said wisely to her foe. "Such a shame."

"But the breeches fit no' so ill on her," Niall answered agreeably. "And she's a thrifty good wife for all of wearing a man's breeches beneath her girtle."

"Aye. The willful lass must have her way—but nae guid'll come of it," Cook prophesied as Lona turned on her heel and marched from the room in a rare show of high dudgeon.

"And it's a daft man wha' says otherwise," Cook warned as Niall chuckled at the retreating figure. She raised her voice and added: "For he'll take tae wife a shrew an he allows it tae long!"

"Have you a toom pantry then? Is your mistress thriftless?" Niall asked, at last removing his hat and cloak and returning to the table.

Cook stared hard at his soiled shirt, but made no direct comment.

"Nay," she answered after a moment, pulling her cakes from the fire and setting them on a platter. Niall thought they smelled delicious. His appetite had been stoked by his labors.

"We have guid care at the mistress's hands. She's

Iona

nae fool. We do prosperously well wi' our wool and whisky, an' there's food aplenty even aen the winter. We get our guid pennysworth frae the Lowlanders come tradin' time. But it's ill for a' that—and nae help was that spunky she wed—neither of them," Cook scolded. "How came ye by such kin?"

"I ken not. Donnell was a true Christiecleet," he admitted, referring to a much-feared bogie used to scare children. The real Christie had been a man of good family but he had still resorted to cannibalism whenever food was scarce, searching the streets with his long hook as he looked for lonely prey. He thought it an excellent description of his cousin, Donnell.

"Some are born like the cat wi' a taste fer fish but nae wanting tae get their feet wet like honest men," Cook said philosophically.

"That was Donnell. He was put out of the oven at an early age for nippin' pies, and he's cut many long lengths off others' leather since. He was his mother's joy and despair. She tried later to be firm with him, but it was a useless endeavor."

"Many a woman gaes running for the spurtle after the pot's boiling over—much guid it does them then, puir souls." The sound of sweet sympathy on Cook's thin lips was an amusing aberration.

"Aye." Since Cook was in a softer humor, Niall changed the subject to something more important; his empty stomach. "They have need of a canny cook that have but an egg for their dinner."

"And ye would wheedle the honey frae the bees, such charming manners ye hae." Cook reached for a small pot and poured out a generous measure of honey.

"Aye, and it's very repentant I am for my wicked

ways!" Niall answered, watching the dark amber pour over the bannocks in a delicious, golden gilding.

Cook chuckled and then rewarded his compliments with the heaped plate of steaming cakes, and the offer of the large chair nearest the hearth. She then pulled up a stool of her own and settled her bulk upon it with many twitches to her numerous shawls.

"Mistress may have a brave heart but she is still only a wee lassie. She cannae gae on carryin' the burthen alone," Cook said this without looking up.

"I ken," Niall answered, perfectly sincere, for he knew better than anyone else that Iona's mistress would not be able to carry on after the English came.

"What's to do? The devil's aen it an' no mistake."

"I am laboring on this difficulty." For once, he meant it in more than the metaphorical sense.

Cook smiled at him, her expression at once benign and grandmotherly. It made Niall pause for a moment as he considered its possible significance. A lesser man would be terrified by the sudden sweetness.

"Then all shall be passing fair. Some more honey wi' yer cakes?" she asked politely. "We have gran honey frae our own bees."

"Aye. Many thanks." He resumed eating but with slightly less enthusiasm.

"Ye'll give me yer vestments for washing. They'll be pure as angels' wings afore the dawn, and naebody the wiser for what ye've been at in those nasty caves. 'Tis best tae disrobe if ye be inclined tae go there often."

Niall blinked, wondering what the cook imagined they had been up to in the dank barrow. He doubted

Iona

that she had guessed the truth, but could hardly believe the other imputation that sprang to mind. Surely one could find a better place to dandle a lass than in a wet cave. Had they no barns on the isle? No sheltered beds of heather where the local lads and lasses pursued their romances?

"Cook—"

"Dinna worry! Mistress nae longer wears the hair. It's married she was, and twice. Ye'r nae despoiling a virgin. Not that I hold wi' hand-fasting," she warned, still smiling with that terrifying benevolence. "We mayn't be dour Calvinists but we are not godless heathens in these isles! So see ye do right by my mistress."

"Cook," he said a second time, but his auditor was not attending to admonitions.

"Aye?"

"It's not as you think," he said firmly.

"Nae? Then how is it? If yer nae trystin' why were ye in the caves for nigh on two hours?" Her benevolent veneer was cracking.

Niall couldn't think of a reasonable answer, so he just glared as Cook fetched herself another wee dram to fend off the cold and retreated to her stool in triumph. Forsooth, but the harridan's tongue was malicious! He concluded that too many meals in her presence could lead a man to chronic dyspepsia.

Bemused and indignant at Niall's behavior, Lona stabbed herself for a second time with her darning needle and tossed the mending aside. She was quite unable to explain her warm reaction to this new MacKay and the strength of the attraction was beginning to alarm her.

She stared into her empty hearth, unaware of the

cold that had invaded her bedchamber while she silently brooded on this question.

It was not his face that appealed so. His features were pleasant but not truly remarkable—except for his smile, which was charm incarnate, she had to admit—but as for his foppish air . . . She didn't allow herself to be deceived by it. This posture of amused languor was carefully cultivated to seduce the unwary. She had seen his true face a time or two, and watched him shift heavy stone with great will and enthusiasm for the better part of an hour without breaking a sweat. No one that well-muscled, -winded and -minded spent all his time languishing in the royal courts of Europe practicing dancing and manners.

She put her chin in the hand that was conveniently at the end of the arm she had propped on her knee, and ignoring the tiny pain in her fingers, she dwelled for a moment on the handsome image of Niall decked in velvet and dancing a gavotte, something that was utterly frowned upon in Puritan Scotland these days. But that thought was not helping her remain stern and resolved, so she then returned her wayward brain to the more fruitful task of enumerating her guest's faults—which were probably legion, she told herself.

Once one peered under the cloak of his disguise and considered Niall MacKay's true state, it seemed downright immoral that, even knowing about his deliberate deceptions, he was still half-able to persuade her that he had no purpose in coming to her isle other than to act the knight errant, rescuing her from vile English machinations and gallantly taking the horrid treasure to the exiled prince.

But she was wiser than that and knew that she

must not be taken in by his buffoonery! Nor amused by it!

Lona sighed and straightened. This resolve was all very well, but it did not seem to be hardening her heart against the thaw that had begun around its edges. And just what she was to do with him or these unwanted, ill-timed fits of fascination she simply did not know; but it seemed almost certain that nothing good could come of them.

In her wildest imaginings she could not see Niall MacKay making his home on her small, cold isle, taking a boat out fishing, tilling the small fields of barley or working in the distillery.

What she could see—and all too vividly—was sitting across from him at the table at night, sharing a meal by candlelight and laughing at his many jests and riddles, or walking hand-in-hand through the heathered hills on the long summer nights that blessed the isle with warm twilights. It was certain heartbreak that lay along the path she was considering, she scolded herself, as sure as the harsh winter would come again to her island. Such foolishness had to end at once!

Lona picked up her mending and began again. Almost immediately she pricked her thumb and dropped another bit of blood onto the linen. The cloth would likely be marked forever, she thought with an exasperated sigh, and so, too, would she. And it was all the fault of charming Niall MacKay who would soon be flitting on to some other foolish flower. It was his nature, no doubt, and destiny's grand plan. Would she deny him these pleasures even if she could?

"Aye, I would." Lona glared at her needle, disgusted at the lovelorn vein of her thoughts. They were bidding fair to become an obsession with her heart. "I must cease this useless musing."

And replace it with what? Wasn't this distraction better than the emptiness of before? Then, strain had dulled her senses and made her think that death was better than the torture of living. And did not Niall's presence in her mind mute the ghostly voices until they were just a distant murmur? She should be grateful that this practiced seducer was reawakening her to the distracting possibility of heartache.

"Gratitude be damned!" Her voice was warlike in the still room, and she was shocked to realize that it was jealousy of his other *inamorata*—past and future—that colored it.

"The faithless rogue." But it was not the familiar despondency she felt when she considered what was denied her. It was something hotter. In a fit of newborn temper, she tossed away her luckless needle. It landed near the hearth and tinkled with soft reproach.

"I vow that I care not what he does!" she told it, knowing that her words were not even within striking distance of the truth.

She dropped her head into her hands and strove for mental order. There were seven disciplines that made up the liberal arts and she had learned them all to varying degrees. Her family had always favored colorful rhetoric to carry the day, and she, quiet logic.

Niall was a practitioner of some talent and used both equally well. She lacked the formality and training of a university education, and she knew she would need to apply herself to the task of staying

Iona

one step ahead of both her guest and her awakening emotions.

Lona rose. She would take up the stitchery again when she was feeling less erratic. For now, she would pursue a more physical activity.

Chapter Four

Niall met Lona's sensible herder, Callum, that same wet afternoon when he went for a constitutional clamber over to the most westerly point of the island. He soon discovered that it was not a part of the isle designed for sauntering—constitutionally or otherwise. In fact, walking there held a positive risk to limb and life, and did nothing aid in his digestion of Cook's thick bannocks.

His aggrieved hostess had been quite understandably surprised when, after his meal, he had announced a sudden desire to go out into the continuing drizzle and tend sheep, but thanks to Cook's ubiquitous presence, Lona had been unable to question him at any length about his true purposes for venturing out again into the cold and damp.

Not that he would escape inquisition indefinitely!

Iona

Lona's fine gray eyes had promised that she would be seeking his company at a more convenient time so that he could explain his erratic comings and goings. And he supposed that he would even be truthful about his plans because—*and what an odd thing to begin doing at this age in my life, telling the truth, forsooth!*—it was time to take her more fully into his confidence.

But first, there were a few things he needed to discover about the isle, for if there was a secondary place of escape, it would somewhat alter his plans—for the better. The one plot he had would not inspire any but an idiot to faith, and he would prefer that Lona MacLean go on believing him confident, intelligent and omniscient. For how difficult it was to woo a maid if she thought her potential suitor was dull-witted or suicidal!

Niall also wished to discover if there was a possible confederate on the isle. Another conspirator, one with a boat for instance, would be a fortuitous find now that he knew for certain that the hounds were closing in. And if that conspirator also happened to be Hector's faithful and resourceful Callum Bethume, so much the better for all of them.

But so far, there had not been a great deal to see along the western promontory beyond more stone—a great deal more stone, gone far too many centuries without the amelioration of any true vegetative cover—and more of the devil sea and moaning wind. Of the loyal Callum, or any other hardy soul, there was no sign.

Niall, whose main desire had been to discover if there was a secondary port of safe landing before he broke his head or ankle, instead found himself distracted by the devilish wind, listening closely among the crevasses whenever he paused to catch his breath.

It was an excellent place for a ghost to hide among the trailings of the monks' many excavations, but it still proved a futile attempt on his part to find where the ghostly whispers originated. Beyond ascertaining that at low tide there was a causeway of sorts composed of giant but much-shattered stones, with dangerous gaps betwixt them where the wind could howl quite effectively in the fosse and where the sea quickly turned and struck back with drowning force, he found it to be a pointless task; one every bit the futile exercise that searching for a second safe port had been. He found no ghostly specter, and unless there was some other path of egress through the giant stone litter, this route across the causeway would be near fatal after nightfall.

The danger was in large part due to the fact that the northwest faces of the sea stones had cracked into countless fissures of various depths under the onslaught of the winter storms that had battered it since the creation. The many, *many* openings that faced the sea were covered over, he discovered quite by accident, with scant bandages of gold and gray lichens and slippery seaweeds which, though gay in color, did little to make secure the fresh earth wounds in the scree, and did a great deal to obscure the old, dangerous scars where some unfortunates, either sheep or men, had likely plummeted to almost certain death among rocks and sea, and then been buried under the loosened scrap stone in a natural bier.

The southeast sides of the boulders were little bet-

Iona

ter, for the many fractures—both new and shallow, and ancient clefts plunging like arrows straight to the stone's cold heart—were buried under a tenacious, stringy moss composed of slippery, conjoined strands that had sewn themselves together in a crazy, concealing quilt through which a careless foot might pass, and the eerie wind could moan unhampered.

"*Gabh eolas Rudh-a-bhaird air.* . . . I couldn't discourage trespass any better had I planned it myself," Niall muttered, falling unknowingly into the habit of the Iona islanders by speaking directly to the ghosts who walked among them. He was watching the moss curtain heave like a forge bellows, in and out with each ghastly, moaning breath of the waves in the causeway. The opening beyond was, fortunately, too small to explore.

Annoyed at the frivolous waste of time, and by then quite damp with drizzle and sea-spray, Niall straightened resolutely and turned back toward the deepening sound with an eye toward the fate of the re-submerging causeway. The uneven stepping stones were briefly exposed during the low tide, and it was from there that the fishermen threw their hemp nets. As a possible point of *rendezvous* it left a great deal to be desired, being both slippery and exposed only twice in a twenty-four hour period, and—as Lona had pointed out—there was no dry crown upon Iona's treacherous causeway.

The boulder path was also near the flensing shed, a very serious drawback as far as Niall was concerned. Even at fifty paces it gave off a disabling smell; an *abattoir* of the sea's dead. But deficiency of pleasant attributes or not, it could well end up being their route of escape if the English came to hunt on Iona without warning. He should make an effort to be grateful for these—though very small—favors.

It was only as he turned from the half-submerged stone steps, handkerchief to nose, that he caught sight of the herder standing a few paces away. Either Niall had carelessly overlooked him some moments before, or the islander had the tread of a hunting cat.

To the average eye, the old man would be an anonymous person, just one of the elderly sheep-watchers of the Highlands, propped up by a stone and staff as he guarded his flock, forgettable—except for one over-large ear that stuck out through his locks like a yard of tin. With his crude clothing that looked a great deal like mice had chewed upon it, and hanks of shaggy white hair that fell over his much-battered brow, he was a fair match for the island's woolly sheep that slumbered atop the flat rock crests and chewed its colored lichens with worn teeth.

It was a wonder that Niall ever recognized the herder as Callum, the stern and dignified soldier who had carried the fatal message to the Scot mission in Holland. It was this same old man who had called both the MacLeans and the MacKays to their diverse parts in the rebellion, when he'd told the delegation that the prince had raised his banner at Glenshiel and was calling Scots to arms. The Iona MacLeans had gone at Falkirk and their prince, and the MacKays—all but Niall—to England to warn George and sue for the best terms of surrender for their clan.

But Niall, being well-versed in the use of disguise, had an uncanny memory for the underlying struc-

Iona

ture of faces, and Callum's entrance into his life just when he had, had guaranteed that he was retained carefully with a few other visages of equal import. And so recognize him Niall did, in spite of the many cruel changes to both his countenance and body. The last time he had seem Callum, the old man had still possessed a matching set of ears and all of his fingers; there had been no scars on his brow.

"And what an interesting coincidence that you should be here, loyal hound," Niall murmured to himself as a sudden breeze buffeted him, carrying his words away. "Perhaps God has shown mercy on his humble toiler."

Of course, he didn't mean anything of the sort. As he had thought earlier when Lona had mentioned the workings of fate, destiny was made by human intervention rather than accident more times than not. That and the fact that the Lord had shown no mercy to Iona so far.

In Callum's proximity he detected the presence of the deceased Hector's fell hand. The last of the MacLean Jacobite martyrs had had a positive genius for bringing disaster to those he loved while he labored to save his prince; it was too much to have hoped that either Callum or Lona would be spared involvement in the end.

The old soldier rather smelled like a sheep, too, Niall noticed, now that the wind changed direction to a course from due north. The joys of bathing were not entirely unknown in the Highlands but not much practiced outside the summer months, except by those who had a death wish, so Niall did not hold this fact against Callum. In truth, he was grateful that if he had to encounter someone he knew on the island, that the someone was a gallant, loyal soldier-turned-herder and not—which was just as likely—another nationless spy-turned-shark-fisherman.

Niall could endure the mild "eau de mutton" for the sake of a little practical help—as long as the wind stayed in the north and away from the flensing shed. He bravely pocketed his handkerchief and prepared to be polite.

Of course, it was probable that there would be more than that one piece of personal unpleasantness to be dealt with before Hector's faithful hound would consent to aid another named MacKay. Understandable though the delay was, since it had probably been Donnell who named Callum Bethume as a conspirator in the treasonous plot as well as killing his master, Niall would rather have been spared the next few moments of time.

But that was not fate's plan for him, and Callum's anger would have to be gotten through as expeditiously as possible, even if it meant more half-truths, sins of omission, and outright lying.

Niall had made a death-bed promise to Karlmann Van de Graaf that he would do everything he could to avert further slaughter in the Highlands, and thereby prevent the spread of religious persecution through the Netherlands. There was also the fact, should he need further goading, that those on Iona were not blessed with an abundance of time in which to indulge in the usual nipping and scarting. Niall feared that the day the seas calmed to even moderate levels, the English would be upon them in force.

"Guid day tae ye," Callum said politely, not bothering to turn his head away from the sea after a first, hard glance at the stranger.

It caused Niall to wonder if the entire branch of

Iona

the island MacLeans were an aberration. Manners for the enemy was not a common reaction among the quarrelsome Scots, and yet all of them, with the exception of Cook, had spoken very fair to him.

"Good day. It has been two years since I saw you last, Callum Bethume. I see you've returned to your mother's people. How fare you these days?"

Callum turned quickly and cocked his one ear forward. He squinted at Niall as though searching his faltering memory for an unfamiliar face. The herder had aged indecently in the last two years, but the air of senility was overdone in one still so spry. Callum's ear had been struck off but not his wits.

And not his courage, or so Niall hoped.

"Come, come," Niall said, with a touch of impatience before remembering how altered his own appearance was from his days in Holland when he'd been masquerading as a French Norman. "No need for the hesitation. I realize that it's hard to sort out friend from foe, but I assure you that I am here on the prince's business . . . whatever I may have been thought to have been doing in Holland back in '45."

Callum did not seem to believe his quick reassurances, and the old man's expression grew dubious instead of forgetful with the introduction of the subject of Holland in 'forty-five.

Niall sighed, assumed an air, and swept off his hat as he made a graceful leg. *"Bonjour, M'sieur. Attendez-moi."*

A count of five was needed for Callum's imagination to replace Niall's missing mustache and supply a black wig, then recognition dawned over the craggy face as the soldier finally placed Niall as a member of a Catholic, Norman delegation to the Hague.

Melanie Jackson

"Ye may hae a guid memory but ye have puir judgement in comin' here if ye are who I ken ye tae be."

"Aye? But then I had little choice in the matter. My cousin—your late and unlamented landlord—was extremely careless with some important information and I am afraid that the Sasannachs are aware that Hector left something valuable here on the island."

Callum's expression grew black as he stared at Niall. Comprehension was written large on the open face, confirming Niall's guess that not everyone on Iona was unaware of Hector's patriotic folly.

"Yer cousin! Ye, a MacKay! But yer name was Flambard—" The gnarled hands tightened on his crook.

"Only in Holland. Here, I am—*alas!*—a MacKay. Unless I've gone reaving," Niall added conscientiously, fastening a weathered eye on the flexing fingers that held the stout staff. There were only seven of them, but they looked quite strong. "Then I choose another name. You weren't thinking of striking me with that thing, were you? It wouldn't be wise."

Callum's wasn't listening to Niall anymore. His face flushed to an angry crimson and he abandoned his ploy of forgetfulness in favor of telling Niall his opinions of Donnell's character and morals. As the herder had enjoyed a varied career as a soldier and had traveled widely, Callum had a variety of languages to call upon when desirous of finding the perfect expression of displeasure. Niall was of the opinion that he didn't miss a single unflattering phrase as he unburdened his feelings about the departed Donnell and the other turncoat MacKays who had descended on Iona after Hector's demise.

Iona

Niall knew that he should call shame upon himself, for he understood every word of the fluent, foreign cursing and even rather enjoyed the comprehensive execration. There was no wrath like that to be found in an enraged Highlander with a taste for hard-drinking in the low company of many nations.

Niall leaned back against a boulder and allowed the tirade to continue unchecked for several long moments. Callum had also been at Culloden and had seen the merciless butchery there; indeed, that was most likely where he had left his missing ear and digits, since he had certainly had all of them in Holland. With such fuel for the fires of hate, it was not surprising that the old man held such heated ill will toward the MacKays, and it seemed best to allow him a free reign of expression before requesting his help. It was the unlanced boil that festered and turned gangrenous. Best to get over this patch of rough ground speedily so that Callum's thoughts hereafter could be devoted to the task of achieving salvation for the isle.

"Aye," Niall interrupted at last, sensing the tirade was running down. Eventually, even a Highlander needed to pause for breath. "I agree completely. Donnell should have been hanged at birth, but my poor aunt is a silly creature and sadly lacking in foresight."

Callum considered Niall's statement, staring at him with a fulminating eye, then said more moderately: "Aye . . . well, some women have these daft fancies for their bairns."

Niall's lips twitched and a great deal of the wrath died in the old man's face as he heard the ridiculous comment with his own large ear.

Melanie Jackson

"So they do. I can't at all imagine why," Niall answered at Flambard's languid best, and was rewarded with a small gleam of amusement in Callum's sharp eyes. Niall's sense of humor was a character flaw among Scots, but it had never proved a detriment to him among any acquaintances other than his patriarchal clan.

"Cha'n ann de mo chuideachd—and yer none of yer cousin's kind. So what wind blew ye here, Flambard or MacKay—or whoever ye be?" the old man asked, as the last of his anger died away. Curiosity replaced suspicion.

Is the whole island blessed with second sight? Niall wondered.

"The same Stuart wind that blew you here has blown me thither and yon these six months past, and now it has blown me hither as well. And very tired of this Stuart wind I am, too." Niall looked up as the sky again began to turn from drizzle to rain. "Another storm? Tell me, does it always rain on this cursed isle?"

"Storm? This is nae but a small squall. Still, best ye step indoors and hae a wee dram tae keep out the cold. A bit of the *uisage beatha* will put a streak of spirit in ye." The herder turned away and began to pick a path over the loose shale. His trudging steps looked weary but he covered a great deal of ground in very little time.

"Excellent notion," Niall approved as he replaced his hat and started after Callum.

It seemed that once again he was to be accepted without further questioning. He made a note to mention, the next time he was on his knees and saying one of his infrequent prayers, that he was truly grateful for the Iona islanders' quick comprehen-

Iona

sion and shrewd judgement of character. Not every man or woman would believe his intent to be pure, but both Callum and Lona had accepted him without a demand for additional—and nearly impossible to supply—proof of good will.

Niall paused and glanced about to see if they were being observed by anyone, and then began a slow stroll toward a pile of rocks Callum called home. It was different from its neighbors only in that it was more or less formed with four distinct sides and had a thick thatch beneath the lichens, and, Niall could finally see, a small curl of gray peat smoke climbing toward a like-colored sky. He had overlooked it completely in his desire to stay away from the shark rot and suspected that Callum had intended it that way.

There was one stone that caught Niall's eye. It was weathered as the others but showed signs of carving, and had a small hole drilled through its center. He had seen such carvings in Ireland. They were holy stones and the finger-sized holes were where the early Gaels would stuff their digits while swearing out pacts and vows.

Callum waited politely until Niall had joined him before pulling back an old, stained pelt that served as a door. They stepped, one at a time, into a cleft that reminded Niall of the barrow where he and Lona had spent the morning, though the cave cottage was altogether more pleasant, being drier and having no disconcerting wind that moaned among its stones. It was not an elegant abode by any standard of measure, the roof was too low for comfort in a tall man, and it possessed many shadowed, dampish corners where toadstools and other fungus might grow unhampered.

Still, it had the basic creature comforts; a shallow inglenook stacked with bricks of peat, a small table, two stools, and a narrow cot laid with two thick blankets and another pelt. Cobbled out of the monastery's stones, the walls looked as old as the Pictish tombs, and as solid. Niall had seen many fortresses not half so well defended.

"I don't suppose that you would care to hasten our meeting of minds along and admit that you are aware of the contents of the casket that Hector left here on the island," Niall inquired of his host. Callum glanced his way with an inquisitive eye but said nothing, so Niall explained: "I cannot help but feel that it wasn't chance alone that brought you here. In fact, I'd wager a packet that it was not. Your father participated with the MacLeans in the uprising of '15 and the Bethumes were ever loyal to the cause of the Stuart princes."

"Nay. Ye have the right of it. 'Twas Hector that brought me here. Mind'ee, he told me nothing certain . . . but I feared it must be here that he hid the treasure. In a sherry cask is it?"

"Ah!"

"Ah, nithing! Look'ee, I dinna return to Iona 'til the autumn past and Hector was then long dead. I thought tae ask Lona about the treasure, but yer cousin was lost soon after and I let the question gae by." Callum's voice was heavy and accented now that the rage had left him. "I kept my mouth shut and my eyes open and my thumb on it, but in truth, I kenned not what tae do. Naebody kens where the prince may be nor where tae search."

The last sentence was an unnecessary reassurance that Callum was not seeking the treasure for personal gain. Niall hadn't thought that he was. The

Iona

Iona MacLeans had proved their loyalty to a man, and they had a sizable portion of graveyard acreage to prove it.

Callum pulled up a rude stool to the fireside and offered it to his guest. He went to fetch a modest helping of the "water of life" from a tiny barrel in the corner and then returned to the warmth of the hearth bearing the cup of good cheer.

"Understandable. Hector's trove is damning enough to take all of you to the gallows of Creiff," Niall said, eyeing the small cask that was almost identical to the one he had exhumed.

"Aye." The old man looked up and smiled sourly. "They must an they wish tae hang us, there being nae trees of guid size aen the isle an' the keep's walls too ill built tae hold up all the sad sinners hereabouts did they sling us o'er the side."

Callum pulled up a second stool and offered Niall the cup. The herder's dram was less generous than Cook's, but Niall admitted that it was just as well that Callum used a parsimonious hand. He already had consumed a dangerous amount of whisky over bannocks and still had a long walk through loose shale back to the keep.

"I fear," Niall began at last when Callum showed no sign of speaking again, "that we may be in some difficulties if we do not remove Hector's treasure at once."

"Aye, difficulties," was the reply to Niall's gross understatement of their problem. "I ken."

"It was no exaggeration of mine when I said that the Sasannachs would come, and soon. Truly, it would be best for everyone here if the treasure was taken to the Continent and briefly displayed in a public manner. Done correctly, it would offer a use-

121

ful, if temporary diversion from your island. It might even help the prince escape by drawing attention abroad."

"That is so." Callum swallowed bravely and smacked his lips. "And how do we gae aboot dragging this herring across the Sasannachs' tracks and leading them astray? It seems a matter o' running for the spurtle after the pot's boiled over."

"We drag with great care if we wish to fool the hounds," Niall said bluntly. "The first step is to send a messenger to France. We must have a French ship for transport and I have one laid on—I hope. She's a small sloop belonging to a *Capitaine* Lestan LaCroix."

"Aye?" Callum was dubious. Like most Scots, he had no liking for foreigners, even Scotland's traditional French allies.

"Aye, of course. The Dutch will not aid us against their ally and the navy will stop any vessel of the Scots."

"That they would," Callum conceded, "did they see one. But think ye, would they see us did we gae at night?"

"Aye. We might be able to leave Iona unmolested but they'll be watching the ports of entry. Remember, Charles is still free. Every ship will be examined by the navy or coast guard before being allowed to pass on into England or France. And any that don't put to will be fired upon, you may be sure."

"Well then, how can a French ship come here? They'll be watching Iona for certain."

"Not from the north," Niall said firmly. "They'll have seen how bad the waters are, and without knowing about the causeway they'll give it up as hopeless and watch from the east and west. The

Iona

Captain'll just have to lay off coast until we get a boat out to him. For that—and to run a message—we need a boat and a boatman from another isle. A good one who is not suspected. I was thinking of the man who brought me here, if he can be trusted to keep a still tongue. No one would be suspicious of a small boat coming to or from Tiree, and from there it may be that he can leave undetected."

"Aye." Callum considered. "Auld Gavin must gae. He's nae love fer the Sasannach and he was born tae the sea. Gavin would dare to bell the cat for a guid cause."

"Did he fight for the prince?"

"Nay," Callum rolled his eyes heavenward as he lied. "His laird, young Duncan's father, forbade it. Gavin was traveling on matters o' business when the battle broke out. It was misfortune that he was in Falkirk when battle began and greatly delayed in his return."

Niall smiled slightly and asked nothing more about Gavin's activities during the rebellion. His own had been less than pristine on occasion, and some completely nefarious. Niall could only applaud the use of sensible caution of silence in this matter. It would not do to enter into a conspiracy with men who had loose tongues.

"And what shall pass after? Do we send round the fiery cross?" Callum asked. "For three failures and a fire make a Scotsman's fortune. Others would come to our aid."

"No. No fiery cross. No fiery peat. We've had our three failures and enough misfortune. We won't drag anyone else into this nasty net."

"What then?"

Niall looked at Callum consideringly and then

decided to answer with the truth. If he kept at it long enough, perhaps the new-sought gift of veracious speech would come naturally to him.

"Have you ever thought of leaving Scotland?" Niall asked gently, not wishing to remind him of the defeat at Culloden and the MacKay's ignominy. "You have been named as a conspirator, you know. And they have long memories in the South."

"Leave? Ye mean go to the colonies?" Callum sounded thoughtful. It was not a new idea; many Scots had gone after the first uprising and again in 'forty-five. In chains and otherwise. "Where? Virginialand?"

"Actually, I was thinking more of the French colonies. New Orleans is nice, I hear." Niall didn't mention the rumor he had heard that the French king had sold the lands to Spain. It would needlessly muddy the waters of thought that swirled around them.

"The French!" Callum said in disgust. "But why?"

"It's warm there and I am weary of rain," Niall answered simply and sincerely. "And so, think on it a while. It may be that Iona is doomed—and the MacLeans with her—whatever course we take. It's best to stay two steps ahead of the hangman's gibbet."

"Aye." Callum's voice was ponderous, his shoulders slumped. "I ken and I've no desire to end on the gallows. But what's tae become of the puir lassie an I go? 'Tis her I fear for. Dae they ken that she hid the treasure aen the isle t'would be a cry of treason and the rope for her."

"Aye, that it would." They stared at one another. No further elaboration was needed. English vengeance was being meted out with a harsh hand

Iona

all over the Highlands, women not excepted. "You may leave Mistress MacLean to me. By one means or another, I'll see that she's safe."

"Set the wind in that quarter? We'll wet thumbs on that," Callum said solemnly, sealing their pact with a heavy swallow of whisky. He added with a fierceness that could not be mistaken for anything other than deadly earnest: "Ye take guid care o' the lassie, MacKay!"

It was an altogether different expression that softened Niall's unusually grim face.

"I shall. Never doubt it." And he would. Niall knew of no way to explain his sudden and overpowering attraction to Lona MacLean. It wasn't that she was pretty, for objectively speaking, he had seen lovelier women and not been smitten—and she was more strong-willed than bonnie anyway. Nor had she used any female wiles to attract him—far from it! She didn't even entirely trust him and wished him gone from her isle.

No, she was not at all in his usual style. For though not a Puritan, she was still a long way from being the hedonist he had become. And though he applauded her blood-curdling courage, such intrepid behavior with the English near to hand made him nearly faint of heart. Lona MacLean would be a most uncomfortable woman for a fribble such as Flambard to live with.

But she would be ideal for Niall MacKay when he went to begin a new and possibly dangerous life in the colonies of the Americas. There her gallantry would stand her in good stead, even if the worry turned his hair to snow while he was keeping abreast of her activities.

Niall felt Callum's deep scrutiny and realized that he was smiling. He shook off his pleasant speculations of the future in favor of returning to the matter at hand.

"What of the others?" Niall asked, staring into the embers and risking a small sip from his mug in honor of his promise. "Will they leave if they have to?"

"I dinna ken." Callum's voice was soft. " 'Tis just Gavin and I that fought with the prince. The rest of the lads that went tae soldier and the lassie's kin are dead, every one. Cook and the crofters may gae tae Tiree should they wish it. They'd be welcomed back tae the fold now that Hector and Wallace are buried."

"That is well," Niall said, much relieved that the islanders would not suffer for Lona's leaving them. "Mind, we may yet see a miracle but—"

"Boot *cha thainig ian glan riamh a' nead a' chlamhain.*" *A clean bird never came out of a kite's nest*, Callum finished. He drained the last of the whisky from his cup.

"Precisely. I fear the taint of treason may stick." Niall took a deep breath and tossed back the rest of his own dram. His eyes began to water but he managed not to disgrace himself with a cough.

"Well, we shall hae a wee search for *anail a' Ghaidheil—air a' mhullach.*" *The Gael's breathing place—on the summit*. Callum rose. "The rain shall pass about dawn. I'll be off tae Tiree with the sun and changing tide. Ye'll hae a letter for me tae take?"

"Aye. From Flambard." Niall rose. He was careful not to straighten completely as some of the rafters were rather low. "Callum?"

"Aye?" The old man picked up the crook in his

Iona

mangled hand and headed out the narrow door. He kept his ear turned in Niall's direction.

"Tell me true." Niall spoke slowly; his tongue had gone suddenly lame. "Do you believe that there are such things as ghosts? On Iona?"

The old man looked uncomfortable as he ushered his guest out into the rain. It was coming down in gray sheets and did nothing to improve the view.

"Well, mostly nae. Ghosts be mainly in the minds of the weak an' daft—wise men and Christians see nae devils. But. . . ."

"But you think that there are ghosts here?" Niall persisted.

"Aye." Callum looked sheepish as he wagged his head. "I canna say for the other places. I saw nae ghosts on Glencoe, though they should walk there. Mayhap because they were guid Christian martyrs wha died. But there be ghosts here on Iona. They are a very restless dead, an like a Lochaber axe when roused on stormy nights. I leave them be—and so should ye, MacKay, fer they've nae love fer the strangers wha come tae our isle."

"Who lives may learn," he muttered.

"Ye think tae tell the lassie that her ghosts are aen her mind?" Callum asked grimly. "She'll not be believing ye, MacKay."

"God forbid! 'Tis not for me for tell your mistress anything . . . yet."

Callum didn't ask him to explain his comment, which was just as well, as Niall supposed that it would be bad form to explain his intentions to anyone in advance of laying them before the island's canny mistress.

Chapter Five

Niall was not unduly startled when Iona's mistress was found to be standing in the middle of his stony path evidently planning to give him a personal escort back to the keep. Her posture was erect and he was sure that her expression under the deep brown hood was as stern as it knew how to be, but some faces simply did not bend themselves well into forbidding lines. *The Lord be praised*! He'd seen enough of soured and weary Scot countenances in the weeks just gone by.

"Good day to you, mistress." Niall looked up at the drizzling sky, then back down at the pink tipped nose that was hiding under the cape's shallow hood. It was to him a countenance wholly beautiful, but she seemed oblivious to cold and flattery alike. He amended: "Perhaps not such a good day. There was no need to come out in the rain. Content you, lass, I have not absconded with Callum's boat and I assure you that I shan't get lost on such a tiny isle."

"I have no fear of that, though it wouldn't be unexpected did Callum toss you into the sea. He is not at all fond of MacKays," she said mildly, eyeing his ungirdled shirt whose loose folds flapped gently when the wind parted his borrowed cloak.

He waited to see if curiosity would get the better of her, but she made no comment on his ruffled attire or the unseemliness of his form of address.

"What!" Niall feigned amazement. Callum's cup of cheer was burning in his veins. Or perhaps it was Mistress Lona's presence that warmed him top to toe. He couldn't tell for certain which lifted his spirits more. Hoping for a smile from her pretty lips, he went on to tease: "That charming, soft-spoken old man? Throw a lone, wandering MacKay into the sea! Never say so, m'dear."

Of course, had he not had his revealing little chat with Callum, he indeed would have suspected that that was how at least one MacKay had ended up in the sea.

Lona snorted at his words, an uneuphonious sound he was growing fond of, and fell into step beside him. The cliff path had widened considerably from the eyelash-wide trail at Callum's hovel, and he suspected that that was why his hostess had chosen it as her place to lie in wait. Stealthy pursuit would be impossible and dangerous anyplace else on the bare isle. It was also difficult to carry out an interrogation while marching single-file in a noisy stone ditch.

"By the bye, m'dear," Niall said, slowing his steps to a stroll and smiling down at her with a show of languid amusement he knew would exasperate her.

Iona

"My aunt wishes to know if you are with child and whether she might have it from you once it's born. You look quite slender to me but if you should happen to be breeding—"

"Niall MacKay!" Her enormous gray eyes turned his way. The pink mouth was held firmly down at the corners.

She was not annoyed then, just startled and disbelieving. He didn't blame her; the question went well beyond gall. But she was such fun to tease that he felt compelled to follow the course.

"You won't sell? Oh! No child to barter? Well then, that bit of business is settled. Perhaps she would be content with a goat to look after; they seem, bairns and animals, very much the same to me. I'll write my aunt this very afternoon. Callum can take the letter for me. Don't look so suspicious, lass. They're fremit friends that canna be fashed o'er sma things," he said, lapsing into broad Lowland speech.

"Och! Mind yer tongue!" But he'd seen the mouth begin to smile before the hood was pulled forward covering completely the evidence of such indulgence.

"They who dwell in glass houses shouldna throw stones," he pointed out righteously. "And mindee, 'tis said that they what have a guid Scot tongue in their head are fit tae rule over the world."

"Oh, aye? And what has the rest of the world to say to this notion, Sir Scot?"

"Why, they approve to a man!" he answered, abandoning the brogue. "Even my old employer said as much. Karlmann Van de Graaf often commented on the fact that where one Englishman or Frenchman might go to earn a fortune, you would find ten Scots were already there collecting up their pennies." Niall reached out a quick hand and guided Lona to the inside of the path. Watching her walk near the cliff's crumbling edge was spoiling his pleasurable digestion of Callum's fine whisky. "The shrewd ones put the coins into their purses and let them alone. It's a fact that Scot pennies breed prolifically if given privacy."

"That is quite enough about breeding," she said firmly. "What then are you saying? Do no lazy Scots go abroad? And are you also greatly laden with pennies?"

Niall clucked his tongue twice and wagged his head chidingly.

"Nay, pennies are heavy things in great numbers. And as for lazy Scots . . . "

Lona stared at him pointedly.

"They all stay home with the fools and cowards," he finished. "That is why I am quite surprised to find you still here." He caught her bare fingers and tucked her hand into the curve of his arm. The resistance in her limb was only very slight. He added outrageously: " 'Tis a pity that kissing was cried down with the shaking of hands. It has put an end to many a simple courtesy and extremely pleasant manner of showing affection."

"Simple courtesy. . . . Aye." Lona was distracted from his first comment about her going abroad as she thought for a moment about her cousins on Tiree. As strict Covenanters, even mothers were forbidden from kissing their children. Niall had only been teasing her again, but she answered seriously: "There's been little joy in Scotland since Cromwell murdered the king."

"Aye, murdering King Charles was a dangerous precedent. 'Tis why I fear for the prince. These En-

Iona

glish have no fear of striking off royal heads. Nor is there likely to be any happiness for the Highlands 'til Tweed and Pausayl meet at Merlin's grave," Niall said, quoting an old proverb.

"It has happened once before," Lona suggested quietly, oddly moved by the slight trace of sorrow in Niall's gentle voice.

"Aye. Under James—and see where that road has led us. From one murdered king to another. We seem to raise them up like human sacrifices and water our battle grounds with their brave blood. Perhaps that is why the Lowlands grow such fruitful crops."

"Aye, the MacLeans, too, have watered the fields of the lands low and high. And MacGregors," she agreed, thinking of the Draconian measures that had been taken against Scotland's oldest clan. The MacGregors had the distinction of being the only clan that the English had tried to exterminate completely—until the Iona MacLeans. A sigh followed and then Lona changed the subject. "Who is this Van de Graaf you speak of with such affection?"

"My mentor," Niall said after a moment. "My employer—perhaps my savior. He found me at a time when I was young and wild, headed for Creiff or Tyburn—and then perdition, if my aunt is to be believed. I held him up one night."

"You *what?*"

"You heard me plain. I had taken to the high toby. Thievery. Reaving without the cattle—heavy, noisome things are cattle. A gentleman's purse, I'd found, was so much easier to carry than cattle or sheep and it seems to me that the principal is the same." Niall pretended not to notice Lona's gasp of horrified laughter, and went on cheerfully:

"Knocked me silly with his cane, he did. Then seeing that I was but a lad, and none too well fed at that, he took me up in his coach by force and kidnapped me away from Scotland to save me from a life of misdeeds. . . . He was a good, shrewd man—even if he wasn't a Scot."

Lona made note of the past tense and then said gently: "You speak of him as you would a father."

"I would that he had been so!"

"You . . . you were not fond of your own father?" she asked, feeling her way carefully in case he still felt grief for his dead parent.

Niall was touched; people did not usually see beyond the part of the social fribble he played so well and often that it was his second skin and soul, and therefore they did not consider him to have deep feelings for anything other than his clothes, gambling and gossip. The role was useful for a spy, but left one feeling quite alone and friendless when traveling abroad.

"Nay. There was not a great deal to be fond of. M'dad died when I was still a babe in arms. My mother took me south when I was five." Niall paused, realizing that he was actually giving a factual history about himself, something he had not done since Karlmann's catechism years ago. After his interrogation, Niall had been ordered to forget his past and concentrate on the morrow and all the days thereafter. Normally such truthful confidences would have made him uneasy, but no such constraint troubled him on this wet afternoon as he paced over the loose stone path with Mistress Lona's hand tucked under his arm. The goddess of unreason was controlling the flux of events; he did not protest but moved where she listed.

Iona

"And your mother? What happened then?"

"I went to school for the first time and found I had a taste for it. When she died, I left university and went back north—rather like Jonah being cast forth from the belly of the whale," he added irrepressibly. "But I was not welcomed by any but my aunt, and she was too greatly taken with her own son to spare much thought for a strange nephew. My only use to them was as a thief. So I left again and took my thievery south where the hazard of my person paid better."

"Donnell was her son?" Lona asked quietly, squeezing his arm in unconscious sympathy. Then added in a distracted voice: "Poor lady. She certainly had a hard bargain there—her son asotted of treasure and bosomed up with malice. Gad! You are worth a hundred score of that heartless bast—um, well, poor soul."

"Donnell was indeed a bad bargain." Niall's lips twitched, but he made no comment on her near slip of tongue. "Poor soul, indeed! She loved him for all of his faults. And that, Mistress Curiosity, is why I went willingly with Karlmann. I grew tired of reaving and the coldness of my kin, and Karlmann's kidnapping gave me another choice of occupation and identity. That is also why I plan to go abroad in the future. I shall do what I reasonably may to put an end to the insanity of these persecutions, but then Niall MacKay is off to warmer, healthier climes where I shall not be troubled with the sounds of strife."

It is a warning, she thought. *Pay heed to it*.

"Where will you go?" The curious question was asked reluctantly. She felt rather like a Puritan observing some fascinating but sinful act from which she could not avert her eyes. Travel for her was simply not to be thought of. The few remaining Iona MacLeans owned her body and soul for the debts of her father and brother. But still, her heart lusted after the forbidden fruit he spoke of so casually.

Niall watched her face and wondered: Did Satan feel as he did every time he tempted an innocent with his heart's secret desires? It would explain his predilection for such activities, for he found the struggle of emotions playing on her face to be quite amusing to watch.

"America. The French colonies—or perhaps the Spanish colonies by now. There was much talk of the king selling them to Spain. No matter. My good Scot tongue serves me well in either language," he finished cheerfully. "And there are plenty of berths on my ship, for any who want to go along. Like Callum, for instance. I think that you must be mistaken about him disliking MacKays."

" 'Twill be a hard life for a while, I imagine," she said, still reluctantly fascinated with the forbidden subject, and growing skilled at ignoring his extraneous comments which, though unseemly, did no harm. "Still, life in the Highlands will have prepared you for difficulties."

Niall decided to dangle a little larger bait in front of his tempted trout to see if she would rise to it.

"Mayhap. But I don't go to my new life as a landless pauper, mistress."

"Nay?" she asked with some surprise. "I thought you feared the weight of all those pennies breeding in your purse. And even an inventive man like yourself cannot take his homeland with him."

"Don't be to certain of that, Mistress. I breed big-

Iona

ger things than pennies. Van de Graaf was, as you say, very much a father to me. We did very well in business, both in Europe and the new world."

"And you helped him? As a partner?"

"As a son, more like. And as his only child, he left it all to me. Niall MacKay, m'dear, is a man of means. It's silver I carry these days." He stopped in the middle of shallow puddle to strike a listening pose as he held up his rather bedraggled sporran to his left ear. "I breed gold and gems and land. A lovely sound it is, too."

Lona made no comment on his further use of an inappropriate endearment, but instead allowed herself to grin at him without her usual restraint. It was impossible not to respond to such buffoonery.

"All in that wee pouch? And here I was, concerned that you coveted my barren rocks and sheep! How foolish I feel."

Niall looked down at the happy face. For the moment, there were no shadows in her magnificent eyes and he saw the woman she would have been had life treated her more kindly. The woman she would be again, if he had any say in Lona MacLean's future.

"You don't look at all foolish. In fact—well, let us say that you would bring a smile to a plaster statue . . . on Sunday . . . in a kirk."

"You, sir, have not been to our kirk. 'Tis so stern that it has frightened the angels away. Not that such frivolous creatures are missed!" Then Lona laughed freely for the first time within his hearing, and the sound was the sweetest music to his newly awakening heart. It carried him so far away from the present place that he forgot about the water seeping into his much abused boots and slipping beneath his unlaced collar.

So distracted was he that his right hand had actually begun to reach for the object of his desire before he was called back to his senses by a gust of particularly cold wind that unsettled his hat.

He rooted his headgear with a hasty hand and then started to lower his arm, but was stopped when Lona took his fingers and raised it once again. She pointed to his sleeve. The lace at the cuff was muddied a distinctive red that came from granite and torn in two places, besides.

"That will need mending and laundering," she scolded. "And you are very fortunate if that is all you have mutilated. Iona is quite dangerous during the rains when there is no grass on the hills. I shall have to see if Cook has a darning needle. I've misplaced my own—" She stopped scolding suddenly and chuckled again.

"And so? This is amusing?" Niall demanded in a plaintive voice, again enchanted by her happiness and willing to play the fool if it earned him another smile. "First I compliment you and you laugh at my praise. Then you see my finest linens are ruined and you laugh some more! 'Tis heartless of you, mistress."

" 'Tis not that. I was just remembering the last time I needed a needle from Cook. It was for Donnell. He had fallen on a path and split his head."

An eyebrow went up. "I am slow today, mistress. I still see no cause for hilarity in the spillage of human gore."

"Ah, well . . . It was not the injury, you see, but Cook. When she heard it was for Donnell, she sent all the way to Iain's cottage to fetch the needle he uses for mending the sailing sheets, claiming that her own had gone astray." Another giggle was barely

Iona

suppressed. "I've seen ribs out of sea gulls that were smaller. Donnell took one look at the needle and went off in a faint."

"Hen-hearted fellow! Imagine that," he said dryly. "I can't think of anything I'd like more than Cook sewing me up with a gull's rib."

"Well, you needn't pull such a face!" Lona said indignantly. "I didn't let her use it. There wasn't any point after he'd fainted," she added under her breath.

Niall laughed too, and resumed walking. The keep was again in sight and looked almost welcoming where the windows shone through the late gloom with a warm, golden light. He was sure he felt this sense of welcome only because Lona MacLean walked at his side.

"And now that you've had a laugh at my expense—" Lona began.

"I rather think it was at Donnell's," he said judiciously.

"—You should be in the proper mood to tell me what you were doing at Callum's cottage."

"Who said that I was at Callum's cottage?"

"No one. But Callum's cottage is all that there is on that side of the island."

"Was I to know this?" he demanded piously. "Aside from that fact, that isn't strictly the truth, you know. There are a great many caves there. I tumbled into several of them, and not always willingly either!"

"Aye? Tumbled, did you? Ah, well! There is also the flensing shed. And what have you been doing these last three hours and more? Playing alone amongst the carcasses and caverns so that you did not notice that darkness was nearly upon you? And I suppose you will tell me that it is not whisky I smell on your breath."

"It is hard to judge the hour," Niall defended himself. "It hasn't stopped raining long enough to guess the time of day. And I was most certainly *not* in the flensing shed. You don't actually keep the carcasses do you?"

"Hmph! Don't think that you can distract me with your silliness. I wish to know what you were doing with Callum—aside from drinking a good many drams and swapping tall tales."

"Why? What knavery do you imagine we could be getting up to? And what is wrong with Callum's whisky? Do you not care for the taste?"

"The imagination falters when I consider what you may be about! And never mind about Callum's whisky. Just answer the question, if you please."

"Or? Methinks I hear a threat hiding behind those pretty teeth!"

"What keen ears you have. Talk or I shall—I shall fall down before your feet in frustration and have a convulsion," she finished direfully. "Now, the answer, and no arggle-barggle please!"

"Why, 'tis a small matter only! I asked Callum to carry a letter for me." Niall eyed her thoughtfully. "A convulsion, did you say?"

"A letter?" Disbelief was plain. "To your worried aunt, no doubt."

"Actually no. If you want the truth—" he said with feigned candor.

"Now, that would be extraordinarily refreshing."

Niall tried to look hurt, but he couldn't manage wounded feelings that moment any better than Lona could a proper scolding.

"I asked him to take a letter to a friend. A French

Iona

friend who just happens to be the captain of a vessel—a rather fleet one."

Lona stopped. Niall also ceased perambulating and turned obligingly.

"This letter is for the . . . " She looked about quickly checking for signs that anyone had drawn too near and might overhear them. A wasted gesture since even the sheep wisely shunned the narrow path during the rain.

"Only in part. You see, O Doubtful One, I actually do have a plan."

"Well, if I have doubts then it is entirely your fault. You haven't explained a blessed thing about your grand plan," she complained, somewhat stung by the criticism. "So, go on. What is the plan with the French captain?"

Niall looked down at Lona. Her smile had gone and she looked suddenly serious and pinched with cold. He reached for her hands, thinking to warm them in his pocket.

"Let us be indoors. We can—"

"Nay." She shook her head but allowed him to clasp her fingers and draw her near. "Cook will find us out if we return to the keep. And I don't trust her not to babble. If we had dunking-stools on the island, she'd have been drowned long since for being a gossip."

Niall glanced up at the darkening sky. Night was beginning to fall in earnest along with the drizzle.

"We can't go back to the caves now. I don't suppose that one of the cottages is empty?" Lona shook her head again. "Then we'll have to wait 'til after supper. When Cook takes herself off—"

"She won't." Lona predicted. "She is like an evil-tempered cat, always underfoot when she's least wanted."

141

Melanie Jackson

"Then I'll come to your chamber once she's abed."

"You'll do nothing of the sort—" Lona began indignantly.

"Do you want to hear my plan tonight or nay? I am willing to wait for the morrow. . . . "

"I am not!" Lona glared at him. "I shall have nightmares about French captains the whole night long."

"Well then?" The sky punctuated his question by opening a new floodgate and letting the heavens fall down upon them. The opportunity for even a brief *tête-à-tête* had ended.

Niall let go of her dainty hands to grab an arm and urged her toward the keep. The leather cloaks the islanders wore repelled moisture, but nothing save a solid roof would protect them from this deluge. Of course, it remained to be seen if Hector's roof was actually solid.

"Oh! Very well, come to my chamber then," she grumbled, matching hurried step for hurried step. "And it will serve you justly if I do have the vapors and faint clean away from being hurried so. 'Tis only water falling from the sky, not boiling oil."

"Surely that would be redundant," he said. "Are not vapors and fainting one and the same?"

"Not at all. Vapors are hysterical, noisome things—like cattle and sheep," she added maliciously. "Fainting is ladylike and quiet."

"Aye? Faint then, if you must do something idiotic. Vapors!" He paused long enough to lift her over a rock with brisk hands that continued to hold her close to his side. "Would they be worse than a convulsion?"

Lona began to laugh, but it was a small sound as she was breathless from rushing uphill and from the surprise of finding Niall's arm about her waist.

Iona

"And would you care if they were? I doubt you'd stop rushing from this rain even if I had all three at once. I've never seen a body avoid water as you do."

"Only cold water. And they must be worse, if they are as noisy as sheep," Niall went on, ignoring her complaints. His breathing was fine. "Who would have thought it? But this just proves that a man's education is never done."

"Nor a woman's," she gasped, as he hauled her into the forecourt at a brisk trot.

"I thought it was a woman's *chores* that were never done."

"That is also a weary fact."

" 'Tis probably for the best." He pulled her toward the narrow door that led into the kitchen. His hat's bent brim was now holding water like a dish. "As the Puritans know: Idle hands are the devil's playground. Especially women's hands."

"Oh!" The last gasp was of amused outrage. Lona's soft, defensive feathers were ruffling again as she prepared for further verbal battle.

"And as for your earlier observation," he went on, after he had slammed the door behind them, and spilled a great deal of water from his hat into his boot as he tipped his head downward to fumble with the bar. "I have not had much experience with feminine carrying on, but I should not think it would engender in me any desire except to escape forthwith. Or—if it was you who was carrying on—to kiss you into silence."

"Kiss me?" He couldn't see her face in the gloom, and that was a pity, for he was willing to bet that it had flushed a lovely shade of pink.

"Aye. Unless you would prefer the usual husbandly thrashing. That also has possibilities."

143

Melanie Jackson

" 'Tis raining Jeddart staffs!" bellowed Cook's voice before Lona was forced to answer his outrageous comment. "An' some daft looby has shut the door. Now the chimbley is a'smokin like Hell on Halloween."

Lona turned and pulled the kitchen door back open. A gust of wind rushed through and pinned the plank to the wall with a final *whap!* She didn't look up at Niall as she tried to slip past him in the tight corridor. Her cheeks were quite pink either from embarrassment or . . .

It was an easy thing to reach out a gentle hand and stop her when she brushed by his side.

"*Whist*, m'dear, dinna be so Sabine. 'Tis teasing I am about the thrashing." He deliberately used the Lowland speech that pricked her. "But don't pout—unless you do want to be kissed. For about that I do not jest."

"Niall. . . . " Her voice was soft but serious, the gray eyes intent as they met his.

"I would never, never . . . " He thought for a moment. "Well, *probably* never, ever thrash you."

"No?" As she looked up at him her expression changed, her voice grew quizzical rather than embarrassed. "Donnell did. Or he tried."

There was a long silence as Niall pulled his ruined hat from his head and poured off the remaining water onto the floor.

Niall reflected that he should not have mentioned the words *husband* and *thrashing* in the same breath. Probably, he should not have mentioned the word *husband* at all.

"I am very glad," Niall said deliberately, his voice as harsh as she had heard it, "that the double-damned villain is rotting on the bottom of the sea. I'd put him there myself if he still lived."

"Niall." She laid a gentle, restraining hand upon his arm—though he could not imagine what he was being restrained from, since Donnell was dead and gone—and smiled tremulously up at him. "Don't think of him. He is gone—and your adoptive father was quite right. Put it behind you now. The poison of the past won't spread to us, if we don't let it."

Then she was by him and hanging her cape up by the hearth, speaking politely to Cook who, being again in bad skin, did not answer in kind.

Niall stood for a moment in the passage collecting himself. He wanted to shed the rest of his anger at Donnell before joining Lona at the blazing hearth. She was correct about leaving behind the poison of the past before it overtook them. However, that was a task easier said than done.

His ladylove was blessed with some sort of inner vision. She seemed, so many times, to look at him and sense the isolation and loneliness that lay beneath his comical demeanor—and understood its potential harm, moreover. Knew it, and named it for the soul-draining thing it was—and instead of being indifferent to the emptiness, as his own kin had been, she was warm and kind to—*well, at best, I am a stranger. At worst, an enemy*. Yet she'd offered her unwanted visitor a place at her table where there was nourishment and light for both his body and his shadowed spirit.

Which was well and good, but Niall wanted very much to make a permanent place for himself at her warm, civilized hearth. He wanted—*nay! needed*—to have the right to always share the fire with her. And not simply because she was a good Christian soul and could do nothing else for her fellow man!

And he would do almost anything to get a place there, he admitted to himself. Since he was nothing if not persistent about achieving his goals, he was willing to expend all his thought and will and passion to convince Lona to trust in him. And orthodoxy and scruples be damned.

To marry another MacKay and leave her world and kin behind, that was what he was planning to ask her to do, and right hastily as well.

It was an astounding, selfish bastard he was at times! But the pursuit of his heart's first true desire had begun in earnest, whether the fair mistress of Iona knew it or not. And he would be satisfied with nothing less than a permanent place in her affections.

Of course, he would have to move so very carefully with his wary plover! It would take time and effort to persuade her to his belief that they were meant for one another, he was unhappily certain. For wise words aside, Donnell had done a thorough job of destroying her faith in men. She would likely resist the twining of hearts that had begun betwixt them.

It was wretched misfortune that time was working so much against them, for her cooperation in this matter was required both for his future personal happiness and for his willy-nilly plot for the safe removal of people and treasure from Iona. Without her whole-hearted help, it would not carry through.

But perhaps this very need for haste could be turned to his favor. . . . A plea for love and loyalty from a MacKay might go unanswered indefinitely. But if she could be persuaded to marry out of duty,

Iona

for the good of her clan, there would be at the least a guarantee of some time together when she could learn to return his regard.

He certainly hoped that his reasonable arguments would quickly compel her, for Lona MacLean was proving to be an endless temptation, and it truly would be best, for the sake of all future relations between them, to get her before a priest—minister, any cleric would do. He'd even settle for a Ru'glen marriage if no man of the cloth could be found—and soon. Else he would surely lose his head and do something unforgivable, such as seducing her like a straw damsel in one of those dank caves!

Resolved to try his strategy as soon as possible, Niall began walking toward the light of the kitchen. The sooner they dined and rendered Cook to Bacchus, the sooner he could slip into his ladylove's private chamber and begin to work his wiles and purge them both of Donnell's lingering poison.

Chapter Six

Lona helped Cook fetch supper and she made certain that no trace of her inner trepidation showed in her face or hands. But it was there, she knew, waiting for an unguarded moment when it might sneak into her head and embarrass her into betraying herself to Cook with some careless word or deed.

She had never intended to be drawn to this man. She would not have been, if he had been merely polite and comely, or a simple, charming flirt.

But Niall MacKay, the self-admitted rogue and gypsy, was much more than that. The foppish nobleman that he showed to the world, and the unrepentant, lonesome boy he still had inside were both endearing parts of his character. They drew her frozen emotions to the fires of life, in spite of her will to the contrary.

But now that she had begun to thaw enough to

Iona

look about with reasoned eyes, it was to find that she was already captured. There was sheer steel underneath Niall's smile. The utter determination that coursed through his character chained her in place at his side even though she did not know what he planned for her, the treasure, or her island.

In truth, she was a willing victim. She felt small and weary; he was a shark among minnows. And the Lord alone knew why, but he seemed determined to draw her to him like a fast flowing river to the open sea. She recognized that she was coveted—and not for Hector's treasure. Donnell had wanted her for that reason and she kenned the difference with Niall immediately and all the way to her soul.

But what then did he seek? For all of his use of the word *husband*, it did not seem likely that this wanderer could want anything beyond the quick kindling of the brief, passionate fire that flamed so easily between them; and yet her deepest instincts said that there was more than dalliance in his devious mind.

Lona watched from the corner of her eye as Niall hung his cloak and hat beside the fire, and sat down to remove his boots. He upended the first one and poured a goodly amount of water onto the flags. His grimace of distaste set her to smiling. He did have charm to spare, and was amusing at a time when she found little reason to smile.

She had expected many things from this MacKay; shrewdness, determination—perhaps even some form of compassion. But not his irreverent and droll sense of the ridiculous for the events that made up so much of human life. And certainly not these unexpected open windows in the wall of his emotional fortress, which showed her some of the pieces of his mind that he probably would rather keep hidden from everyone.

She sighed and turned away.

It was the nature of such wandering beasts to travel ever onward—and travel he certainly would, as soon as this treasure was seen to. His will was committed to it; she'd seen that much through the inadvertent breach in his wall. She had heard it in his words and was well warned.

And she also was a great fool for wishing that it could be otherwise. Or that she might go with him.... And perhaps she was an even greater fool for considering the thought that she might surrender to her captor and allow herself the indulgence of a brief, passionate kindling before he went on his way.

Loneliness had been a constant bedfellow. Could she blamed for wishing for another?

Niall came calling that night on stealthy tiptoes that passed Cook's room with extraordinary care, the flame on his lamp turned nearly all the way down so he did not wake her with the light.

He found his ladylove waiting patiently by a warm hearth that did not smoke too terribly in spite of the firmly closed shutters that held back the rain. It brought him satisfaction to see that she was busily employed, mending his torn shirt with a moderate-sized needle.

He closed the chamber door softly behind him and shot the bolt. It had been waxed recently—perhaps that very afternoon—and moved with smooth silence.

Niall began to relax with the first obstacle overcome without mishap. Sneaking about was second nature for him, but not into widowed ladies' bed-

Iona

chambers when his hostess had to be blackmailed into issuing an invitation. And particularly not into ladies'—widowed or otherwise—bedchambers for purposes unamorous.

Or, at least partly unamorous.

Lona unbent her head from her task long enough to give him a small smile, but then resumed plying the needle with great diligence. Perhaps the dim light required her extraordinary attention to the rent linen. Or perhaps she was shy to be alone with him in her bedchamber after their conversation that afternoon.

"And so?" she asked, her voice calm and revealing nothing of her inner thoughts. "You will tell me about this grand plan whilst I finish this sleeve."

"Aye. If I must" He made his tone reluctant as he blew out the small flame of his lamp. Feigning reluctance was difficult when he was near bursting with the need to have the matter of their future settled between them.

The answer caused Lona to again lift her head and study his face with her serious, all-seeing eyes. He hoped that the tiny light from the flickering fire revealed nothing of his stronger emotions that must surely be betraying themselves in small ways: a too-heated regard, a pulse that pounded visibly beneath the collar of his shirt. And then there was her uncanny knowledge.

He also hoped that just this once her second sight failed her, and she did not ken how manipulative he was being.

You should be hanged for a wolf, Niall MacKay! said the voice in his head. He couldn't disagree, but it didn't sway him from his pursuit. Only boldness would win the day—and win the day he felt he must, or perish.

"Speak then. Do not hold back any detail for fear of alarming me. I have long been aware that moving this treasure would be a risky enterprise. Or is it about the treasure that you wish to speak?" she asked quietly.

"The treasure? Oh, aye. 'Tis not that which holds my tongue, mistress, but fear that you will greatly dislike my plan. I think perhaps you shall—and I find that this all but unmans me."

That at least was half-truth.

"I cannot say whether I will like your plan or nay," Lona replied with exasperation, not noticeably moved to softness by his false confession. "You have not yet told me enough to cause either like or dislike—only a great deal of alarm. And as for your being unmanned," Lona snorted. "I should live to see such a day!"

Niall walked two steps nearer his doubting mistress and knelt by the fire. He did not touch her, but only looked into her face, as though trying to read what her answer would be. The tension from his body could be felt in the air around them as if it poured off of him and into the small atmosphere of her chamber.

Lona grew nervous under the sudden scrutiny and tried to imagine what he could suggest that would be so horrible that he could feel any fear of speaking. Surely even a lustful propositioning would not tongue-tie him so.

"Just tell me," she whispered, reaching out a hand. Had she complete misread him? Her emotions had lately been so unsettled by this man that it might well be that her intuition that had erred.

Iona

Niall glanced about the chamber while framing his words. The room had none of its owner's pleasant aspect. It was murky with shadows beyond the fire's small radius, and contained a cot, two uncomfortable chairs and a plain table fit tightly into its ill-proportioned walls. He saw no wardrobe, but a large oak trunk rested at the foot of the bed upon whose top there rested a plain brown pitcher and bowl.

He saw that the shutters in her chamber fit no better than the ones in his own chamber and let in an uncomfortable amount of fog that made the fire's wavering shadows dance grotesquely where light and dew met in combat in the corners of the room.

The only ornamentation was in the lively colors of the plaid spread upon the cot, and a rather hideous effigy of Saint Columba carved in a piece of driftwood. It was not the place that a romantic man—or even a man of only moderate sensibilities—would choose to propose marriage to his future wife.

But as no ideal locale existed anywhere on the isle, and for the moment they at least had warmth and privacy, Niall decided to screw up his courage and make his—most likely unwelcome—offer.

Niall turned back to Lona who waited with outstretched hand. He spoke simply. "Will you marry me, mistress?"

Niall's question was asked in a tone so mild and at odds with his intense regard as to be incongruous. Lona blinked and swallowed.

"What?" she asked stupidly, feeling her heart leap as it understood his question. Her arm dropped but Niall's left hand closed over her own before she could withdraw it to the safety of her lap. "*Marry you, Niall MacKay, is it? Oh, is that all?*"

"Aye." His lips broke discipline and twitched once. "That is all. How very maladroit of me to break it to you this way. I can only say in my defense that great need has made me clumsy."

That was complete truth!

"That is your plan? I marry you? Then what? You and I remove the treasure and sail to paradise?" She glared at him, feeling an odd relief that he offered marriage. She felt something else besides. Her instincts were rolling over in agitation and her pulse quickened while she tried to identify what she was feeling. She said quickly: "For this simple-minded plot you have left me stewing in nerves all this long evening!"

Niall ceased smiling. He stood up and paced away from her, but the room was small and he could not go very far before reaching the wall.

"Aye. That is my simple-minded plan. Think on it before you answer," he said quickly as if truly fearing a refusal. "If we married, it would mean a journey to Tiree—before venturing to paradise, I fear. Though I should like to visit there eventually."

Lona said nothing, just continued to stare at him with an expression somewhere between disbelief and outrage. Did she think he was mocking her with this talk of the future?

"Mistress," Niall sighed. Since she did not appear capable of drawing the proper, wise conclusion about his plan, he gave his trout a little more line to play with. "On such a joyous occasion it would not be unusual if everyone on the isle made the journey, as well. There might be several boats that went with us."

The voice was calm and reasonable, but Lona's heart pounded harder with each word. She felt

Iona

slightly dizzy. It had not been lust which moved him then, but only duty. She had been fooled by his attentive mask into believing that he wanted her for herself.

"Aye . . . " she managed to say, hoping that she hid her foolish disappointment from his searching eyes. For months she had kept all her thoughts deep inside. Now Niall MacKay was turning them outside where she—and he—might examine them. She was not pleased to have herself scrutinized in this manner, but it was important that she put her feelings to one side and listen without prejudice to what he had to say. She strove for calm and reason. "Go on."

"We would also wish to bring a feast with us—and some of Iona's famous whisky in its distinctive sherry casks."

"Ah!" The tone was at once comprehensive and Niall ceased pacing to look again at his love's face. He couldn't read it—damn the *faint light*!—but she seemed unnaturally calm and inanimate.

"That is shrewd, Niall. From Tiree, it would be an easy matter to move some cargo to your friend's ship." Now her voice was also brisk and removed of emotion. It was the voice of yesterday when he was simply another unwanted invader. It displeased him.

"Aye. It would also be easy for Callum to go aboard," Niall answered while considering the unwelcome change in his ladylove. He was not able to guess at its cause; there were so many unpleasant possibilities to choose from.

"And you also," she said softly.

"Of course. And my wife as well. Though not immediately. That would cause a great deal of suspicion and bring attention to the ship." Niall waited for some comment or sign until he was unable to wait anymore. "So what say you, mistress? Will you go with me to a brand new world and a brand new life?"

"I?" The voice was surprised.

"Of course *you*!" Now he sounded as exasperated as she had been. "Or do you think me such a bastard that I would take the treasure and abandon you here?"

His eyes burned and made heat course through her. But it wasn't only anger that made them hot. The fire of passion she had for a moment doubted beckoned once again. Apparently Niall MacKay was able to cleanly separate his duty from other emotions. Like desire.

Desire. Lona swallowed uneasily. There was no talk of love; not even a pretense. And fires—even passionate ones—consumed everything: peat, wood, human flesh and emotion. If she went into this conflagration he offered would her spirit be reborn as the Phoenix? Or would she become a burnt offering?

She had to be like Niall and separate the two things in her mind. He desired her, but that did not mean that he wanted an outlaw wife hung like a mill stone around his neck. He was making a noble gesture for the sake of duty; so would she.

"I . . . I cannot go. What of the isle?" Lona bit her lip and looked away from temptation.

Niall frowned at her answer.

"What of the isle," he repeated.

The isle, yes. She had almost forgotten that she had an obligation here. But it was more truthful to say that she had just decided that she would not go with this man simply because he lusted, and duty said he must make an offer. She had her pride, too,

Iona

and she did not want to be married again for any reason other than because she loved and was loved in return. Even all-consuming lust was not sufficient reason to enter a union. Indeed, it was a strong argument against the plan, as it clouded her thinking at a time when she needed to see her way clearly.

"I have a duty here."

Niall's face turned hard as granite.

"The isle is doomed—and everyone on her. That is why they must be got off of it before the weather moderates." The voice was still low, but had turned relentless. He would offer her no false comfort. "The Sasannach will come, m'dear, and believe me, mistress, you do not want to be waiting when they arrive."

Lona was silent as she ran a finger over the carefully seamed cuff and contemplated his words. Niall took it as a good sign that she did not argue with his assessment of Iona's future, but the feeling persisted that with every word he spoke, Lona was moving farther from him in spirit and thought, becoming inscrutable and *female*.

That afternoon's teasing aside, he did not think that she would ever indulge in hysterical convulsions no matter how great her fear. He had been sincere when he'd called her shrewd, and she had had long practice at facing hard quandaries alone, but that did not mean that she did not have other defenses against emotional raiders, which in a sense he was. A defensive wall was going up against him and quickly.

"I do not see that a marriage is actually necessary," she said at last, fitting another stone in place on the barricades. "Once the treasure is gone—"

"Once the treasure is gone there will be a great many suspicions," he interrupted. The voice was quiet but grim. And logical. He used it like a battering ram against this new barrier. "And reprisals against any that are proved to have acted in collusion with the prince are assured. The MacLeans of Tiree took no part in the late rebellion. Do you wish to drag them into harm's way at this late date by implicating them in your escape? And if they are implicated, where will your people go to find a new home? Mull offers no havens."

"I know this." Lona set her needle aside, but she still did not look up. Her voice was suffocated. "It seems rather a large sacrifice you make for us, Niall MacKay. To take a rebel traitor to wife at this 'late date. . . . ' Trust me when I say that this kind of marriage never prospers. And frankly, I am greatly wearied of performing this particular duty for my clan."

Niall's face grew even grimmer at her words, but she did not see the darkening of his expression for her head never lifted from her mending to look at him.

"I am more than willing to do this," he assured her gently, beginning to understand the depth of her hesitation if not the reason for it. He wished that he was able to declare his feelings, but feared that she would be completely disbelieving. " 'Tis not duty for me but my heart's greatest desire. And you are no traitor, mistress of Iona. The rebel MacLeans betrayed no one."

"Niall," she whispered, her voice inexpressibly weary. "I know not what to do. Your words are comforting, but you can't want a MacLean for a wife."

"Do you truly doubt that I want you?" He wondered if he should admit to her that the lusts of his body had nearly subdued his brain.

"No. But that does not mean that you want a *wife*. If you had desired a wife, you would have wed before now."

"I have not previously needed a woman in this way." Niall explained as he searched for a believable argument. It was difficult when he did not understand it himself. "I have always enjoyed ladies' company—women were made for love, after all. But I have never sought one out for counsel or mental companionship. That I sought from other men— and damned few of them. But I have somehow found this need of companionship and mind met in you. Believe me, it is not *duty* that asks for your hand. It is a man who wishes for your company as he begins a new life."

Lona swallowed twice and finally looked up. He spoke the truth, but since her eyes remained so sad Niall had to think that she did not believe him. So when she finally answered him, her quiet words of agreement came as a surprise.

"Very well, Niall MacKay. I will marry you. But I have two conditions to add to our . . . bargain."

"Aye?" He kept his eagerness in check. For a bride-to-be she did not look in the least joyous, and he did not care for the word *bargain* when applied to their future union.

"First, I need a little time . . . to make plans for my kin. If what you say is true then when they go to Tiree they are leaving here forever—"

"Aye. I ken. But we cannot delay too long," he warned, understanding that her wish for delay was not only for the benefit of her clan. "Ten days I can give you—twelve at the most. The time for safety is very short."

"I also ken, but I must have some time to prepare." Lona tucked the needle into her spindle of thread and set the shirt aside. "My other condition—"

"Aye?"

"Is that we swear to release each other from this marriage if . . . "

"If?" he asked harshly, not at all pleased with the notion that she might want her freedom. Something quite large was troubling her, obviously. No Catholic would ask for a divorce—or annulment—unless she was tormented by some spiritual demons.

He wondered if one of the demons was named Donnell MacKay and if he had done more than "wearied her of performing this particular duty." How cruel a monster had Donnell been to his wife? A pointless question surely. He'd betrayed her brother, beaten her and murdered her kin. Nothing else was required to give her a horror of sharing his bed. He was right to have kept a silence about his own wild desire. He would have to be certain not to frighten her with his own many impure impulses.

"If either of us should feel it was necessary to . . . to . . . "

The answer was unenlightening, and Niall fumed in silence while he debated the wisdom of demanding that she name her reservations plainly so that he might combat them immediately.

"I ken your meaning, mistress," he said at last, unable to find the will to ask the cruel question of his ladylove. There had not been time to teach her to trust before demanding her hand. He would have to leave her with her wall intact or risk a refusal. "Very

Iona

well then, I agree to your terms."

He was lying through his teeth; the only thing that would force him from Lona's side was a call from the hereafter. And he would personally dispose of every last demon that bothered her, if he had to woo her a twelve-month with sonnets and posies of rare flowers. He'd shower her with wealth. He would even rid the world of every turncoat MacKay that had set foot on her isle if that was what was needed to give her peace.

After this wedding was done he would convince her of his feeling and he swore silently that he would never lie to her again.

Niall took her slim, chilled fingers into his hand and raised them to his warming lips. Fire seared ice and promised without words that there would be great heat between them at the time he called her wife. Great pleasure and no *duty*.

Her delicate fingers trembled in his and she turned her face away. Was it fear? Or passion? Even Lona could not have said for certain what shook her so.

Niall knelt and slowly lowered his lips to her trembling mouth. He paused only a breath away.

"I would seal this pact with a kiss."

"Do you seek permission?" she whispered.

"Nay. I just wonder if I should risk it." Somehow, there was humor in his voice.

"Is it such a risk?" she asked, wistful.

"Aye. Your presence greatly effects my reason and balance." He caressed her cheek. "And I also desire your willing trust."

Yes, and he wanted to be trusted in so many ways. She didn't know if she should give trust in any way except the one to which she had no alternative.

Melanie Jackson

"I had thought you possessed of a harder head, one not turned by a comely face," she said lightly.

"Aye, so had I. But I was in error." He closed the distance, setting the seal on their bargain.

It began as a light kiss—just a gentle brush of the lips. Then Lona made a languid sigh and relaxed into his embrace. Niall immediately found that the emotions coursing through him were less romantic and more forceful than he had anticipated.

They were, in fact, primeval. So much so, that in an instant, he was near the end of his self-control. He was ready to pull her to floor and have his way with her. Such naked impulses would never do! She needed to be treated gently, not ravaged by another MacKay.

Niall groaned and jerked himself away. She, arms still twined about his neck, urged him to return. With deep regret, he forcibly set her aside. He did not want to make love to his future wife in this ghost-haunted hovel, with memories of Donnell hanging in the air and nosy Cook sniffing at the door.

"Damnation!" he muttered.

"Niall?" When he did not answer, her softly dazed expression grew wooden. "I suppose I should thank you for your gentlemanly impulses. I am sorry that you are disappointed."

"Indeed you should be thankful, Mistress," he growled, disliking her expressionless voice, but unable to change it at that moment. Niall made an effort to smile. "I am not disappointed. Far from it! And so for both our sakes, I shall leave now."

"But certainly. Pray leave at once. I would not want honest emotion to overpower your good sense." She shoved his shirt at him. Her tone was

Iona

peevish and made him grin in spite of his frustration.

"I make you my most abject apologies, m'dear. That was ill-done of me. If it pleases you to know it, I'll admit that I shall probably regret that noble impulse for some time to come." Niall tucked his mended shirt beneath his arm and relit his lantern. "Still, I think it important that you come to know me a little better before we *know* one another better."

"Hmph!" Lona rose to her feet. "Have done with apologies and regrets, and please just go before Cook finds you here. I've no wish to be pilloried without the chance to commit the sin."

He looked reproachfully at her but was met with a frown of acute vexation. The languorous mood was indeed shattered past repair. He took up his lamp and went to the door.

"Very well, Mistress, I shall leave now and without further ado." He drew back the bolt and turned to face her. "But think on me tonight when you go to your—prayers."

The door closed softly behind him and Lona sank back into her chair. Her hands were shaking.

Think on him! It was a totally unnecessary exhortation. It was all she had done since his arrival.

Chapter Seven

Lona made an effort to calm herself. After Niall departed her chamber, she followed her usual evening ritual of combing out and then plaiting her hair. But though she pretended absorption with the task, her inner thoughts were not deceived by her busy fingers. She had for a moment—*unbelievably*—forgotten that Niall had multifarious reasons for coming to the isle; none of which included taking a wife or even a lover. Her overwhelming attraction for this man had subdued her senses. The inattentive slip left her shaken.

The important question was, *Had it been a ruse*? Had he guessed her feelings and used them to persuade her to his purpose?

She couldn't answer dispassionately when her mind's eye still saw Niall's gaze glittering down at her. She felt the lingering print of his hands on her skin, and she had to admit that she would have gladly assented to his lovemaking if he had not pulled back when he did.

Why had he pulled back? Had he concluded that it was risk that would, in the long run, turn her against him? Or might he not have truly suffered from a sudden, and unexpected, gentlemanly impulse?

She didn't know, and might never know. The only sensible course to follow was to err on the side of caution.

Lona stifled a sigh and crawled beneath her coverlet. To err was human. So, she had been momentarily weak and taken a few offered kisses from a very charming man. She would simply draw a lesson from this unfortunate incident and see to it that Niall did not share any more intemperate kisses with her.

She frowned when her stupid heart laughed at this wise resolution.

Lona worried her lower lip and finally admitted that the task might prove an impossible one if Niall began an earnest wooing. He was sly and audacious, and quite adept at getting what he wanted. And her earlier, inexplicable jealousy of the unknown women that had shared his life told her that her heart had not waited for logic's consent before caring. She was now vulnerable to him in a manner that had never troubled her before.

She was, in point of fact, in imminent hazard of surrendering caution in spite of the apprehensions that his presence awoke in her mind. Such was the tenacity of the heart's hope for a better life.

"Niall," she sighed. "Why did you have to be a MacKay? And a charming one at that. It makes trusting very hard. And without trust, what hope has love?"

Would *he* ever speak of love? she wondered whimsically, settling under the covers. And if he did, could she risk his kisses then?

And when they were married? The sensible question killed whimsy. Would she be able to resist his siren call? She'd have no right to refuse his kisses then. No, nor anything else he desired as long as he remained with her.

Lona rolled onto her side and pulled the linens over her head. She was feeling harried. She needed to detach from her troubles and consider them one at a time.

Her first concern was the treasure—and she had decided to trust Niall to get it away from the isle by shipping it to Tiree with a cargo of whisky. It was a reasonable decision since he had to remove the treasure somehow—whatever he ultimately did with it.

Marriage, if it ever happened, was another matter. That she did not have as much faith in. It might be that such a union could be avoided, and if the opportunity presented itself—Lona's lips trembled, but she faced the dilemma squarely—then Niall might very well avail himself of the chance at freedom. Especially if he had the treasure stowed safely away. And wasn't that what she wanted? To be married only for reasons of—*what had he said?*—counsel and companionship.

Nay! said her heart. *For love and only for love.*

"Columba's nightgown!" she swore, preferring oaths to tears and knowing that the tears were close. "'Tis not likely that he'll love me—or any other woman. Trust him, but don't desire him so!"

And wasn't that a nice discrimination! She would reluctantly trust him with the treasure and—by

Iona

extension—her family's safety, but not with her heart.

And with good reason! For if such misfortune happened, and Niall left her behind, she did not need the misery of broken promises compounded with heartbreak and pregnancy. It would be too great a cross to bear.

The wind moaned, sounding for all the world like a crying child. Lona sat up and listened. Perhaps the cat . . .

But no further weeping came, just wind and a patter of rain. Lona snuggled back under the covers.

Pregnancy.

Lona rolled back onto her back and stared at the ceiling, watching absently as the fire's dying shadows danced over the stone. The sea wind breathed heavily outside her shutter, but after months of practice Lona was able to ignore its usual low whispers.

It was all Niall's nonsensical talk of breeding that had put this notion into her head! Lona closed her eyes against it. But the idea was snugly wedged in her thoughts and refused to let her sleep.

A babe. From Niall. Would that be such a bad thing? If the threat to Iona was lifted and she was allowed to live in peace? Would not a child compensate for being abandoned?

She considered what might come of taking Niall as a lover and her skin became dewy with perspiration. She laid a hand on her belly and considered the idea. As her imaginings grew heated, her breathing became agitated and her nerves trilled ecstatically.

The wind outside began to chorus loudly.

They could have a child, she was certain. Union

between them would bear fruit. Hadn't she been dreaming of late of a a babe in a cradle?

"Go to sleep," she scolded herself.

The wind gave a low, voiceless chuckle.

A while on, she decided that, storm or no, it was too hot to sleep. Lona kicked fretfully at the coverlet, not caring for the restlessness in her blood that made her over-warm even on a cold eve. She had never been troubled by such feelings before, not even when she first approached the marriage bed.

Was this what had been lacking with her other husbands? The desire for children?

Or just plain desire for a man? Niall's kisses disturbed her, there was no doubt. Their fiery nature had incinerated the memories of every marital unpleasantness that had gone before. Nothing in her previous life had prepared her for these sensations. She brooded on this new phenomenon, not consciously realizing that for the first time in years she had failed to pay attention to the chattering of Iona's mournful ghosts.

Niall lay abed in his own chamber staring at nothing in particular. He had no fire's shadows to watch while he pondered the day's events.

Pledging his troth to his ladylove was not quite the idyll he had imagined it would be. Whoever would have thought that kissing one's affianced bride would be hurtful? Though, it was not the kisses that had turned painful, only the cessation.

Had he been a gallant fool? If he had persisted, taken advantage of her dazed pliancy, would he now be spending the dark hours in cozy intimacy with his beloved? If he returned to her this night, would she take him in?

Iona

It was a tempting thought, and she was so tantalizingly near to hand. Her proximity made the blood race in his veins.

Ah! But would she have come to her senses after a moment more and kicked up an unholy din? Ordered him to begone, and to take his proposal with him? She had been quite annoyed with him when he'd departed, and his own impulsively begun—and then aborted—lovemaking did not exactly cover him in romantic glory. It was the act of a scurrilous knave.

Niall sighed. His pretty Scot was not accustomed to riotous living. He should know better than to urge an immoral liaison. Even with the bonds of matrimony, it could take her a long while to trust another MacKay.

Yet, he thought, it was not hopeless. She burned when he touched her. The natural impulses were unspoiled. It was only the circumstance that disturbed her.

Niall began to feel more cheerful and relaxed.

At certain moments, it seemed that she was even coquettish with him. A flirtation was a long step from being caught in the throes of deeper passion, but given the circumstances—and his damned name—it was more than he could have reasonably hoped for.

He was a monster of selfishness to be discontented and impatient with the time she needed to relearn trust. Niall resolved that he would do better at playing the gentleman on the morrow.

Niall fell into a light slumber with his baser nature discoursing against his better intentions.

Around him were the scents of a tropical night, a heavy perfume that drugged the senses. The fresh linens beneath his body were cool and fine—woven of silk, perhaps—but still he was heated by his lover's nearness.

Knowing what he would find, Niall turned on his side and reached for the delicate form beside him.

Lona moaned softly in her sleep and rolled toward the wall. Her hands reached toward an empty space, yet her mind supplied her with an image of—

Niall. He had come back to her and a strange, perfumed summer had followed him. Heady scents filled the warm night air that belonged to some enchanted land.

He leaned over her, this man who was her chosen lover. His dark hair tumbled down over his breast. His lovely form was marred by faint scars, but far from detracting from his appeal, they caused a desire in her to touch and heal.

She reached out a hand, fearful that the dream would dissolve with contact, but her fingers rested against a solid wall of muscled chest wherein his strong heart was beating.

Faster it beat and faster, yet he made no move to come to her. He was leaving the choice to her. Just as he had earlier.

Understanding that she would have to make some sign, she looked into his taut face and nodded.

Niall's eyes blazed with pleasure as she gave silent assent.

Niall's breath rushed out into the cold darkness where the wind muttered in the chimney. He was caught in his dream and temporarily unaware of the winter chill that hovered in the ugly chamber.

Iona

He rose up on elbow to study her face. He could kiss her, yes. But would she grant him his greatest desire?

Lona's hand approached him with hesitantly. He wanted to pull her to him, to overwhelm her, but he could not. He was helpless, mute. Until she broke the spell, all he could do was to urge her silently to grant him leave.

He watched her expression in the silvered moonlight that bathed the bed in eerie radiance, but left the rest of the room in shadow. Anticipation was agony. What if she never—

He sighed as her warm fingers touched his breast and she at last nodded her head. Now he could touch her! Make her his own.

Joy rushed through him.

Lona pushed at the smothering covers that restrained her limbs, kicking them to lay tumbled on the floor. At the shutters, the wind held a loquacious discourse.

Her woolen nightrail had disappeared. In its place was a gown of the sheerest silk unlike any she had ever seen. But even this beautiful softness was annoying, a bothersome layer that separated her from Niall. She did not protest when he loosened the ties and folded it from her shoulder and down over her breast. The heat in his hands was vital and alive, and it drove off the cold that had been living in her bones.

Niall frowned in his sleep, feeling an unpleasant chill at his back. He did not want her to hear the moaning of the wind lest it call her back from his arms.

He moved to shield Lona from the invading winter

breeze. His lips brushed her hair. Then her throat. Then her breasts. He was awed at her pale beauty, humbled and grateful that she came to him with certainty and grace.

He leaned over her, slowly drawing the rail aside, reveling in the unveiling of this vivacious treasure. His heart squeezed painfully as he was overcome with exultation. The time had come.

Lona stirred beneath him. She flung her arms wide and—

Lona flung out a hand, tossing the last of the covers aside and cried out as her knuckles grazed against the icy stone floor.

In an instant, Niall and the beautiful night disappeared into the cold drafts and shadows that filled her bedchamber.

She sat upright, for a moment unable to reconcile reality with the beautiful dream. Sleep had taken her to another, warmer place and she had finally met her lover, the dream man who had haunted her night-thoughts for the last year and more. And there had been complete love and trust between them—not like here.

Her heart and temples pounded. Her chin dropped down onto her breast and she tried to calm her hurried breathing. She resisted the urge to both weep and curse at the revealing dream that had fled before she had the chance to know Niall as a lover.

Outside, the wind chattered excitedly.

Niall also came awake, his mood equally distressed and foul. Was he to be denied her even in his dreams?

He reached for the bedside table, struck a tinder

Iona

and kindled the flame of his lamp. He began rapidly donning attire against the room's chill and then went to the chimney flags. He had yet to use the hearth in this chamber and was dubious of its ability to draw. Yet, a quick check of the ceiling showed no accumulation of soot, so he decided to risk building a fire.

Stacking the peat was a long enterprise, but he was reasonably certain that sleep had abandoned him for the time being, and as he still needed to compose several lengthy epistles for Callum, a fire to ward off the chill was a necessity, else his shaking hands and turgid ink would ruin Flambard's flamboyant fist.

Unsmiling, Niall set out his supplies. The quill was sharp but he found that the parchment had been water-stained and creased during its travels. The ink, as he had feared, was cold and thick but improved after warming on the hearth for a time, and he was able to write with something approaching his usual adeptness.

Lona paced about her chamber with her hands clapped over her ears. She muttered imprecations at the whispering wind, but still it chattered. She feared that she would have to resort to whisky if she was to have any sleep.

"Go away!" she pleaded plainly. "You are making me mad. I shall end crazed and howling—and so shall Niall."

And for a wonder, the noisy breeze departed.

Lona blinked, unused to the silence and privacy.

"Am I truly alone?" There was a distant singing of unknown voices, but none within the keep.

She was alone. They had granted her privacy for . . . whatever she wished to do.

Melanie Jackson

What did she wish?

Lona hesitated for a moment, but finally, she opened her door and peered along the passage towards Niall's room. She would have to go that way if she wanted the water of life. The soporific was sitting in the kitchen . . . if that was what she wanted.

As she had anticipated, a dim light shone from under Niall's door and with only one panel left to separate them, she could plainly hear the soft sounds of him moving about his bed chamber. Clearly, he was awake.

She closed her eyes and leaned against the cold wall.

Did she want the whisky? Or should she go to him? Inquire why he was wakeful so late in the night?

Lona sighed ruefully, admitting that this was not the reason for her visit. Curiosity about his activities she had aplenty, but her other feelings were less noble and altruistic. Especially the one that kept her pulse racing, and that was what had her ghosting down the corridor past Cook's darkened room and scratching on the panel with nervous fingers. She wanted to know if Niall had dreamed. And if so, if he had dreamed of her.

There was a slight noise as Niall unbolted his door, and she was a little startled to be greeted by her husband-to-be with a long dirk in his hand. He hadn't been carrying a weapon in her dream and it rather spoiled the image of an eager lover, for it suggested to even the meanest intelligence that he did not presently have gentle thoughts in mind.

However, he seemed gratifyingly pleased and startled by her arrival. After setting the knife aside,

Iona

he quickly drew her to a chair by the fire. He took her candle from her trembling hand, snuffed the wick with finger and thumb and set it aside.

His light touch was solicitous. She found that she liked being the object of his gallantry. No man had ever treated her as treasure—a queen. Without a doubt, she could grow to enjoy being treated as the most fragile of flowers. If only she could be certain that Niall would remain her champion.

"Lona, m'dear, is something amiss? You are trembling." He fetched a coverlet from his pallet to tuck around her, but transferred his quizzical gaze back to her face as soon as the task was done.

She loved the sound of her name on his lips, and for the moment, Lona was pleased that she had stifled her long-held notions of propriety. She relaxed into her modest throne.

"Beyond what is always amiss?" she asked with a small smile, grateful that he was not undressed as he had been in her dreams. His fully clothed presence was disturbing enough to her feeble senses. "Nay. I just could not sleep and thought that perhaps this would be a good time to talk. We parted rather abruptly this evening."

"I see." Niall walked back to the table where he had been writing and stared down at the sheaves of parchment. He frowned. Lona had the impression that he was not actually looking at the documents and was answering her at random when he said: "You wish to talk?"

"Aye. Talk . . . Hold a conversation. Enjoy social discourse. Gossip, even." He turned to stare. She chided: "You do converse, Niall MacKay. I've heard you."

"Conversation! I recall it now." He laughed softly,

Melanie Jackson

putting aside whatever thought had been distracting him.

He drew up a stool and joined her at the hearth. He was careful that their legs did not touch, but even through the coverlet, Lona could feel his heat, stronger than the fire on the flags. The distraction scattered her wits and made her forget what she had planned to say. Her lips parted, but no words came forth.

Niall stared at her lips for a long moment, and then sighed. He leaned back, lacing his long fingers around one knee and holding tight as though he did not trust them if they remained unfettered.

"Some other mason laid these flags and constructed this chimney," he observed with a grin, rescuing her from her conversational difficulties. "It draws well enough to suck the noisome drafts away. I've never heard such chattering winds."

"Aye." She smiled gratefully for the harmless observation. "Callum laid the stones. He is a better builder than Hector or my father."

"A very talented man is Callum Bethume," Niall agreed, smiling, but watching her intently.

"Aye, he is that. I am grateful for him."

A silence fell. She sensed that Niall was restraining himself from discussing some topic, and she very much wondered what the subject might be. She could think of no subtle way to ask if the ghosts had sent him dreams, too.

"Would you care to play a hand of piquet while we visit?" Niall asked politely, as though sensing her turmoil, and pulling still farther away in the mistaken belief that distance would calm her.

He turned to stare at his small valise where it sat

Iona

under the table. The withdrawal of his gaze left her bereft, but able to speak coherently.

"You have cards?" she asked. "In Scotland?"

"Aye. Travel can be tedious at times," he explained, as one duty-bound to make polite conversation with an unexpected guest. She was both grateful and annoyed to be treated thusly. He went on: "It is particularly so in foreign climes. I find that a game of whist not only breaks the tedium, but finds friends—or at least companions—for the night."

"I see." And she did. Loneliness recognized its own kind when they met. "I fear that I am an indifferent card-player. I do not care for games of chance. Life is gamble enough for me."

Niall's answering smile was wry. He glanced at her briefly and made another attempt at conversation.

"I would offer you refreshment, but alas I have none. And I am not certain what to offer a lady at this hour of the night. If you were a man, brandy or port perhaps, but a lady—"

"Rum punch, I believe, is customary," she suggested.

"Certainly not!" But his eyes twinkled. "Not until we are married, in any event."

"Well, I thank you for the thought, but I do not often drink either. I fear that I would be a poor partner for you." Lona was beginning to feel self-conscious, sitting in her nightgown while they talked of nothing. This encounter was not proceeding as smoothly as she had hoped.

"You might be a poor choice for cards and befuddled carousing, perhaps. But in every other way, you suit me admirably." His tone was bantering, flirtatious, unalarming. It invited her participation.

Melanie Jackson

"That is a very gallant, yet reckless assumption," she said quietly. It took an effort to resist his charm, and she was not certain why she did. The only reason was that it was important for her to have truth from him.

"Is it?"

"Aye. After all, sir, you know little about me. I might be a Puritan. Or worse."

"True, true.... Ah, is there anything worse than a Puritan? Never mind. I feel confident that my ignorance shall be remedied with time. However, my instincts—which are excellent, by the way—tell me that you are perfectly suited to be my *companion*. I trust my lucky impulses. And you should trust them, too, since they so closely concern you."

She smiled reluctantly.

"You are kindness itself, guest Niall. I might trust, if I thought that you were sincere."

"You wound me, Mistress. When have I not been sincere? Question me at will. I shall answer." Niall's voice sounded as candid as his words.

She gave in to curiosity.

"Tell me then, how is it that you have escaped marriage all these years? Are the foreign lasses immune to your abundant charm?"

Up went the mobile eyebrow. Did he sense the jealousy lingering behind the question? Or was he merely surprised that she would unbend far enough to ask? She hoped it was the latter.

"Nay. But Flambard was usually fleet of foot. And for those misguided enough to give chase, he had an impenetrable hedge of vice about him." Niall's voice was suddenly gay. "It suited him better than thorny virtue, you see."

"Indeed? And it kept the women away?"

Iona

"Certainly. At least the respectable ones." He grinned fleetingly. "Not all courts are as dour as the Hanovers', but they have some limited standards of deportment. Flambard routinely practiced six of the seven Sins of Virtue and several vices never mentioned in the Bible. I fear it scared away the faint of heart. Fortunately, you possess the courage of any ten men. You're staring, Mistress."

Lona blushed at the reminder but did not look away.

"My apologies. I was attempting to determine which of the Biblically approved seven vices you shied away from. *Sloth* was the one exception, I suppose." She gestured to his elegant attire.

"Just so." Niall smoothed a hand down his coated sleeve, as though admiring the texture. It was a foppish trick and made her snort with scorn even though she knew it was done for her amusement.

"I find it difficult to believe that you ever felt *envy* either."

"Well now, there you are mistaken." He looked up, his eyes dancing. "I find that I am quite damnably envious of your shift and robe."

"Whyever for?" she asked, looking down at the plain woolens. "Your brocade is much grander and more costly."

"I envy it, Mistress, that it may rest close to you in sleep while I am consigned to this dingy chamber. At least for the present."

Lona felt a darker blush stain her cheeks and hoped that it was not apparent in the weak light. The world of light flirtation was so removed from her orbit that she was at a momentary loss to know how to reply to Niall's direct bantering.

Nor did she have any ready plan for how to deal

with the warmth coursing through her at his careless words. Plainly, she needed to make an effort to calm her leaping senses before he recognized what her racing pulse betokened, but she was uncertain of how it was to be done when he was determined to flirt with her.

"I think, sir, that you must also be a liar."

"Flambard was. Compulsively so," Niall agreed, not one whit abashed by the accusation. "But here, with you, I am as honest as the day is long."

"That answer is no help. You might now be lying about lying. And at present our days are none too long. That leaves a great deal of darkness to be dishonest in."

"I would never lie to you, Mistress. The rogue Flambard was left in France. 'Tis I, a fellow Scot who addresses you." Niall strove manfully to look innocent of anything except patriotism, and he nearly succeeded. "Mine whole being is dedicated to—"

There was a faint noise from the hall. He broke off abruptly to listen. When the scuffle came again, he rose swiftly and went to the door. He drew his knife and then opened the panel.

"Who is there?" The hard voice did not belong to the Niall who had just addressed her. It was a dangerous stranger who peered into the dark.

There was no spoken answer, just a second rustle in the darkness beyond.

"Stand fast!" Niall commanded. There was a sharp creak from the right side of the corridor and Niall jumped through the dark opening to give chase.

"Wait!" she called softly, fearful of waking any of the others who might be sleeping in the keep, and

Iona

having her bed-ready presence discovered in Niall's chamber.

It was a short chase. There was a heavy thud and then some creative swearing in the French tongue that told her Niall had met up with the barrel at the base of the stairs and was thankfully alive to regret it.

Lona threw off her tangled cover, took up the lamp and went to give aid. Cook's door remained tightly, damningly, shut through all the noise.

"Oh, no." Lona stared at the unmoving panel. "She wasn't!"

"Filons avant!" Niall swore.

Lona turned from Cook's door and headed for the stairs. By the time she had journeyed half a dozen steps into the passage, Niall regained the upper corridor and was approaching with a steady, if limping, gait. He had one hand up over his forehead, attempting to staunch a flow of blood; the other still clutched his unbloodied knife.

He hurried her back into his chamber, turned and bolted the door. His actions were unnecessarily forceful and suggested a high degree of annoyance.

"Niall?" she asked softly, feeling both alarm and amusement. "Are you much hurt?"

"Whoever it was escaped. Damnation!" he swore as a red stream slipped down his cheek. Niall tossed his knife aside and pulled a handkerchief from his pocket. He started to blot up the blood.

"Sit here," she instructed, indicating the chair by the fire. "Let me see what you have done to yourself. I suppose that your nimble hoof slipped on the stair."

"Done to myself!" he repeated indignantly, ignoring her reference to his possible cloven-hoofed status. "There was a trap laid on."

"Aye, I know. I believe it is the barrel that Cook puts out at night to catch the rain."

Niall stared at her from the one eye not covered by his makeshift bandage. The one-eyed gaze held both disbelief and annoyance.

"The roof leaks," she explained.

"But only at night?" he asked, sarcastic. "I saw no barrel there during the day, and it rained from dawn onward."

"No, but we can deal with any excess rainfall during the daylight. If it were to come over storming in the night, the whole hearth might flood and make a dreadful mess before we awoke in the morning. 'Tis just a precaution she takes in winter."

"Are you saying that the *downstairs* leaks with such regularity that you need must leave a barrel out nightly?" He was still disbelieving.

"Well," Lona took over the chore of folding the hankie, deftly pressing it into the cut on his scalp. She tried to ignore that she was standing close enough to Niall to feel his breath between her breasts, but there was no resisting the temptation to smoothe his wayward locks before firming the pressure on his small wound. "The upstairs does leak, as well."

She jerked her head at the bucket in the corner that also served as a chamber pot.

"It isn't so bad now, but in the winter a bad storm turns out the mice and rats. They make a dreadful noise when the cat catches them."

"The cat." Niall relaxed against her and began to laugh softly. Tension melted from his body and he slumped toward her. She was so startled by the contact that she nearly dropped the kerchief. "Let me guess. I was making up the final act of the parade of the cat who was chasing a rat who was hunting grain in the kitchen."

"In a manner of speaking." Lona avoided his gaze as he tipped up his head to smile his devastating smile.

"I suppose I should be grateful that Cook hadn't left out a rack of antlers or a bayonet. The dark down there is as absolute as a coal pit." He laughed again. "The cat! Mistress, your island has shattered my nerves. When I didn't hear the door open, or feel the hurricane wind in the kitchen, I was nearly convinced that I was chasing a ghost."

Lona debated about mentioning the hidden passage to the cliff where she had confronted Donnell. She decided to preserve silence on that subject, not wishing to bring the subject of Donnell into their conversation. Yet, she felt that she must warn Niall of what might well await him on the morrow if her suspicions of Cook were true.

"I hope that you were earnest in your proposal of marriage," she began gently.

"Of course. I shouldn't have suggested it otherwise. But why do you ask, my sweet?" Niall continued to smile, but a cautious, questioning look had entered his eyes.

"Because I think that the others know of our conversation."

"I am pleased to have it so. But how would they know of our private conversation?" He turned his head and glanced at the door.

She cleared her throat. "I strongly suspect that you were actually chasing Cook. Not the cat. Or a specter."

Niall sat up again quickly, his smile wiped clean. Lona told herself that she was grateful for the modesty of the separation.

"Cook! I don't believe it. She's too fat to be creeping about in the night. It's indecent. We didn't speak of anything—inappropriate." His voice held a note of exasperation, and Lona had to bite her lip to keep from smiling.

"That is a matter of opinion. And Cook's not always polite. I've never caught her, but somehow, she always manages to know what goes on at night. It can only be from spying," she muttered.

"But—"

"She is light sleeper, and she never stirred when the barrel went over. If she was in her chamber, she would have heard and come scolding."

"But how did she escape the keep? I swear she did not use the kitchen door." Niall was now more suspicious than exasperated. His hands tightened on her waist.

"There is another door at the back. She may have gone out there."

He thought about that.

"For what purpose did she spy upon us?" he demanded. "And why flee into the night?"

"Because you chased her," Lona suggested. "And to spread the glad tidings that I have gone to visit your bedchamber in the middle of the night and therefore must intend to wed again."

He stared at her, his expression arrested.

"This needn't worry you," she said tightly. "It changes nothing. Our arrangements can go on as planned. Eventually, everyone will understand that it wasn't—that we weren't trysting. That it was all a ruse."

Iona

He continued to stare, saying nothing to affirm or contradict her words. Lona's heart had just begun its plummet to the depths of despair when he said: "I wonder if that's what happened to Donnell. If she's that fast of foot and quiet . . ."

"Donnell!" Lona stiffened. "Cook did not push Donnell off the cliff. *Ow!*" she exclaimed as his fingers tightened beneath her ribs.

Niall growled and relaxed his grip. Lona knew that their lighthearted flirtation had come to an end, shattered this time by Cook's heavy-footed intrusion. And the renewed speculation of how Donnell had died. It was unfortunate that she had not had the chance to ask him about his dreams.

It was probably for the best, she instructed her too-susceptible heart. But its sorrowful throbbing suggested that it did not agree.

Lona glanced at Niall, and finding his eyes upon her, she turned her face away before it betrayed her.

"She's lucky I didn't catch her." He spoke mildly. "I might have, if I had not been distracted."

"Indeed." Lona looked over at his business-like dirk. The unadorned steel was smooth and sharp. "And by what were you distracted?"

"By you." Niall turned his face into her warmth, leaning into the valley of her breasts. This time there was no mistaking the deliberateness of his actions.

"By me?" she asked, her heart beginning to gallop under his lips, which she could feel, fabric or no. "But I was nowhere near you."

"Aye. And that was what had me distracted," he said.

Lona could not be certain, due to the thickness of her gown and robe, but she suspected that he was nuzzling her breasts, as well.

"Concern about our marriage is taking up much of my attention," he complained.

"I am a trifle concerned myself," she managed.

"Aye. But you needn't be." Niall reached up. He stroked her cheek with a long finger, his gaze almost wistful as he studied her face. Almost. There was something else there, as well. The passionate fires had been banked down, but they were still burning. And beyond that, there were questions forming in his nimble brain. Questions that hadn't been there when he'd been flirting with her.

Lona couldn't answer them because she was no more certain now than the day before that she could completely trust his charming words or deeds. Especially if Donnell's fate did matter to him.

"I think that you are not much hurt," she finally managed after a swallow or two, preparing to step away from the cage of his thighs. "Unless you have sustained other injuries, I shall leave—"

Faster than a lightning strike, his arm was about her waist. It was hard as steel.

"Niall!" she croaked.

"I feel faint," he complained, but the arm relaxed and then slipped completely away. He sighed. "It is not kind to make a grown man coax and wheedle for a little more of your time, mistress."

Lona looked again at the lethal-looking dirk gleaming on the table. It was a reminder of the violence that surrounded them. Her future stretched before her, but she could not yet see her way past the coming storms and sorrows.

She needed more time.

"Tell me, Niall," she asked quietly. "Do you always answer your door with weapon in hand? Or is it only my isle that is so honored? And who came to the door tonight? Flambard or MacKay?"

"Neither. Both. Pray forgive me, mistress. My life has recently been too precarious for the regular use of manners." He followed her gaze to the dirk on the table. He answered shortly, no doubt irritated that he had betrayed himself with the use of naked strength when he wished her to think him charmingly helpless. "I no longer take foolish chances with my life."

Lona laughed without amusement.

"Then what are you doing on Iona?"

He didn't answer her question for a long moment, but his eyes fairly smoldered as they looked up at her.

"I'm doing more than I had ever planned on, m'dear." A dangerous smile slashed his face. "I knew that I wouldn't be able to discharge my task without some danger. But, mistress, I never reckoned on finding you."

"I—here." She pulled the stained handkerchief away. Her hands showed a fine tremor. "Your wound has stopped bleeding."

"My thanks for your assistance." His voice was polite, but Lona was certain that he was fighting the urge to pull her back into his arms.

That she wanted to be there only proved that it was time for her to depart. Lona stepped away from Niall, waiting for him to protest again, but he did nothing. She walked to the door unmolested and drew back the bolt with a shaking hand. For a certainty, it was time that she effaced herself.

"You might attempt to redirect mine erring footsteps instead of fleeing, m'dear," he suggested softly. "I am educable."

Melanie Jackson

"Direct them where? Down the narrow path of virtue? That is too great an undertaking for this hour." She looked back reluctantly and offered a smile.

He shrugged. "Whither thou goest, mistress. I shall swiftly follow."

"I am going back to my own chamber to try and recapture my sleep. I suggest that you not follow me there. I think that we have given Cook enough grist for the rumor mill for one evening."

"And methinks the lassie is a coward to flee before the gossip's word," Niall taunted softly, but he was laughing with his eyes.

"I'm not a coward. I am practicing prudence," she said firmly, taking another step toward her freedom.

"Mistress Prudence, you never did say why you came here tonight."

"I was feeling momentarily intrepid." Another step of retreat brought her to the edge of the darkness. She had forgotten to bring her candle, but she did not return to Niall's side to fetch it.

"If you are still feeling intrepid, mistress," Niall's amused voice held her checked in mid-flight. "You might dream of me."

Intrepid? Lona nearly laughed. She was giddy and crazed, more like!

"I already have, Niall MacKay," she whispered, pulling the door shut behind her.

Chapter Eight

Niall was growing quite skilled at clinging to the slippery scree. This was an excellent advent because falling into the sea would be rather more embarrassing—and probably fatal—than falling into a rain barrel at the foot of a blunted stair.

His choice of scrambles was limited by circumstance. Clouds partly obscured the moon, leaving light enough to show Niall the path to Callum's abode, but not the lesser sheep tracks he'd explored during the daylight hours. The only other available trail from the back of the keep went through the herber and down to the beach where Gavin had landed, and he had no desire go there just now, however sweet the smell of newly crushed thyme was floating on the island's night wind.

Niall paused for a moment to catch his breath and listen for the stealthy sounds of pursuit, but the racket from below was of such percussive violence that nothing much could be heard above the clap of large waves hitting unforgiving stone. There was, at the moment, no beach for a prowler—or the gossiping cook—to hide upon. Satisfied that he was not in danger of being followed by anyone from below, Niall aimed his restless footsteps down the path to Callum's hovel.

The smell of herbs died away swiftly and soon the night air was filled with salt tang and unpleasant moanings, but Niall was physically unmolested except for a small gorse bush that loomed suddenly out of the darkness and twitched in an alarming manner when the wind bent its wooden spine. Fortunately, for his already wounded dignity, Niall recognized the bush for what it was before he plunged his dirk into the inanimate object and attempted to wrestle it to the ground.

His own exasperated groan joined others in the chilly, air.

Those who knew Flambard would have expected him to turn this midnight farce into a merry jest. But instead of being amused at the evening's mishaps, the moonlight showed Niall's mouth shut in a straight line, his pleasant face unusually hard.

His earlier buffoonery while chasing Cook—which had not shown him to great advantage with his future bride—was still a pointed reminder that while he was busy playing the gallant with the isle's mistress, the golden mist of his future was threatened by omnipresent danger, and that he could not afford a protracted distraction until the danger was diverted or rendered harmless. It followed, inevitably, that since Mistress Lona would continue to distract him, it behooved him to dispose of the

Iona

approaching menace as swiftly as was possible. Hence the midnight visit to Callum Bethume.

Niall stepped around the hunched bush with care and continued on his way. He trod the narrowing path with caution, but no particular quiet, as little could be heard above the island's mutterings and the sea's cold, tidal assault.

The walk from the parting of the beach path was a short one and presently he arrived at the configuration of boulders that marked Callum's humble abode. A feeble glimmer of lantern light showed round the hide door, telling any observant passerby that Callum was in—and hopefully in a mood for receiving visitors.

Niall puzzled for a moment at the door, pondering the etiquette of seeking admission when there was no panel to tap upon, but before he could decide on any alternative to knuckles on wood, the salt-stiff hide was pulled aside and a fully dressed Callum was looming in the doorway.

Niall noticed that he also had a dirk in hand, and wished that his wary love might be there to see that he was not the only suspicious resident of the isle.

"Good evening," Niall said politely, his own weapon carefully stowed.

Callum snorted and rolled an eye heavenward. He consulted a moment with the sky and then shook his head.

"Is it now? And I thought it was coomin' down cold." He lowered the knife and jerked his head in invitation, stepping away from the narrow opening.

Niall stepped inside and shrugged off his damp cloak that was by now nearly as stiff as the hide door behind him. Half of his attention was focused on Callum's weapon.

The tiny room was comfortably warm and tidy, and made only slightly redolent by the tallow dip burning on the table. Niall sniffed the atmosphere experimentally and shuddered. The best to be said of the odor was that it was not shark oil. It was, however, too cold to leave the skin parted to the evening air while he visited. Niall resigned himself. He wouldn't enjoy the experience, but would endure it for a while.

"And why are ye not lying down in yer bed? Is ought amiss with yer lodgings?" Callum's dry question suggested that Cook had already sent round the fiery cross. Niall accepted that the bubble of his vanity was being pricked, and got on with his business.

"That malevolent old woman is what is amiss. I take it that she has already been here."

"Aye, she came tae call." His tone suggested that the situation was exquisitely humorous.

"Of course she has. What else would the old witch be doing in the middle of the night but flitting on her broomstick?" He didn't add that if it was the heart benevolent and kind that most resembled God, then Cook's doubtless belonged to the devil. For some reason, the other islanders seemed to like the horrid woman and Niall was about to sue for a favor.

"Muckle she may grieve ye, but she uses a useful sharp eye."

"Indeed." Niall resisted the urge to touch his sore forehead. That was a very tangible bit of grief that she had already caused him.

"Well, ye cannae hope she'll turn a blind eye tae this callin' on the mistress and sinking into dissipation. And speaking of the blind—" Callum scrutinized his countenance, and then gave particular

Iona

study to Niall's hair. Obviously, his swift ablutions had been inadequate because Callum saw immediately that something was wrong. "I do nae like tae mention it, but ye look a wee bit pale. Pull up and set, and I'll poor ye a dram o' some gran' whisky if yer wishful of snorting a bit."

"A grand one, is it?" Niall took a stool. There was a slightly upward tilt to his mouth when he asked: "Tell me, Callum, have you ever drunk a bad whisky?"

"Ach, no. I cannae say tha' I have. But there's good whisky an' better whisky—an' I tell ye, this is the greatest." Callum set a generous mug before Niall, and waited anxiously while he sampled it.

The cup reeked. Which wasn't an entirely bad thing when the competing smells were tallow and unwashed sheep-herder.

Niall picked up the mug. He had a moment's foreboding, remembering the strength of Callum's earlier hospitality. *But faint heart ne'er won fair lady*! Niall set the rim to his lips while Callum watched anxiously from under his tufted eyebrows. The thought of poison again reared its ugly head, but having committed to a conspiracy that would end in his death should Callum betray him, he supposed that it mattered little if he died now or later. He had to trust sometime; why not this night and this man?

And surely Callum would not ruin an entire barrel of whisky just to dispose of one MacKay.

He sipped cautiously at the golden brew and gave a small grunt of pleasure. It was pure smoke and had a bite, but still managed to go down smoothly. It was indeed a grand whisky, and Niall suspected that it was all the sweeter for having escaped the malt tax.

Melanie Jackson

"I'd offer ye someitt tae eat, but I think yer hunger cannae be fed anywhere but the keep—if Cook's got the right of it." Callum barely interrupted his volubility by upending his mug and downing the contents without pausing for breath.

Niall blinked a little at the blunt speech. He was still a little out of the custom of frankness.

"You are remarkably quick to leap to conclusion. We might well have just been plotting treason," he complained, waiting for the paralysis that must surely strike Callum following the rapid consumption of a quantity of liquid fire. But as Callum continued to sit at ease, Niall went on: "However, as it happens, my intentions are honorable. All of them. I just wish that your mistress had believed me before Cook forced her hand."

"I wadnae know about all of that, but ye shouldnae lump them all together. I ken that ye possess a loyal and true heart, but 'tis for the lassie tae be deciding if ye get anything besides bannocks." Callum returned to the cask and when he retook his seat there was a second full mug cradled in his mauled hands. Niall could only marvel and conclude that Ionans must have uncommonly hard heads.

"So do I believe this. In spite of any tales that Cook has carried, I've offered marriage to your mistress—and what's more, she's accepted," Niall informed his host. "The old haggis needn't have embarrassed her in this manner."

"Aye? She's agreed? Why then are ye in bad skin, MacKay?" Callum cogitated a moment and then chuckled. "Is she nae acting like marriage to ye is the Promised Land?"

Iona

"I'm not in bad skin. I'm in bad graces. And Cook has made it worse."

Callum chuckled some more, but he was understanding. "Nay. Ye worry for naught. The mistress fancies ye. 'Tis regular caution only. Lad, 'tis a fact that she's been married afore. . . . And a solemn event is a marriage. Ye've been spared it sae far, have ye?"

"Aye. For too long, I think. I've lost the way of honest persuasion," he said morosely. "I've near had to blackmail and threaten her into it."

"Yer a bit impulsive, laddie." Callum added kindly: "There is nae such a hurry about this as the other thing. Give her some time tae think on it. She'll decide on being wifed o'er being widowed."

"But there is a need for haste. I've refined the plan, and we've little time to carry it off."

"Have ye?" Callum sobered.

"Aye. And it will involve those on the other isle. Particularly, young Duncan."

"The gowk! Puff'd up with false pride."

"It matters not. He'll cooperate all unknowing. Hist ye, whilst I explain." Niall proceeded to clarify the details of his nefarious plot and the arduous labor it would entail if all Iona was to be spared from the English. It was a simple task in conception, but they would need the entire island's hands turned to the effort.

"So, that's the way of it," Callum said slowly. He stared at the table for so long that Niall, too, felt compelled to examine the surface. Of course, there was nothing amiss. Nothing beautiful or eye-catching either. Whatever Callum was examining, it was something only he could see.

Melanie Jackson

"I hope this is the best way. Indeed, it is the only way that I perceive. I'm just grateful that Cook didn't overhear this part. This is one tale that must be kept mum."

Callum asked without looking up: "Ye ever play chess, MacKay?"

"Aye." Niall waited.

"Then ye'll ken that yer coomin' tae the end game."

"Check and mate," he agreed.

"The lassie doesnae play chess. Ye must teach her about it, and soon."

"Aye. If we have time for it." Niall rubbed his neck. "Though I wish it were possible to practice noblesse oblige, I cannot risk her neck by obeying every gentlemanly dictum. The English are not playing by established rules, and neither are we. All I can do is hope that time and circumstance will teach her to trust in me. . . . Perhaps saving the lives of everyone on the isle will begin the process."

"It may."

"Let us hope—and plan carefully. It would not do to leave the task half-done. We could easily be caught in a net of our own weaving and then the whole island would suffer for it."

"Aye." Callum tried to sound optimistic. "Well, take up yer cup. The whisky will make ye feel well-loved."

Niall snorted. It was a bad habit he had acquired from the islanders.

"Toss your cup off if you must, but I have a long walk back to my cold, cold bed. I think I'll just sneak up on this a little at a time."

"MacKay!" Callum looked shocked. "Ye've been in the South too long. It's made ye soft and cautious like. That's just a drop tae keep out the cold."

Iona

"Aye. That it has been. A long time. I haven't been home since I was lad." Niall took another sip and suddenly he began to smile. Perhaps it was the spirit's fiery influence, but the ridiculousness of his situation appealed to his sense of humor.

Over the course of the years, through careful grooming and education, Niall had created the perfect, sophisticated persona. Flambard was a gentleman of means who lived in luxury and was jealous of his creature comforts. Flambard was as far removed the wild Highland boy Niall had been in his youth as it was possible to be.

Yet, here he was back in Scotland, sitting in a stone hovel and falling back on the old Highland expediency of drinking whisky for his breakfast. He was also in more danger than the reckless Flambard had ever been while traversing about Europe for his adopted parent. Destiny was an ironic jade!

Niall caught sight of fresh stains and a tear on his cuff. He laughed softly. Another of his fine shirts was headed for the boiling pot and Mistress Lona's needle. Flambard would have been in high dudgeon at the abuse of his wardrobe, but Niall MacKay didn't care a bit. He was shedding Flambard's civilized skin in favor of a tougher hide.

There was something about Iona—and all of Scotland—with its constant uncertainty, discomfort and hazard, that made a man careless of the hard-won dignity that was valued elsewhere. As an instance of uncertainty, he could not have guessed a fortnight ago that he would be sitting in a cave with a rebel crofter, drinking malt and lamenting the sweet pangs of his first true love.

" 'Tis love ye feel?" Callum asked, causing Niall to realize that he had spoken his thoughts aloud.

Melanie Jackson

"Aye. Love and I are not well-acquainted, but I believe it is my affliction." Niall took another swallow of the liquid smoke. He added to himself: "And if it's not, it's something so near it that I'll never know otherwise."

Callum's glance was eloquent with understanding.

"A'right. Ye've two troubles. We'll begin wi' the Sasannach as they're less bothersome." Callum added a few pithy observations about the English buzzards who flew over the land.

Niall smiled. If he remained long on the isle, he would be proficient in several new forms of vulgarity.

"As tae the other . . . Well, laddie, the Lord fills a man with blood an' sweat—an' a need fer women . . . an' whisky," he added, after a moment's consideration. "They—the women—are made bonnie fer a reason. 'Tis the Lord's plan for the continuation of our kind."

"Aye." And Lona was quite tiresomely bonnie. Just thinking about her caused an emotional storm to arise in his breast. Continuing his kind with her would be a pleasure, if she let it.

"An' man has just as much appeal tae the lassies."

"Let us pray so." Niall said softly. "And that she is content to let me manage this affair without a great deal of interference and foot-dragging." Niall's face was a little grim as he contemplated the hardhearted measures he might have to employ to ensure Lona's safety. He didn't want her to see him as a naked aggressor and begin comparing him with Donnell. "Aye, I do most sincerely hope that she never finds that I am in truth as ruthless as my double-damned cousin, for she will never trust me an she does."

Iona

"Are ye so ruthless?" Callum asked without any great concern.

"Aye. And then some."

"That is nae such a bad happenstance, MacKay. A ruthless man is needed aen our isle."

"Aye. But Mistress Lona is bound to view a ruthless man as making a devil of a husband." Niall finished his drink, and he turned his head experimentally. It did not topple from his shoulders, which led him to believe that whichever version of the water of life that Callum was serving, it had not been brewed on Iona.

"Ye'll care fer the lass? Be patient if she comes over daft and female-like?" Callum insisted.

Niall smiled at the unflattering assessment of his future bride's nerves.

"She'll have all her heart desires—or as much as I can give her. And she may ride roughshod all over my life and heart—once we're safely away from this isle," he assured Callum.

"She'll nae doubt enjoy that," he said comfortably.

"No doubt." Niall changed the subject. "Will there be any trouble procuring Gavin's services?"

"Nay. He'll give aid an' gladly so."

"Good." Niall stood up. He was relieved at his upright position. It confirmed his theory of the whisky's safer origins until he heard himself ask: "Callum, if a man is filled with blood and sweat, what then is a woman filled with?"

Callum finished his own mug and rose to his feet without a single stagger or weave.

"Wi' paradise, lad, and maybe yer salvation."

"Salvation . . . For the second time in my life?" Niall's quick smile was whimsical. "I am growing

Melanie Jackson

maudlin. So I believe that this is an auspicious moment for our parting."

He pulled several sheets of folded parchment from his pocket and laid them of the table. Only one of them was sealed. Callum glanced down and frowned.

"That's them?"

"Aye. Do make an effort to keep them from Cook's greedy eyes. Such small things, these papers, but they could get us all hanged."

"Aye. I'll take great care," he answered, scooping up the letters and shoving them into his own pouch.

"Have a pleasant—if long and wet—day."

"Yer day'll be long as well, MacKay, if drier. I hope ye are a social beast for the kin are likely cooming tae call at first light."

"Aye. Thanks to Cook."

Niall nodded politely to his host, stepped out gladly into the freshening air, and began a slow and careful stroll back to the dark keep where his possible salvation—and paradise—lay slumbering abed.

Or would she be awake, worrying about the morrow's advent?

He considered laying in wait for the malevolent creature who was the cause of tomorrow's embarrassment—Lona's embarrassment, not his own. For himself, and for the sake of his insane plan, he had to be glad that Cook had forced his love's cautious hand.

Given that small mitigation, and the fact that he was more than ready to seek the warmth of his cot, he decided against catching the gossip and throwing her into the sea as punishment for her moonlight flitting.

Niall smiled nastily. Anyway, he could always

Iona

strangle Cook in the morning—providing Mistress Lona did not perform the task herself.

Lona was abed, but not slumbering. A very unpleasant thought had occurred to her upon returning to her chamber, and it had destroyed her ability to sleep.

In the haste and shock of Niall's planning, Lona had forgotten about Donnell. But now that she had been given a brief respite, his shade had moved into view and blotted out her sunny horizon.

Niall's words about Cook's possible involvement in Donnell's death proved that the dead man was still in Niall's thoughts. Eventually, if they married, she would have to tell Niall the truth of what had happened to his cousin.

And then he might hate her. He was a man of sensitivity and would most likely be repelled by her actions—however justified they had been.

The thought of Niall's revulsion and hatred was one cross too many for her to bear. Lona turned her face into the scratchy blankets and wept.

Chapter Nine

That most punctual of Iona's guests, the sun, arrived the next morning bright and—to Lona's thoughts—far too early. Her eyelids drooped as she listened to the wind blustering at her shutters and Cook banging pots about in the kitchen. She was exhausted after her night of passionate, futile weeping, but the dawn waited for no man—and certainly no woman! Lona grimaced at the ceiling but pushed her blankets aside without further delay.

The face in her hand mirror was of a woman sorely tried and Lona replaced the glass hastily, face-down on the table. It was difficult enough to encounter the morning with optimism and cheer after a long night absent of repose. She didn't need the looking glass's bleak taunts added to her woes.

Lona pulled the twine from her braid and shook her hair loose. The best that she could hope to man-

Iona

age that dawn was a polite placidity and a degree of neatness. Niall would probably not be deceived into thinking that all was well, but it would do for the others—they were, after all, expecting her to be showing the signs of dissipated revelry.

There were a great many things that she would have to do in the next precious few days, all of them either difficult, unpleasant or both. But, "suffice it unto the day, the troubles therein," she reminded herself as she combed out her hair with long, soothing strokes that were a form of meditation. She would surmount these tribulations as she had all the others that had faced the isle. The device was to tackle the troubles singly and not allow their collective size and numbers to overwhelm her reason. The islanders would accept MacKay if they were handled with care and tact.

She neatened her clothing and straightened the bed as she did every morning, and thus spiritually fortified by the morning routine, Lona pulled open her door and went out to partake of the early air.

She suffered her first reverse in the kitchen. If there was any justice, Cook likewise would have shown a haggard countenance and bloodshot eyes, but she was her usual, actively disagreeable self as she fussed over the kitchen hearth and sniffed meaningfully about the mistress's late rising. She also muttered darkly about Niall being abed at this late hour, and speculated about what the other islanders would have to say about the coincidence.

Lona came close to boxing Cook's ears for the last remark—since if there was any speculation on the island it came from her own gossiping tongue—and she said as much through clenched teeth and fists.

Cook shrugged and replied smugly that it mattered not how rumors began, the result would still be the same: a wedding.

"You're proud of yourself, aren't you? But do you seriously believe that you could trap the MacKay by compromising me with this unproven gossip?"

"If he's a man of guid character—"

"Aye. If he is, it might work. But what has led you to believe that Niall MacKay *is* a man of good character?"

"Are ye witless? The man isnae like his wicked kin." Cook snorted at the idea.

"Much you know," Lona answered crossly, even if she was secretly pleased by Cook's favorable evaluation of Niall's personality.

"Well, we shall see. The others will be waiting tae see what ye say about this. Sae make haste."

Lona wanted to argue the point, but even the kitchen cat's yellow gaze seemed unusually inquisitive as it stared from its customary place at the hearth.

Lona decided that she needed more armor before facing an island full of persons who believed that she had passed the previous night wallowing in sin with another MacKay. She refrained from heeding Cook's grumbled warnings about the time, and instead carried a brass can of hot water back to her chamber and indulged in a warm basin bath.

After a time of quiet, where she breathed in the fumes of steeping heather she'd tossed in the can, Lona decided that she was prepared to gird up her loins and face Niall and the others. She would not enjoy the morning and its inquisitive visitors, but the day was as comfortable and civilized as it was going to get with a MacKay in the keep, Cook in the

Iona

kitchen, a cursed treasure in a barrow, and English vultures circling the isle.

She found Niall was up, shaved and manicured, and awaiting her at the kitchen's small table. He smiled warmly as she entered the room and rose up from his stool to guide her to the board as though he expected her footsteps to falter. Unlike yestereve, Lona did not enjoy the show of sweet solicitude.

"Many thanks," she managed politely, even though her jaws were tight.

Niall smiled widely. Though she admired his handsome face, the cheerful, rested countenance rankled. No true son of Caledonia was this joyful on a wintery morning.

"Good morning, Mistress. It seems that we have only light showers and wind to plague us this day."

"How fortunate for us," she replied sardonically. "Do you plan to be out of doors a long while this morning?"

Cook pushed between them and placed a dish on the table. Lona's nose wrinkled. She couldn't help but notice that Cook was reeking of thyme. She looked at the hem of the old woman's skirts and found it grimed with haulms. Lona's lips tightened. The exit from the monk's tunnel opened up at the edge of a bed of the wild herb. The twigs were as damning as a confession.

"I rather expect so." Niall answered calmly but his expression grew slightly wary as he took in her swollen eyes and fixed expression. He suggested gently: "Will you not break your fast? Cook has made bannocks. Don't fret about the smell. She did not add any thyme to the honey."

Lona nodded tightly and allowed Niall to seat her

at the table. His elaborate courtesies almost made her smile, in spite of having a heart bowed down with woe and a tongue that was itching for an opportunity to flay Cook's broad hide.

"Mistress, I would not care to trouble you, but I need must borrow Callum to deliver some letters for me. I hope that you can spare him."

"That is fine talking, sir, when you know full well that you don't care one whit if you trouble me," she said crossly.

"But, m'dear, how can you say so?" Niall captured her hand. He was less lover-like than chiding. She noticed then the bruise just under his barbered locks and reminded herself that she was not the only one who would suffer for Cook's gossip. They also had a duty to perform and it required that she play a sweeter role.

"My apologies, Niall," she said quietly. "I am not my best this morning."

"Alack! And just when you've made me the happiest of men, mistress. Perhaps I can spread the cheer while you rest. Why Cook was just offering her congratulations. I'm sure that you'll be pleased by her approval. The rest of your people will wish to hear our news as well. And, of course, I wish to inform my own family of the joyous event."

Lona tried to think of an appropriate comment that was both polite and truthful, but failed to do so. She contented herself with a fleeting touch of his bruised brow—a kind gesture which surprised Niall into blinking—and glaring at Cook with an evil eye.

"Poor Niall. Iona has been unkind to both your person and your wardrobe." Cook snorted and Lona scowled horribly at her broad backside. She said

Iona

loudly: "I am ashamed at the inhospitable welcome you have received on my isle."

"Cheer up, lass. We can always drown her in the sea on the way to Tiree," Niall whispered while pressing a swift kiss into her captured palm. He went on in a normal voice. "Finish your meal and I'll be on my way rejoicing. Don't worry that you'll be left to cope with all the details of the wedding, for I have them well in hand."

"I never doubted it," she answered ironically, tucking her tingling hand out of sight. "But haste ye back, Niall MacKay. We have much to speak of yet."

"Never fear. I shall return forthwith." Niall pulled on his much-used cape, stopped at the table to recapture her hand and press a kiss into her wrist, and then was off into the wet morn.

Cook *harrumphed* triumphantly and stomped out of the kitchen before Lona could belabor her.

Lona ate without enthusiasm and found that she was growing drowsy sitting by the fire. She decided not to wait for Niall to return and explain his plans. There was much work that needed to be accomplished in the few free days they had remaining. She could not afford to waste any time, not even on the lingering enjoyment of Niall's farewell kiss.

It seemed to a bewildered Lona in the days that followed Niall's proposal that the whole of Iona followed the charming MacKay like bespelled rats after the *Daoine Shi*—the fairy pied-piper—dancing all the way to Tiree. All that was needed for Niall to work his spell upon the islanders was the invocation of that most powerful of charms, the wedding feast. From the first incantation of those powerful words it took only ten days for the enthralled Ionans to arrange the grandest MacLean nuptials of two decades.

And there was none of the expected grumbling about the indecency of marrying less than a year into her widowhood either, Lona thought indignantly as she accepted her second score of congratulations from her besotted kinsmen.

Niall had wasted no time in carrying forth with his plan. She heard from Cook that Callum was sent off post-haste with Niall's letters—mere hours after Lona accepted Niall's unromantic proposal.

Lona was not surprised at her news. Callum went as Niall had planned the previous day, sailing off on the morning tide, but carrying with him the additional two harmless missives from *Niall MacKay*.

One innocent message was to Niall's family in the North whom, Niall admitted privately, would be very surprised to hear from him.

Lona gave in to momentary curiosity and asked what they would think of the news. She feared that they would not like it, but Niall said that he was indifferent. He conceded that they might well write to condemn him for the moral aberration of stealing Donnell's wife and property by marrying his deplorable rebel wife—and perhaps to scold him for not sending a purse home with his letter. But as they would not be on the isle to receive any chiding responses, he didn't propose to worry himself about the matter—and neither should she. Her own kin's reaction was of more immediate importance.

Niall needn't have worried. The other document was written for the easy consumption of any interested parties on Tiree, and was rather heavier since it contained both a fat purse of silver and a polite

Iona

letter to the principal of Tiree outlining his intention to marry the mistress of Iona. The two parchments copied out in Niall's bold hand and signed with his rightful name were handled quite openly, stared at by many, and read greedily by the few who were able—and nosy enough—to demand a wee peep before Callum got off the island.

There were several of these hardy, curious souls who came out at dawn to see the herder off to Tiree, as news of Niall's plans to marry Lona had swept over the island as quickly as Cook could carry it through the dark and rain, and it drew the old gossips like bees to heather. No work of fiction had ever been so greedily consumed.

They both spent several moments silently contemplating the third—and most important—of Niall's letters. Lost in the folds of Callum's thick cloak and wrapped in oiled-skin, the last epistle, the one from Flambard to a certain French captain, was carried with greater care. It had been hidden there by Callum with the firm intention that it be passed to old Gavin one dark night—and not discussed with another soul in the isles. Or so they prayed.

The story about the purse of silver served as a grand divertissement, but it also had the added effect of bringing to the keep an amazingly large assortment of the less curious and hardy persons whom had missed Callum's dawn departure. Niall was introduced to them, one by one, by a very quiet Lona who dispensed whisky and bannocks with a steady hand as she greeted the thronging horde.

Niall hadn't realized until that evening, when the masses had subsided with the sun, that there were so many souls on Iona that he hadn't yet met and who would need transport to Tiree when the time came to leave. Where they had been hiding themselves he could hardly imagine, for it did not seem possible that fifty-odd persons could be crowded into the few cottages that made up the tiny hamlet near the keep.

He finally concluded that they must live in the caves and barrows the way Callum did; it would help explain the feeling he always had when walking about that he was closely observed by hidden eyes. That was a marginally more comforting thought than the notion of Lona's Pictish ghosts following him about with the wind.

Niall also discovered something more about his bride, as well. Even making every allowance for unity in the face of another MacKay, it soon became apparent that Lona MacLean was held in near mystical esteem by the Ionans. Her stewardship of the island had extended far beyond the role of landlord to tenant, and had crossed into the realm of a chieftain ruling a clan.

The true oddity of the arrangement was that few of the strangely assorted Ionans were blood kin to her. Their only commonality was that they all had their backs to the wall and that there was no place else to go. They were poor, landless, and broken, collected up by Wallace and Hector to fight in the prince's war, but ministered to in the aftermath of the rebellion—and right well—by Mistress Lona.

The sense of duty and obligation on both sides made the success of his endeavor all the more critical. If he failed to bring the Ionans off safely, his bride would likely never be able to forgive him—or herself—for failing them.

Feeling grim and determined, Niall set to work with a will.

Iona

The wedding could actually have been accomplished in only three days since no banns were required on Tiree and all that was needed for passage was a moderate sea—and Heaven knew that Ionans were willing! But Niall had to allow sufficient time for Gavin to track down LaCroix on Mull and get back to Tiree; also he wanted as reasonable a span as he could arrange for the Ionans to gather their possessions and finish their soft, loomed cloths which they could sell later that summer when the need for money was upon them. Things were going to be a lot harder for the old ones when Lona was gone, and they would need every bit of silver they could earn before moving on to new lives.

A reasonable wait was also one of the two conditions of acceptance that Lona had imposed on their marriage, and since he had absolutely no intention of honoring the other codicil, he did his best to keep faith on his first promise.

Still, though Niall had agreed readily to delay the wedding as long as possible, he was always aware that on the other side of the narrow line they walked was the inevitable fact that at any day the weather could moderate sufficiently for the English to arrive on Iona. So, safety of person was weighed against the safety of future economics. . . . Should they drag the Ionans away from their isle to save them from the physical prisons of the English, only to condemn them to the prison of poverty?

Lona said nay. And she continued to say it every time he asked.

In exasperation, five days after he had made his reluctant promise of time, Niall looked out at the humming, happy islanders and offered to dower the entire island, if they would only make haste to leave the isle for the comparative safety of Tiree.

Lona said nay to that also.

He demanded if she thought he was not good for the debt, and she had answered sadly that there would not be time for her people to discover that he was. And in any event, the islanders would not accept money from a MacKay's hands.

Charity might begin at home, but obviously it could not come from a MacKay. The bridegroom ground his teeth in frustration at the continuing lack of trust on his bride's part, but he was running out of clever ideas to demonstrate his honor and loyalty.

After that daunting conversation, Niall said nothing more to his bride-to-be about paying for the islanders' safety, though he silently damned the stiff-necked pride that was the bane of the island Scots. And the Highland Scots. And the Lowland Scots. Counting the days until the necessary tasks were done, and watching both the weather and his ladylove for sign of improvement of temperament was not a conundrum he enjoyed in the slightest.

For the first time in his life, Niall prayed for inclement weather. He prayed for other things as well, mostly for inner fortitude because he continued to dream of his ladylove with distressing regularity and in intimate, colorful detail that was more than mortal flesh and blood should be called upon to bear.

He was frustrated on another front as well. Niall's usual skill at the cat-and-rat game had abandoned him. The silent waiting exhausted his usually limitless patience, and he found himself shifting whisky barrels with Callum and Iain as an anodyne to the

Iona

restlessness that grew every day that passed and Gavin was not heard from.

Almost, he looked forward to tearing down the treasure's cairn for a second time and loading the cask into a boat that could take the damning evidence away from Iona. And he might have done it in spite of his better judgement but for Callum's calming presence and repeated urges to wait on Gavin.

The quiet herder had returned swiftly from his errand to Tiree. He was big with news. The Principal MacLean, Duncan, had charged Callum with the message that he was sending a small fleet to carry the Ionans—and as much whisky as they would care to bring—to his isle, where a large wedding feast was even now being planned in the bridal couple's honor. Kin from Mull and the mainland would attend, as well. The missing Gavin had been sent to invite them.

In a hasty aside, Callum warned Niall that three Englishmen were already ensconced in the manor house on Tiree; they had been sent on from the MacLeans of Mull after visiting the other isles in LaCroix's wake.

Cottan dearg—redcoats—spies they were, he warned Niall, his large jaw out-thrust. Boggles, the light infantry of Satan. His missing fingers were prickling with ghostly admonitions.

Niall didn't need any ghostly prickling to warn him of the Englishmen's likely purpose in visiting Tiree. This development was not unexpected, but it did make the situation slightly more difficult and a great deal more dangerous. He could only hope that the islanders' innocent delight in squandering his money while planning their mistress's wedding would be sufficient to screen his true plans from prying eyes, and that LaCroix had not betrayed himself to the Sasannachs who were likely only waiting for the weather to moderate before forging on to the ghost isle to hunt for the fugitive prince and his missing treasury.

Niall came to Lona's chamber again that night to tell her in private of what had occurred on Tiree, and what he feared might be the Sasannachs' purpose in visiting all the western isles.

She took the news with her habitual calm, though she was troubled that so many kin were gathering on the isle; they had not done this for the other two weddings and she did not know how to interpret this action. It could simply be that after the long winter, the MacLeans were ready for a feast. Or it might betoken something much more sinister—especially if the prince had escaped from Skye. Perhaps Gavin would bring them further news.

Niall bit back his more blasphemous words, refrained from kissing his ladylove into insensibility and thereby hopefully extracting a promise of haste, and left her chamber by only the greatest effort of will—and the knowledge that Cook very likely had her ear pressed to the door. He still had no proof that she had spied upon them, but how else could the sly boots have known of his proposal of marriage before he'd been 'round to see Callum? He had not forgotten the unlikely smell of thyme that had lingered in the air when he took his midnight stroll, or the fact that Cook had appeared the next morning with the same herb clinging to her skirts.

Niall scowled at the mystery of how she had escaped the keep without his detection, and then he shifted a great deal more whisky in the cold drizzle

Iona

to work off his fresh accumulation of frustrations.

He would have preferred to shelter Lona from the worry of the British presence so near to Iona, but his second-sighted love was too adept at learning the truth to leave such an advent long undiscovered, and he was trying very hard to be completely honest in his dealings with her. The period of his casual deceptions was over and done with; from here on, he was only Niall MacKay, a man honest as the day—and night—was long.

Then ill-fortune struck the island. The sheltering rains began to slacken. Niall's patience also began to slacken and he again urged haste. Confronting Lona over a cozy supper of potato soup, he stated finally that they dared not delay their bridals beyond Saturday next or LaCroix's presence would certainly be noted and cause suspicion among the English. The blockade could be summoned at any moment if the seas were calm enough for travel between the mainland and Mull.

Sensing that her reprieve had come to an end, and that Niall was sufficiently concerned to effect her removal willy-nilly did she not cooperate, Lona relented.

Saturday was agreed upon as the day of departure and all efforts to be prepared for the wedding were redoubled. Callum returned to Tiree with another letter and jingling purse for Duncan.

In the days that followed, Callum, Niall and Lona might have had worry in their hearts, but the other islanders were ecstatic at the prospect of the wedding feast. They dragged out their finest clothes, polished up their pipes and fiddles, and began to practice their airs and dances. There was a joy in the wet atmosphere that had not been felt on the isle since Lona's first wedding, before the troubles of '45 and the prince's rebellion.

Niall even heard some jokes issuing from the old, wrinkled faces that had almost forgotten how to smile, and he tried to share their innocent enjoyment of his hurried wooing and the plans for his nuptials. And at moments he did feel pleasure. The old, worn story of the dog who ate the bagpipes because there was both meat and music in the meal had made his lips twitch.

Callum's description of a Highlander chiding a pastor for walking abroad on the Sabbath actually made him laugh—Niall could not resist the image of the stern Covenanter saying to the erring minister: "Aye, the Laird did walk abroad on the Sabbath and I never thought any the more of him for doing it."

Even Lona managed a small smile when the story was repeated to her by Cook, who could not resist stealing Callum's thunder by rushing the tale ahead of him, but almost immediately she fretted aloud to Niall that they could not tell her kin to take all their possessions with them when they left for Tiree.

He consoled her with the possibility that they could return after the English had gone from her isle and collect their few meager bits of furniture and the all-important looms.

She was frustrated by his answer but had to agree to leave it at that; their total ignorance meant total innocence in their actions. Innocence would be their only reprieve from suspicion and questioning, short of an incriminating flight from the isles, and most of the islanders were too old and set in their ways to contemplate beginning a new life in some other land.

Iona

The interval to the week's end crawled for the impatient Niall, but this time the hours of waiting rushed on the fleetest wing for Lona, as the days for her people on Iona counted down to the final one. So involved was she with this happenstance, that she was very nearly able to push from her mind all thought of what her new life might be, either with Niall, or more likely, without.

The ever-present thought of Donnell's fate and the confession that must be made caused a certain lowness of spirit, but Lona kept herself so occupied that she had little time to pay it heed except in the dark of night when she was all alone. Then, disinclined or not, she was forced to think on what would happen when she confessed her deed. Some days her imagination said that Niall would forgive her for what she had done. On others, he turned from her in disgust and loathing.

But whatever her waking thoughts, in her dreams she imagined having a child. The compelling, lifelike image of the dark-haired babe in the bedside cradle haunted her even after waking.

In her sleep Niall came and gave her a babe, night after night. He made love to her in many places and at many times of day, and always it was warm and the breezes that swirled around them were scented with exotic flowers rather than briny sea.

Niall was never rough with her as Donnell had been, and always awaited her consent before coming to her bed. She knew his body well by now, his smell and taste, and passionate expressions of pleasure and love—and yet, he had not in actual fact done more than kiss her hand since the night when he proposed their union.

Melanie Jackson

Lona did not know if it was the ghosts who sent these dreams or her own lonely imagination, but hour by hour they wore down her resistance in both mind and heart until she was almost desperate for the reality of making love with Niall MacKay—regardless of the consequences.

Chapter Ten

Lona had no time on her wedding morn to say a proper farewell to kings Duncan and MacBeth, and the others buried on the isle. She rose in darkness to bathe and dress, but the isle was far from still as the singing Ionans came by torchlight to board Duncan's fleet of ferries. There was no wind whispering their royal blessings from the dark cliffs, yet Lona was sure they heard the islanders' happiness and that they wished them all godspeed, whilst she closed all the shutters for a final time and scattered the fires' embers in the keep's already cooling hearths.

She was standing alone in the darkened kitchen watching the red sparks blink out one by one, remembering her mother as a young woman just come to the isle after the failure of the first uprising had sent them from their home among the

Protestant MacLeans. Lona had been four and Hector eight when Wallace had brought his family to Iona. A youthful Lorna MacLean had been seated on a bench next to Cook who'd also been younger then. She had not been aware of her quiet daughter's presence hovering outside the door when she'd said quietly that Hell must be just like this empty, ill-laid kitchen, a barren place without a fire in its hearth and the larder swept bare by cruel fate.

Lona had been frightened then, but now she did not think that the empty, echoing kitchen was so much like Hell as a lonely stone grave.

Melancholia might have overshadowed her as she stood in the dark with her private ghosts, had she not heard Gavin's cheery voice in the forecourt raised in silly song.

> *Gavin MacLean's m'name*
> *an' Scotland's m'nation.*
> *Tiree's m'home*
> *an' Heaven's m'destination.*

"The guid Laird'll spare ye a while yet. He's in nae great haste to see ye," Cook interjected sharply.

Guessing at the cause of the old woman's cross reply, Gavin went on in a teasing sing-song:

> *O the stormy sea, it vexes me*
> *The waves they drive me mad.*
> *Up an' doon, I pull my oars*
> *an' sailing's just as bad.*

Iona

"Ye witless graybeard—" Cook screeched, affronted at the taunt to her seamanship, which widely was known to be very poor.

Lona quickly abandoned the shadowy kitchen and her ghosts, and went out to the courtyard to keep the peace. Gavin in high spirits needed looking after for he would tease Cook until she assaulted him. Much as she might want to, Lona had no time to brood over the abandonment of her isle; fate was marching on to Tiree and she had been chosen as the standard-bearer.

She had one bad moment before they boarded when the kitchen cat came down to the beach to see them off, and she realized that they were leaving her behind on the empty island.

"Niall," she whispered, distressed, looking into the cat's calm eyes.

"I know, m'dear, but we can't take her," he said gently, his own voice hushed. Niall squeezed her hand. "Don't fret. Gavin will come back for her. I'd take her now, but how would we explain her presence to the others?"

Lona shook her head. It couldn't be done. If they took the moggie, they might as well hire a crier to announce their plans for permanent departure. The cat would have to remain behind with the sheep and the crying birds.

Her heart misgave her, but she allowed Niall to lead her away from the lonely feline who sat on the beach, watching in stillness until they were well away.

The actual crossing to the flat isle of Tiree began before true dawn on her wedding day and was an easy one, blessed with a golden sunrise, as they neared the larger isle and calmer waters, than they had seen in an eight-month. Everyone huddled about Lona in Gavin's boat said that it was a good omen; but she looked at Niall's closed face where he stood at the prow watching the lightening horizon with a weathered eye, and knew that a slackening of the rough seas was as ill an omen as they could possibly have.

Lona turned from her husband-to-be and looked over the curving bow at the stern, past her gabbling kin and Gavin's solid shoulders, to the smaller boat where Callum toiled alone. He was hauling Iona's remaining stores of whisky and his aged keel rode low in the choppy water.

There had been talk about this decision to move the whisky so early in the spring and in a lone ship. Lona had told everyone that Niall had found a French buyer for their life water, but that it would all have to go at once and be loaded at sea, for the other vessel was too large for Tiree's tiny dock. It was that or lose their contract with the foreign gentleman.

The fact that their whisky would not go to the hated English had cheered the cautious ones enough to pass her half-truth as a suitable explanation for the unusual and hurried arrangements. Lona was shrewd, they knew, and they trusted her to see them right. She found her lie of omission was a bitter bile to swallow.

Lona watched in the dawn light as Callum handled the laden boat with consummate skill. The old man's limbs seemed strung together out of the hardest hemp rope sewn over with the toughest hide the sea could cure, but still his joints must feel the strain of hauling his burden by the strength of his oars. The wallowing boat was difficult to control all alone and there was no wind for a sail. Every minute it fell farther behind the others.

Iona

Lona had wanted to send another man along to help him, but Callum had refused point-blank. She understood his reasons. If they were stopped and searched, and the treasure was found aboard, anyone on the boat immediately would be executed. Callum refused to play God with another's life, and in truth, she did not know who she could ask to man the boat without telling him of the genuineness of the danger. Iain would certainly have volunteered, but he was so very frail and old. They were all very gallant and very old.

For one treasonous moment, Lona wished that Callum's boat would overturn and that the cursed treasure would be lost in the sea; but then she remembered the rest of the cargo that he carried. That whisky was going to pay for a new life for her people by giving them a start on Tiree. They would not be coming to the isle as beggared kin, but as people of at least minimal means who could pay their way until it was safe to return to their own isle.

Thinking of those minimal means, Lona looked over at the third boat in their tiny flotilla. It was carrying every last bit of woven goods that the women could finish. Again there had been some puzzlement about her haste and constant toil at the looms—asking the old ones to weave late into the evening by lantern light while refusing to spare time for the sewing of a bridal dress—but she told them again that there would be buyers on Tiree come for the wedding, people other than the English that she would prefer to sell their cloth to.

And again the women had all agreed to her plan and had set to work with a will—even Cook who usually avoided the *other wabsters* as being beneath her notice.

Melanie Jackson

Thinking of her old nemesis, Lona turned sideways to take another unobtrusive peep at the Old Mother Demdike who was squatting on her stout haunches in the bottom of the boat and muttering darkly. Cook did not care for ocean travel, but even less did she care to have her sea-weakness commented upon.

She was wearing her Sunday finery, a cloak of leprous green and brown that matched her current nauseated complexion, and when she occasionally thrust her face from under her hood to gulp some sea air, she looked a great deal like some sly, malicious toad peering out from under a pile of moldy leaves.

Reassured that Cook was still breathing and coping with their journey in her own peculiar fashion, Lona turned her worried thoughts inward and struggled to maintain her air of calm. The dreaded hour of confrontation approached and she was losing her blessed calm.

They arrived on Tiree in good time and without mishap. No one seemed to notice as they set all but Callum's boat ashore on the cockle-shell beach so similar to Iona's, that the bride was in a less than celebratory frame of mind.

That was due mainly to Niall, who was giving a fine performance as a lusty, joyous groom as he strolled through the small town calling out salutations. It was a spectacle sufficiently attention-calling to take all eyes from the somber bride—and even from a bonny prince with a coronation parade, had such a train been nearby.

Illumined by a rare day of sun, her husband-to-be looked like an effete butterfly as he spun and danced on the green path that led through the village,

Iona

dressed in his bright blue cloak and colorful court clothes, greeting their guests—people hardly known to him from his brief stay—with generous Highland effusion. Niall was preparing to lead them a merry dance, and she prayed that she was not mistaken in him and that he raced toward freedom, and not greed or the Hanover king. Of course, regardless of where the chase ended, the fox was out of its earth and running; the race against the Sasannach had begun.

She was lightheaded with worry. Lona ducked her chin and feeling wan, she tried to pinch some color into her cheeks. The withdrawal of attention from the bride was well-timed. It had been shock enough for Lona to step out onto the shore of Tiree and find the warm sun awaited her. A year had passed since her last visit, and she noted with a briery pang that the miraculous phenomenon of spring had come again to the larger isle.

The bare winter ground had been covered with a soft fur of new green grass and a few bluebells had begun to bloom in sheltered places in the rocks. Soft sunlight shone like a benediction on the new fields where tiny lambs gamboled. The isle had put on its wedding clothes for them. Even the deeply bitten stone that made up the gray village, pitted by a century of wind-borne sand and reflected as lighter shadows in the few lingering, tarry puddles, wore an air of gaiety under its mantle of early blooming heather.

She drank in the beauty, but it was not enough to warm the cold inside her.

Duncan came down from the manor to greet them, the household led out in force by the young principal of Tiree. Her cousin was of medium height and carried himself well—and was every inch a Lowland stranger. He was wearing a new dignity with his white-linen shirt, made from a cloth that dazzled the eye with its purity and was trimmed out in a Flemish lace and belted over French trews. He also carried embroidered gauntlets and a lace handkerchief in his left hand.

Lona again had to conceal her shock. The last time she had seen Duncan he had been arrayed in a rather shabby MacLean plaid, worn as a show of support for the prince under whom his father would not fight. Today he looked like a prosperous, Lowland foreigner.

"Shuis slo slumus sheen!" Mine is yours and yours is mine—he called out in awkward Gaelic, embracing Niall as he would a brother before turning to buss his cousin.

She accepted the embrace but quickly stepped away from Duncan, feeling like a pariah and having no taste for stray kisses, even from kin.

Looking about at her milling clan—sadly short of so many familiar faces—Lona saw that all of the remaining men were dressed as Duncan was, and she realized in a final manner that Hector's cause was truly lost in the isles. The clan had been all but destroyed by the second rebellion for the bonnie prince, all signs of it obliterated by death and the fear of reprisals against Hector's remaining kin. They should be left to rest in peace; not forced to play host to the woman who was a reminder of all their suffering.

"A glorious day it is for me to take a wife," Niall agreed.

It was indeed a glorious day for a wedding; and the bride didn't seem able to feel a thing except

Iona

numbing anxiety that she had brought another curse into the MacLeans' midst by trying to return the prince's money.

Her stomach quaked. For the sake of her remaining kin, the prince's treasure should have been left in its grave—and patriotism be damned! Instead it would be trundled ashore with the other food and drink for the feast; a bit of treasonous poison among their sumptuous banquet meats.

And if the English had found the grave? What would have happened then? Have you the right to save Iona by endangering Tiree? asked her conscience.

Lona rubbed a finger between her troubled brows. She didn't know any longer which was the right thing to do.

The Tiree women surrounded her at once, babbling happily about the feast to come. Lona was not an innocent maid going to the altar for the first time, so many of the wedding rituals would be overlooked. Due to their haste, there had been no time to embroider linens or stitch a bridal gown. Lona would have to wear the soft plaid wool that had come from her own loom, died to match the summer heather and threaded with a white-striped border as pure as an angel's halo.

Though a fine dress and the virgin's veil was missing, still the women wished to comb her hair and weave some flowers in it before they went to the kirk. Lona was content to let them do this for her. Her one admitted vanity was her hair, thick and black like raven's wing, which she wanted to display favorably for her new groom so that he would not be shamed by the bride for whom he was endangering himself.

Lona knew that she and Niall were to have a

Covenanter wedding. The fiddler's bitch had sniffed them out and the gossips on Mull were determined to have their way in this. The first MacLean wedding after the rebellion would not be a Catholic one; not when the enemy was near and hunting Jacobite sympathizers.

She did not care, Lona told herself, for Niall did not. Her groom claimed that he would gladly be married by a Hebrew rabbi, if that was all they could find, but Lona suspected that it was only his exquisite manners that led him to say such gallant things. For surely a man who had never been married before would wish his wedding to be in the church of his own faith.

Of course, Niall didn't have a faith, not truly. He had been baptized as a Catholic, as she had been, but in many ways that boy MacKay was long disappeared from the man who bore the same name.

He had told her more about himself in the days before their wedding, small snippets of his checkered career, and she knew that he had worn many different identities while both spying and conducting business for his philanthropist employer. In his various roles he had worshipped at many faiths in many nations. He could play the Puritan bridegroom with ease.

The fact of his religious fecklessness didn't bother her as it probably ought; she felt no horror at his fall from grace by this idolatrous blasphemy. Perhaps that was because she had fallen so far from faith and grace herself that she did not mind being among the heathen ghosts or even marrying a man who felt no need for divine grace.

Entering another church was surely less offensive to God than her own grievous trespasses.

Iona

It was a sin, the church said, to take another's life.

It was also a sin, she felt in her angry, blaspheming heart, that the Lord had so abandoned her that she had had to sin to save her family's lives. The fact that Donnell had fallen off the red granite cliff without being pushed did not excuse her, not according to either her own church or the Covenanter's kirk—for was it not true that those who sinned with the heart were as guilty as those who did the deed? Nor had she repented her act in the days that followed or even confessed it.

Aye, by the church's definition of sin she was very far from grace. It was best for Niall that they were not marrying in the true faith with such a stain upon her soul. Because of marrying as a Protestant, a divorce or annulment might even be attained at a later time if that was what Niall should want.

He might very well be compelled to it when she told him of his cousin's true fate, which she would have to do someday. She might not confess her deeds to a priest, but her honest heart demanded that she tell the truth to Niall. But what then would become of her marriage? . . . Hadn't she been unable to remain in a marriage with a man who had her kin's blood upon his hands? Would her husband feel any differently than she had? He was not impervious to her charms, so she indulged the optimism that he might care enough to forgive her but . . .

Lona swallowed hard. It made her ill to the stomach to think that Donnell's poisoned intent could spread even from the grave. Was he one of the ghosts now? Had he sent her dreams of Niall—luring her into false hope?

A cold fist squeezed her heart as she thought on this, and one of the women noticed her sudden pallor. She exclaimed worriedly about the heat and Lona forced herself to straighten and smile reassuringly at the concerned faces. She would not own up to feeling either fear or fatigue.

Her marriage might be a hollow sham, but she would not present a betraying, pallid countenance to the world. She must appear gay or at least content at these nuptials or their plot would not have a hope of succeeding. Their act had been set in motion and could not be called back. She and Niall had no choice now; the Sasannach's were here and must be duped. For everyone's sake, they had to stay calm.

If luck did not turn against them, they would carry the day. For Flambard, duping the others would be simplicity itself. He was inclined to dissimulation and masquerade, and had spent years honing his skills before the most critical of audiences. She would place her dependence upon Niall's ingenuity and guile, and Callum's steady wits.

And Iona's whisky, of course. Today it truly was the water of life. By sundown everyone on the island needed to be drunk and lost in revelry; everyone accept Callum, Gavin and Capitaine LaCroix, who were to transfer the last piece of cargo to his ship under the cover of darkness. The ship and its whisky already would have been searched by the diligent coast guard because it had been told openly by her captain of her early morning sailing. They hoped that the small cask mixed among the other barrels that were brought to the feast would be unmolested.

Niall would have sent the Frenchman on his way to France this very night, but their actions needed to appear innocent and natural. That was why they

Iona

could not themselves immediately flee Tiree. The bluff must run its full course if those left behind were to be spared suspicion in later days. They would honeymoon on Tiree for another ten days and then depart.

Lona scolded herself. She already had risked so much to protect Hector's last gift to his prince, she must not fail now because of nerves or some silly dream of a romantic love, and how it might die unborn when Niall discovered the truth about his wife and his cousin. Yet panic threatened to seize her foolish heart, and it was panic at both the English presence and at losing Niall.

Unable to stand the gaiety, she slipped away from the other women for a few private moments, and was glad to find the old library was unattended. Even as a child she had found a great deal of comfort was to be had among the leather tomes, stacked a score high on the deep shelves. Many of the illuminated manuscripts drawn by Saint Columba on Iona had found their way here when Iona was abandoned centuries ago. They were her favorites, though she treasured the many books Duncan's father had added to his collection when they became less rare: the works of Plato and Aristotle. A folio of plays by the English Shakespeare. A disputed copy of a Gaelic Bible. This place of accumulated wisdom was her chapel, her sanctuary.

She selected a book at random and seated herself on one of a pair of oaken settees that flanked the inglenook, and rested her feat on a fine Persian rug. There was even a large tabby cat asleep near the fire to lend a touch of domestic comfort and keep her company in her vigil.

Melanie Jackson

She should have been completely at ease but wasn't, and couldn't be until the treasure—and the English—were gone from the isles.

The English! She did not know how to think of the enemy, to judge their strength and intelligence. If the treasure was found on Tiree, would they revere this library enough to loot its books? Or would they burn it to the ground? No need to ask what they would do to the people, but to the property? Were they that vengeful?

Lona stared at the book in her hands. It was a collection of devotions from Saint Columba. That in itself was almost a treason. It was to be hoped that none of the English spies knew Gaelic.

Lona scanned the shelves with a concerned eye. Because of the Sasannach libels about the Scots' native stupidity and ignorance, many Englishmen would be surprised by the scope of the island MacLeans' library. And many of them would be shocked by the Catholic content of it. True, it was Celtic Catholicism and not the hated Roman Papisim, but it would still alarm the average, uneducated Presbyterian or Episcopals to be among so many forbidden works. That Duncan had left the door unsecured against intruders suggested that he was careless, or that his unwanted English guests were illiterate.

She decided to concentrate on the latter possibility and to take that as a good omen, a sure sign that they would be able to outwit such men. Finally, she felt a slight lightening of the burden in her heart. Hope was a buoyant quality of spirit that simply refused to drown, no matter how deep her sorrows. And a fortunate thing that was, too, given the occasion. She soon would have to set about making herself agreeable to those who hunted them, for they likely would attend the celebration.

Lona was all-too-soon found in her retreat, and she was forced to surrender her tome to a scolding aunt as they made their way to the approved chapel. Fortunately, she had by then regained some peace of mind and was able to smile at the strange women milling before her as they twitched her skirt into place and gave her a posy of flowers.

The wedding procession inside the kirk was got underway with little fanfare, the only formal touch being Duncan's elegant escort. It was only moments until she was facing the throngs of the new strange faces of distant MacLean relatives, for the aisle of the low, stone kirk was a short one and allowed her no comforting distance from the congregation. She looked, too, for British spies, but as they all dressed alike now, the Scots and the English, and the Sasannach carried no outward mark of their unpleasant office, she was unable to sort out friend from foe.

The new Tiree kirk had little to recommend itself to Catholics. It eschewed ornamentation just as its stern parishioners did, and on this day it was grossly overcrowded with foreign MacLeans who pressed together, shoulder to shoulder, like the coffled slaves who filled the bellies of British ships traveling to the New World in that distasteful triangle of slaves, molasses and rum.

Lona found herself staring at the ugly altar and thinking irreverent thoughts, such as: *Surely the Holy spirit has never filled such an ugly house of worship. And, God, Himself, could find no glory here.*

In spite of her sacrilegious sentiment, Lona managed to play her part well. No one guessed that she was less modest than subdued by the weight of her worries, and disdainful of the architecture. She appeared demure.

With the part of mind that had been given over to thoughts of her new husband, she could only marvel at Niall's ability to portray an innocent man, all but delirious with happiness to be wed to his sweetheart. Everyone was fooled. Even she almost believed his smiles and caresses. Almost. Had she not heard his proposal of their union so calmly laid out in terms of survival and logic, she would have believed his performance completely and had her silly heart broken for her pains.

As it was, a part of herself she held aloof and disbelieving from every word he said. She needed her mental wall, for her body refused to remain cold in his charming presence. It responded to the physical lust that Niall undoubtedly felt for her, even there in the cold, disapproving church of the Covenanters. When their hands touched, her pulse grew tumultuous.

Once the sober ritual of Puritan marriage had been properly observed, the alien folk who shared her name returned to the manor where the bridal repast had been laid on a long table.

A faint crease showed between Lona's brows as she was led to do honors at the table. The feast was a surprise. There were fowl, stuffed with grain and roasted in butter laid beside platters of fish in oyster sauce, and mussels boiled in wine. Next were herring fillets stewed with apples, gherkins and red cabbage. There was potted hare.

Tiree had no fatted calf to kill, but some spring lambs had been sacrificed for the table. Lona stared, amazed. There were turnips and potatoes, and

Iona

boiled salad of spinach with cauliflower and leeks garnished with boiled eggs.

There had been time to obtain brawn, though where they had found a boar to pickle she could not guess. The pig looked quite handsome with the cheesecloth rolled down and its body nested in a bed of rosemary. Its tusked face wore a smile of approval at the apple stuffed in its jaws.

She saw no sign of the ungodly minced pies, but there were elegant cakes as large as her palm made with fine milled flour, fat currants, precious nutmeg and iced with sparkling sugar.

The islands had not seen such a sumptuous feast in many a year, and she realized that Niall must have sent Gavin off to the mainland for supplies, thus providing him with a legitimate reason for leaving the isles.

It was a great honor, and a great ruse, but all Lona could think of was the obscenity of feeding like English lords when so many were dying of starvation throughout Scotland. She ate because the role required it, but all was as ashes in her mouth.

She wondered how the others fared as they faced the groaning board. The natives, those of conscience, must be torn. On the one hand, as good Puritan moralists they had to deplore the grandiose display of wealth from a turncoat MacKay. On the other hand, it would not do to have their visitors— unwanted or not—think that the MacLeans of Tiree were negligible personages.

And the winter just past *had* been long and filled with deprivation.

Lona smiled inwardly as they fell upon the food. They had obviously decided to enjoy the brief mortification of the flesh that the MacKay money had brought to Tiree. Their consciences could smite them later—provided that their morals could recall anything after the consumption of the free-flowing Ionan whisky to expatiate upon.

She personally doubted that the folk from Mull and Tiree would be able to recall much beyond the ceremony itself, and if they did, it would be from behind a hazy veil. They did not, as the Ionans did, practice moderation in their consumption, and they were unused to the power of the *uisge beatha* of the ghost isle.

Lona turned, and Niall, feeling her eyes upon him, looked her way. She nodded slightly at the ravening horde and received an answering smile.

"God bless the whisky and the Scots' thirst," he murmured quietly.

"Let us pray that the English are likewise led astray."

An immodest level of feasting was done from the dishes of good cheer—and a great deal of drinking from the barrels that were broken open and passed around from one end of the table to other in the manner of a medieval revel. There was none of the merry sports of dicing or masques that the unholy English delighted in, but the islandmen were still partial to a restrained revel or two after they had filled their empty bellies.

Temporarily replete of meat and drink, the Iona musicians brought forth their instruments and set about making music for the celebration. There would be piping and dancing to chase away the melancholy of the past years—and if they were mistaken for Christians instead of Puritans by the men from Mull and Tiree, at least the English visitors to

Iona

the islands would not see their gambols as the act of high treason that the Covenanters thought it to be.

Duncan stood clumsily. His thin face was slightly flushed with drink. He raised a cup and proclaimed: "Good drink have we, and good meat. A fire and kin to bring cheer. Prithee, make no more ado. Let the music begin!"

The musicians needed no further encouragement.

The cheerful tunes of pipes and fiddles held the Mull Covenanters in thrall. They had not heard the lively jigs of the Irish for many long years and were uncertain of how to react to cheerful songs like *"Nigham Donne na Bual."*

However stunned the Tiree and Mull MacLeans were by the raucous music, their English "guests" heartily approved of the gay holiday. They had not, so far, enjoyed their stay in the northern climes where the people had proved as cold as the winter, and they were relieved to at last be in a place of comfort and good cheer where no one made any mention of that troublesome prince of the Jacobites. To show their appreciation, the Sasannachs tapped their toes and hummed to Gaelic words they didn't comprehend, and drank and drank and drank.

Iona had been presented to the three young men who stayed in the manor house with Duncan, the ones who supposedly were spies sent to find Prince Charles if he was lurking in the isles.

The three Englishmen she did meet bowed low over her hand. They were very pleasant and polite in a backward way, hardly what she would have assumed an enemy soldier to be. They did not seem the specie of humankind who went about the pursuit of others with unflagging zeal and a remorseless adherence to some political plan. She was grateful for that, because it made it easier for her to forget the danger they represented and to play the part of the happy bride who faced no bar to future peace and security.

There was a fourth *cotton dearg* also on the isle, Duncan said with a sneer as he led her away from the Sasannachs. He was just newly arrived, but a very stern individual and held himself back from the *"muckle mirth and meal"* of the jolly celebration. To think that there was any man so saintly that he found the Covenanters too gay!

Duncan's description of the last man conjured to Lona's mind a picture of an old gray-bearded prophet so tired of travel that he preferred a nap to noisy revels, and this image did much to reassure her of the English's ineffectualness. Perhaps their venture had not turned unlucky after all.

Feeling for the first time that perhaps all would be well, Lona allowed herself to accept a modest measure of whisky from Duncan's hand. She even relaxed back into her carven chair and smiled at her new husband as he played with her hand beneath the table and swapped travel tales with the unknown lady on his right. A Mull cousin, no doubt, but Lona did not recognize her young face.

Meanwhile, Niall was truly enjoying himself—this in spite of the jeopardous English presence at their table. It seemed to him that a lifetime of exile had passed since he had feasted among Scots and listened to the sweet, sad music of home.

As the Norman Flambard—*never as a MacKay*—he had visited the assembly close in Edinburgh in the happier days before '45 and the rebellion. As he listened to the musicians' rude sawing, he recalled a

Iona

favorite country dance they'd played there on days when dancing lessons were given. He smiled at his happy remembrance of childhood and nodded politely to his companion without hearing her words.

In no other country did they love dance like the Scots. It had been taught to all the children and youths in the days before Cromwell's Puritans had deemed it a sin to make merry in any way. He had a dim memory of his own mother pulling him into a circle and showing him the simple steps of a country dance. How she had smiled then! So happy and proud of her young son. . . .

In a sudden rush of unexplainable feeling, Niall was moved by the desire to once more play and dance the old songs that were filling up his head. This might be his one chance to do this sentimental deed before he left the *hieland* life forever behind him and he wished to seize the day.

It was silly mawkishness, he supposed, or too much of Iona's whisky, but just one time before he departed his homeland, he wanted to play a jig while standing on Scotland's soil and to dance and sing her songs as a *hieland* MacKay.

Demanding a fiddle from the resting Iain, Niall jumped to his feet and took up a position at the head of their impromptu orchestra. In the midst of much encouraging laughter and applause, he began to bow out a blithe "Circassiun Circle."

With cries of delight, the Iona MacLeans rushed for an open place on the floor, and soon many of the elder MacLeans of Tiree had joined them in the dance. Even dour Cook was happily hobbling about like a daft, fat fairy affected with the gout. Niall's great charm of manner had again carried the day.

Melanie Jackson

Lona watched with proud eyes as Niall played on and politely refused Duncan's invitation to dance. Her cousin was never light on his feet and he already had had a great deal to drink. She was more than contented to stay at the table and she watch the stray sunlight play over Niall's happy features. He looked like a dark-haired angel bathing in its radiance and she was glad that he had found some joy in the day.

As afternoon wore into evening, the country dances and jigs were replaced with older songs, some sad, some happy, but all beautiful because of the passion Niall's clever fingers put into them. Iain's old fiddle seemed to sob and laugh and cheer all at her husband's bidding.

Niall even tempted fate by singing a new Lowland ballad about two Jacobites who were longing to return to Scotland at the end of the war. One man was free but the other condemned, and faced with knowledge that he would never see his true love again, the condemned man sent a message to her with the free lad who would return home to Loch Lomond.

By the end of the sad tale, his audience—even the Englishmen—was singing loudly and snuffling into their sleeves and pocket linens as they shed maudlin tears into their whisky.

Feeling that perhaps it was an inappropriately somber note for a wedding feast, Niall shook himself from the embrace of his darker emotions. Noticing that the light had shifted greatly to the west, he turned casually to the large, leaded window that faced the westward sea and looked at the setting sun.

Down the table three seats on, Lona saw Callum

Iona

straighten and set his mug before him on the table. He also stared at the window.

Night had not yet fallen and so the Sabbath had not officially begun, Niall commented to Iain in a carrying voice. There was time for another toast and a song.

He turned back to the room, saluted his bride with a call for another drink—which he did not partake of, she noticed—and then he launched himself into a happy air called "Blackthorn Stick."

Revelry was restored and no one except Lona and Niall noticed when Callum and Gavin disappeared in Lestan LaCroix's unobtrusive wake.

A tiring Niall hoped that the three were swift with their task. The sun was almost down and people would begin to wonder why the groom was playing at the fiddle and drinking whisky instead of claiming his new bride.

Niall wondered about that himself. He was a man of concentration and will. He did not confuse his roles or purposes. But several times that day he had actually forgotten about the cursed treasure stowed in the back of manor's rapidly depleting larder, and simply marveled at the fact that it was his wedding day and that he was welcomed among these Scots.

He also found himself thinking at odd moments, that from this morn forward he would call Lona MacLean—No! Lona *MacKay*—his lawful wife.

Which led to a rather vexing question: Bound only by a Covenanter's ceremony, did Lona consider him to be her lawful husband?

The troubling question went unanswered, and not being at all certain about how to approach his new bride on this their wedding night if she felt otherwise, he found himself sitting with the orchestra, playing the fiddle, singing scurrilous songs, drinking whisky, and fretting in a wholly alien manner.

Then, feeling an odd prickling in the flesh of his nape that betokened a hard and hostile stare, Niall looked over his right shoulder at the somberly clad man who entered from the back of the hall where he stayed, watching fiercely from the shadows. The new arrival looked like a swarthy gargoyle escaped from a French cathedral parapet—one of Satan's lesser demons whose face was carved from mottled gray stone—and he wore all the arrogance of a Roman emperor.

Unfortunately, it was not only an ugly face but an ugly face Flambard knew all too well.

Niall instantaneously forgot all about his other woes as he recognized the fourth English "guest" that had avoided most of the feast. Hudson Coldsmith, known among the rebellion's survivors as the *Hoodie Craw*—the carrion crow—both for his profession, which had him often at the gallows picking over the dead, but also for his repellant personality and grim appearance.

Niall cursed inwardly. The Black Death, forty days of Biblical rain, or even Satan himself would be more welcome in a Scot home. Coldsmith's presence was doubly damning here because he had met Flambard on one particularly memorable occasion. He might well remember Niall as the Catholic gentleman who had aided in the escape of a French spy from the port of Dover by offering the runaway man passage on his ship . . . and by flattening Coldsmith's inept guardsman when they'd attempted to board the *Wybrzeze*, as his vessel was then called.

They had a fresh worry now, one that went beyond seeing to the disposal of the prince's trea-

Iona

sure. So many questions were raised by the Hoodie Craw's appearance on tiny Tiree. The English's chief hunter should be busy in the Highlands where the prince and his remaining supporters were said to be hiding from Cumberland.

Unless he had received word that the prince had escaped from Skye? It was an unanswerable question, but Niall pondered it anyway as it could affect his calculations. It was too late to alter the disposition of the treasure, but it might have bearing on when he could take Lona away.

Niall wondered also if his coming to the isles was the reason why the MacLeans had traveled to Tiree *en force*. To offer some protection of numbers perhaps? . . . Which did beg the question of whether they and young Duncan knew of the treasure's existence? Had the young MacLean summoned the English to Tiree in the hope of currying favor by either turning it over to the Sasannachs and proving his innocence thereby, or did he mean to allow them to search Iona for something he knew was no longer on the isle, and so clear his name in that manner?

Or had Duncan a mind to keep the treasure for his own use, and to use the Jacobite hunter to remove his rivals from the isle without bloodying his own hands? It would not be the first time such a thing had happened.

If Duncan did know of the treasure—and Niall was not certain that he did—then the young MacLean was either an ignorant fool for inviting Coldsmith into his home, or he was a blackmailed coward in the pay of the English and a willing Judas of his own kin.

In either event, he would not be saved by this ploy if the treasure was found on Tiree. One tiny hint of anything that could be construed as proof of collusion and Duncan would be taken to the gallows along with everyone else in the manor. Another MacLean isle would be forfeited to the bloody English crown.

Niall looked at his new bride, so beautiful and so sober as she looked out at her guests, and thought that he would give a great deal to know which person her fairy-sight said Duncan MacLean really was. Niall hoped sincerely the lad was an innocent dupe of the executioner's, for then he and the other isle MacLeans might still be saved from this folly.

But if Duncan MacLean was a Judas and had betrayed them to the *Hoodie Craw* . . . Niall's hands tightened on his bow and fragile fiddle's neck.

It would not bode well of the MacKay's future relationship with the Clan MacLean if he was obliged to kill the young heir of Tiree while a guest in his home. But kill Duncan he would, if it was necessary to protect Lona and the rest of the Iona MacLeans from the fate that would be assigned them by the *Hoodie Craw* should a greedy Duncan betray his people to the English scourge.

Chapter Eleven

Unlike the other revelers, Lona had been watching Niall's performance with great and sober attention and therefore saw his slight stiffening when the man in black came into the hall. An immediate and atavistic alarm tightened the muscles of her neck at the sight of the grim shadow darkening the door.

Reacting to her nerves' violent hailing with a long-practiced caution, she forced herself to turn slowly, and lean only slightly to the left to gain her cousin's attention in a insouciant manner that drew no comment from her neighbors at the table.

"Duncan," she said softly, twitching his cuff. "Who is that man hiding in the shadows?"

"Hiding? Who . . . " Duncan looked around owlishly. He had been indulging heavily in Iona's favorite liquid. "Ah! His name is Hudson Coldsmith. He's another damned servant of the Sasannach

Melanie Jackson

Mammon—buttoned up the back like Achmohoy's dog and the more pious for it."

"The *Hoodie Craw!* Why is he here?" Alarm traveled from her neck down her spine. Like the Israelites, the Scots were subjected to the wrath of their own Sasannach Philistines, and this creature in black was their own Goliath. The tyrannical John Knox would have been appalled by Coldsmith's cruelty.

"Looking for Jacobite rebels to take off to Lawnmarket. Don't fret. He'll find no rebels here." Her cousin's contempt was evident.

Lona knew that Duncan had no patience with ascetics. To starve oneself because there was no bread was the lot of the Highlander; moderation for one's religion was stupidity. But he was still very young and Lona did not think he yet understood about the remorseless forces that drove religious zeal.

Lona did understand it. She had lived with zealots all of her life and knew well to what extremes they would go to prove their loyalty to God or prince. Leeches did not adhere half so tenaciously.

Heart athunder, Lona constrained herself to lean back in her chair in an assumption of ease. She hoped her face was not as pale as she feared it might be.

As though guessing her distress at the crow's entrance, Niall looked her way once and gave a slight shake of his head. She was a little reassured by the gesture until she remembered that they were effectively trapped in the hall until Callum and Gavin returned from stowing the treasure. Niall didn't mean that they were safe, only that she shouldn't act precipitously. Any unusual action on the part of the

Iona

bride would be noticed immediately, even by drunken revelers.

She looked again at the leaded window above her husband's head. There was a creeping stain of dark clouds spreading over the western horizon, swallowing up the copper light of the setting sun. It was not a fierce storm, just some rain and a bit of wind; and nothing that would delay Capitaine LaCroix's departure if he chose to leave under its concealing cloak.

It was nothing that would delay the English from calling on Iona either, she realized. Not that it mattered now that the treasure was gone, unless . . .

She glanced again Hudson Coldsmith. He looked a great deal like his namesake, the carrion crow, just perching and waiting for some disaster or mistake so that he could swoop down and feed on their misery. And he kept staring at Niall, head cocked as if searching his vile little brain for where he'd seen this particular prey before.

Cold dread filled her stomach. *He knows Niall from somewhere.* And since he cared for nothing but Catholic rebels, the knowledge could not be safe for her husband. She had to do something to turn the crow's attention away from Niall!

Feeling once again that she was calamity-driven to desperate measures, Lona forced herself to her feet with suddenly clumsy arms and legs. Immediately she was the center of all eyes, including Hudson Coldsmith's. Her lips parted ready to speak words of defense, but her mind and tongue were blanketed with wordless anxiety and would not do her panicked bidding.

"The bride wishes to speak!" Iain's voice was cheerful. "Do you have a request of us, lassie?"

"Play 'My Love's Bonny When He Smiles At Me,'" she heard herself say.

A cheer went up.

"Will ye sing for us, lassie?" Iain demanded. "It's a grand voice she has, sae sweet and pure. Come and give us a song."

Sing? She couldn't!

Then she looked again at the crow staring at her with his hot eyes. He was another Donnell. Another endless fount of poison that would keep welling up from his rotten soul and flush them out into the open if he was not distracted from his vigil.

And Callum would be back soon. And Gavin. It was quite likely that they would be recognized as rebels from the wounds they bore; from there it was a short step from forced questioning to the discovery that Callum was named traitor for his part in the rebellion. The two would walk in all unaware of their danger, if the crow's attention was not diverted while they were warned.

"Aye. I'll sing for thee, Iain." Lona stepped away from the table and walked over to the old man on limbs made of wood.

Niall had handed Iain his fiddle and stepped casually away. He was whispering to Cook as he held out his goblet, as if asking for more drink.

"If you will play for me, kind sir?" She forced herself to smile.

"Gladly, lassie." Iain picked up his bow and drew it once to check the tuning on the strings. Evidently satisfied, he said: "At yer pleasure."

Lona turned to face the room, praying that her voice would not betray her with fearful warbling. Then Niall was behind her, his strong hands at rest on her shoulders giving her strength and warmth.

Iona

All at once, she had the answer to the largest question that had plagued her since his arrival on her isle. She wondered how she could have ever doubted—even for an instant—that Niall MacKay was an honorable man.

"Do you mind another voice, m'dear? I've always fancied singing this tune with a beautiful woman at my side. And none could be lovelier than my new bonnie bride."

This brought a cheer.

"Nay," she answered, though she did in fact mind that he was again the center of attention. Lona forced herself to keep smiling. Niall being recognized by Coldsmith was likely of less danger than Callum and Gavin walking into the hall unaware. At least, that was what she told her nervous heart that was panicking on Niall's behalf.

"Shall we then?" Niall nodded to Iain, and he struck the first pure note on the taut strings as Cook scurried from the room under the cover of lifted goblets and a fresh round of cheers.

Lona didn't bother to hide her grim smile. Cook was an evil-tempered, drunken, sneaking, thorn in her side, but at that moment Lona was simply glad that the fat fairy could move as quickly and quietly as she did.

Knowing that Cook had escaped the hall without drawing Coldsmith's eye eased some of the constriction in her throat, and she found that she could actually sing and enjoy it. The pleasure sprung from the irony of the moment and she knew that Niall shared it. Everyone else thought that she and her husband were singing a last romantic duet before the Sabbath as the final rays of the sun disappeared from the sky; only they knew that they were committing an act of rebellious treason by stopping up the ears and eyes of the Sasannachs' sniffing hound with Scottish music.

They retired from the festivities soon after their duet. There was much cheering as the bridal couple left the room, but no embarrassing procession to the bedchamber door and no rude jesting about the wedding night.

The moment that they were behind stout wood, Niall dropped his arm from her waist and went to the casement. He pulled back the time-worn tapestry drape and opened the narrow leaded pane that faced the sea. Lona joined him and together they searched the dark horizon for the outline of Capitaine LaCroix's ship.

"There!" Niall sighed into the freshening wind. "I feared that he might have taken alarm and decided to flee. He may yet."

"We wait for Callum and Gavin?" she asked in the softest of whispers, very aware that there might be other ears listening. "Dare they come so close to the house with the English crow nearby?"

"Aye. There's little risk this night with so many of the folk drunk and walking abroad. It would be hard for anyone to know who is whom—especially in the night."

"But not the *Hoodie Craw*. He'll not be drunk." She shuddered and crossed her arms against the cold that seemed to come both from without and within when she thought of his cruel face.

"Nay. Not Coldsmith. A bit of joy might ruin his sour countenance and then he'd look less holy. These Puritans!" Niall threw up his hands. His voice was unusually bitter. "Everyone else is content to

Iona

suffer for his religion when God sends trials his way. Why must these whey-faced reformers seek persecution out? And then inflict it on others!"

"Possibly because no one would bother with them otherwise." With a last look at the shadowy harbor, Lona pulled away from the window. "It is not easy to be martyred these days, you know. Not when you are on the victorious side. One must be as Perpetua and seek it out."

"Possibly. Though I suspect that we've willing martyrs aplenty gathered here on the isle." Lona wondered if he realized that he was speaking as a Scot and not as the disinterested third party he had thought himself to be when he'd arrived two weeks before.

"Aye. Far too many." And she feared for them all.

Niall also came away from the cold air, but he did not close the casement completely since he did not want Gavin or Callum raising the house with loud hails when they came to report.

Lona selected a comfortable brocade chair arranged near the generous fire, and Niall soon joined her at the hearth. He appeared both distracted and irritated as he swung a booted foot and drummed restless fingers on the beautifully stitched arms. Probably he wished that he was free to be out hunting in the night.

She stared at the semi-recumbent form, studying the planes of his face, now familiar and beloved, by the fire's glowing light. It was not easy to read his expression with his head turned half-away and bathed in flickering shadows.

Beloved, she had called his face. *Be-loved . . . Love?* Lona looked away from the countenance that moved her heart and studied instead the long fingers that played with the lacings on his coat and fidgeted with its fringe.

Love. She had been married twice before. And she had dreamed of Niall nightly, making love in some wonderful paradise. So it was curious that she had not thought of this moment sensibly ahead of this night. There was some excuse for Donnell—she had been shocked with sudden grief and had not known him at all—but what about the first time she'd married? Why hadn't she thought about love then?

Because she hadn't known what it was. Because she had had escape from Iona on her mind, not romance.

Did she feel love now?

It was a word with as many meanings as the colors of a rainbow. It could mean lust, passion, adoration, affection. It was also a word that would be used by many of her kin for the honor and respect that could be engendered by the sterile agreement of a practical marriage—just like the one she had contracted two years ago.

And again this time?

No! This time it was different. It was her heart making decisions, not her head. It was a triumph of feeling over reason. And it was confounding—terrifying—exasperating that she did not know herself as well as she had always assumed. Why did this epiphany have to occur at this moment of great danger?

She was sure that Niall felt some mixture of these emotions, too, but even if the resulting brew from them was a strong feeling of liking or affection, it was not enough for her now. For the first time in her life she wanted something that was more than the

Iona

sum total of all those nice words. She wanted love. Love that the bards and *seinneadairs* sang of.

Lona closed her eyes against the knowledge and tried not to sigh or beat her head against the chair's back in an expression of her own frustration.

What a splendid time she had chosen to have this revelation! There was the need for confession about Donnell's grim end hanging overheard like the proverbial sword of Damocles, and Satan's light infantry—as Callum called the English hounds—sniffing through the house for rebels and traitors while a traitor's treasure was stowed just offshore, and she and her new husband—who might or might not wish to continue to be espoused to her—were on the brink of fleeing to the New World with all their bridges burning behind them. . . . *It had to be fate, that malicious harridan, up to her old tricks again!*

"Such a heavy sigh, m'dear." Lona cracked an eye. Niall's shrewd gaze was on her face. His hands had stilled. "Is there something troubling you?"

Lona laughed softly but without pleasure. Niall did have a wonderful sense of the ridiculous, but she thought that nothing could amuse her tonight, not even his artful use of massive understatement.

"Other than the obvious things like the *Hoodie Craw* attending on Duncan?" An uncomfortable pause ensued as he did not answer the dangerous question. "Well, perhaps. But I am not certain that this is the time for large confessions. We have rather a lot to worry us as is."

"Confession is said to be good for the soul. I have never found that to be particularly true—at least, not until I had met you. Now I am quite comfortable with telling the truth." Niall looked away politely as she absorbed the compliment and wrestled with its implications. "I also have things of import to discuss, but I can be a gentleman and let you precede me."

"I . . . I hate to muddy the waters just now," she said, swallowing uneasily. "Perhaps later . . . ?"

Niall studied her. From her glossy black locks to her delicate fingers and toes, she was a sight to take a man's breath away. It was only her beautiful gray eyes with their troubled gaze that detracted from the fantasy that she was an innocent maid, created by the gods for no other purpose than pursuing earthly pleasures.

But those great gray eyes were indeed troubled as they examined her life's companion, and he sought to soothe their distress.

"Shall I make this easy for you, m'dear? I think I know what troubles you."

"You do?" she asked in surprise, sitting forward in her chair.

"Certainly. I am not entirely lacking in wits, in spite of my rather lame plan to remove that cursed treasure. I should have been here last fall," he said to himself, again distracted.

"And you are not upset about Donnell?"

"Donnell?" The hazel eyes focused again on her face. The abstraction fell from his voice. "What . . . ? Ah! So that is what worries you? Don't give it another thought. How did Shakespeare say it? 'Nothing so became his life but the leaving of it. . . . ' That was from *Macbeth*. How appropriate," he murmured.

Lona picked up the fire-iron to prod at the burning peat. The attention was unnecessary but habitual as the fires in her keep never burned well.

Iona

"It does not disturb you that he was assisted to his leave-taking?" She did not look his way as he thought about his answer.

"Nay. But I will admit to a definite curiosity about how it all came about. Was it Callum after all who chucked him in the deep? Or our lightfooted Cook?"

Lona's head jerked around. The hand on the poker was clenched tight.

"Callum?"

"Aye, Callum. Was he the one to *assist* Donnell over the side?"

"Nay." Her voice was quiet. "So you did not know—"

"And don't care!" he assured her swiftly. Whatever distant place his thoughts had been before, he was with her completely now, his gaze sharp and steady.

"Truly?" she asked, wistful.

"Tell me nothing if you prefer not. I suppose it is too soon for trust to have grown between us, try as I might to reassure you," he added to himself, in a voice that was unusually grim.

"I do trust you." Lona put up the iron and drew a deep breath. She stared into Niall's kind eyes, willing him to belief and understanding. "It was the ghosts that told me how . . . and I did it, Niall. *I* did it, not Callum. Not Cook. *I* put on Hector's clothes and confronted Donnell out on the cliff walk. . . . He was drunk. He panicked and ran—and the sea got him."

"The *ghosts* told you . . ." Niall sounded mildly incredulous. Then with growing anger: "Did the ghosts fail to mention that it might be dangerous to confront that double-damned bastard out on the cliff walk? Did this simple fact never occur to you? Good God, woman! What if he had attacked you? Donnell was a strong brute."

"Of course it occurred to me! That's why I brought a claymore," she defended, surprised at the direction of his anger. "And you needn't tell me of his strength. I knew it all too well."

"I see." Niall stood abruptly and took a turn about the room. When he spoke again there was amusement in his voice. And disbelief. He said: "Do you know, m'dear, that your confession about Donnell is in actuality less alarming that what I wish to discuss?"

"It is?" Lona felt almost dizzy. Was it safe for her to feel relief? Was he absolving her that easily? "What could be . . . What is it you wished to discuss?"

"Our marriage," he answered.

It was indeed too soon for her to be feeling relief, she realized with a painful new twist at her heart. Lona drew a deep breath and tried to fortify her newly opened heart. Habit came to her aid.

"Yes? And what of it?" she asked steadily, calmly.

"Lestan is a Catholic," Niall said unexpectedly. "If it would put you more at ease, Capitaine LaCroix can marry us again as soon as we're at sea. Or we can go to France and find a holy father to say the words over us. But, Lona, you must understand—*and believe*—with or without the blessing of the Church, you are my wife."

She blinked at him and then began to smile. She had not thought to be amused by anything that day, but Niall's words had eased some of the tightness from around her beleaguered heart. If he wished to marry her again in their own faith, he could not be upset about Donnell.

"Are you certain that it is not a spring madness that will soon pass off? This desire you have for a rebel

Iona

wife?" she asked softly, aware of the opened casement, but unable to stop the pleasurable question.

"I pray not." He returned to her side and knelt there. His eyes were shining and there was a smile at his lips. "If this be madness, Mistress, then I am greatly enjoying my insanity."

Lona took his offered hand and he quickly laced their fingers. He was very warm and close, quite near enough for their lips to meet if . . .

"Lona—" But at that moment there came a hiss from beneath the open casement.

Niall ducked his head and then rose swiftly. Lona swallowed her disappointment and followed him to the window. Gavin was below. The north wind tugged steadily at the hem of his dark cloak and disturbed what remained of his grizzled locks.

"What word?" Niall asked softly.

"We're a' set but canna depart 'til the tide. 'Tis a dangerous business, the *Hoodie Craw* being here. I like it not."

"Nor I. But you and Callum must be away with the tide regardless."

"Aye. That's a' well and guid. But Callum is of the notion that ye'd best be away with us. Seems yer Flambard was up tae nae guid during the rebellion and was named as a foreign spy by the Sasannach."

Niall's teeth flashed. "That he was—and worse! Still, the case has not altered. You and Callum must be away with the dawn. We're none of us safe until that damn cask is gone."

"Well, lookee, MacKay. I am nae in the army now." The Lowland accent grew with his agitation. "And I dinna take orders from any man. So, here is our plan. We'll away with the tide, but we're going nae further than o'er the horizon. We'll wait at the causeway on Iona for a day and a night more. Iain kens the place. If nae message comes, then we'll away the morn after. But I like not the chance of the *Hoodie Craw* bein' here and will use a caution!"

"Very well," Niall agreed, surprising Gavin greatly. The old man had been preparing himself for the next verbal assault and ended up expelling half his breath in a startled puff when argument proved unnecessary. "I like it not either, and I cannot take chances with Lona's life. Can you see Iain tonight? I dare not leave the room myself in case there is a watch in the hall."

"Aye. He's already been told and is prepared tae give aid." Gavin's accent was immediately moderated.

"Good. If all is well on the morrow, then you get off with the tide and we'll see you in France in less than a fortnight."

"Aye . . . And Mary of the sweet son protect you from all sides until then."

"Amen to that, and thanks for the prayers."

"Fare ye well, Mistress," Gavin called softly, speaking to Lona for the first time. "And six loads of burial clay on the *Hoodie Craw*."

Lona raised a hand in salute but did not try to answer. Her throat was again tight with alarm. How could she have forgotten that carrion crow was hunting them? It was stupidly careless of her.

"Niall," she began to remonstrate. "I would not go without you—"

"I believe, m'dear" —Niall said, fastening the casement and pulling the tapestry back into place—"that this is an appropriate moment to think up some alternative plans in the event that our good fortune deserts us." He turned from the window and looked down at her with a gleaming eye. "But first, there is one other matter . . . "

"Niall?" she repeated, her earlier lecture forgotten when she looked into his face and saw the man of her dreams looking back.

He was coatless, then shirtless, and finally breechless. The tense, wary look had faded from his face. He—*her husband*—stretched full length on Duncan's bed. Propped on an elbow, he watched with unblinking enjoyment as she shed her outer woolen raiment. "Would you consider it evidence of my lax morals and licentious habits if I confessed a desire to see you dressed in darkest velvet—and undressed in a shift of the thinnest red silk?" The honest humor of the question, along with the absurdly matter-of-fact tone that he used, lapped against her heart in a warm wave. This was Niall, her *kind, loyal* Niall—and all was well.

"Probably. Is it very fun being licentious?" she asked wistfully, pulling the short, woolen veil from her hair. The last minute addition of the traditional covering had made her grimace. It reminded her too much of a novice's veil or the uniform of the nuns—appropriate enough for her cloistered life, she supposed, but not at all alluring on a wedding night when the groom yearns for red silk.

"It has its moments," he admitted.

"I've always wondered if it was." She tossed the offending scrap aside.

Niall laughed softly and held out a hand. "Mistress Lona, Van de Graaf told me that I would find a treasure on Iona—and how right he was. . . . No, don't bother with the shift, lass. Leave something for me to unwrap."

Melanie Jackson

He sat up and reached out a long-fingered hand. His arms, as she knew, were very strong, but his entire length was lean and ligamented with lengths of brawny sinews. In the soft light of fire, she saw about his person the scattering of assorted scars and especially on his naked chest, small ones that had come from cuts; a musket ball had pierced his pale flesh at one shoulder and left a puckered crater behind it. The marks proclaimed the truth she had suspected all along; her husband was actually a soldier masquerading in a courtier's ruffled coat.

Then she was distracted from all sensible thought. His fingers were feverishly warm against her skin as he pulled her closer.

The mattress rustled softly as she knelt upon it. A pleasantly sharp smell rose from the bedding. The tick had been laid with dried lavender and verbena within the linen cloth.

His hand moved up her wrist and found the pulse that beat there. It was light and fast, also feverish. *Mild fear*, she thought, *does indeed lend spice*.

Her shift was simple, white, decorated only with pin-tucks. Mercifully the night chill was held at bay by the hearth stones that breathed warmth into the spring air. The flags would keep them in comfort while they spent the sweet hours before dawn with each other. At dawn they would begin waiting on fate, waiting on the weather, waiting on the tides. . . . But not yet. They would have this short time together.

He was silent as he cast her shift aside, almost greedy with his burning fingers against her skin as he removed the last bit of clothing. She shivered her way down into the bedding where he burned beside her warm as any fire could ever be.

Iona

The covers he put aside and then lay back with her. The smell of lavender was strong as he slipped an arm beneath her head, and with his other hand, pulled her into the curve of his body. She slipped her own free arm about his waist and absorbed some of his heat into her chilled bones.

"More comfortable, lass?"

"Wonderful," she answered in a voice that was almost drowsy. Surely she had done this a thousand times before—then she realized that she had. In her dreams. They had prepared her and she felt as though she had always been in Niall's arms, just as the winter rain must feel when it returned to the sea or the heather blooming once again under the summer sun.

"I wish you had been here last winter," she murmured. "I was so often cold."

Niall's shoulders shook. "So do I wish it, Mistress. But we'll pass the next one in greater comfort."

"Do you truly think so, Niall?"

"Aye." He glanced once at the window.

"Is there a moon yet?" she asked, turning her head to the casement, still worried about Callum and Gavin and the time before the dawn tide. "How is it now? Has it set?"

" 'Tis fuzzy with cloud and growing dark. Minute by minute the light grows less. Soon it will be black and safe for the hunted ones out on the sea. They'll be safe away." He spoke soothingly, like a mother's soft lullaby, or the calmest sea upon a flat shoreline.

Some of the tension slackened and her breathing grew more deep. She turned her cheek into their mattress and found Niall's dark hair. It was thick and soft, smelling sweetly of the summer lavender in their bed. She kissed it lightly, thinking of her dreams and welcoming the distraction from her other troubling thoughts.

In the cold hours just before dawn broke, it was hard to be brave. She knew from experience that it was the time when dark deeds were done; thievery, murder. They were hours when she had the least resistance to her fears and when the ghosts whispered to her about dark things.

For Callum and Gavin, the hours of darkness were a blessing; but for her and Niall, the possible danger hunting in the dark just before dawn could come creeping upon them all too soon. There was no safety on the isle while the *Hoodie Craw* scavenged nearby. But this time, it was different. Niall was at her side. She wasn't facing cruel fate alone.

"Enough, love. You brood, not sleep . . . And if it is not rest you crave . . . " Niall loomed over her, shifting her easily onto her back. A light finger traced the line of her shoulder down the curve of her breast.

"I see that you have not lost the art of making yourself agreeable," she whispered, an involuntary tremor passing through her body.

Niall grinned down impudently. "Some things, Mistress, a man never forgets."

"Aye, and thank the Lord for it," she muttered into his chest.

Niall heard her and laughed.

Passion, newly awakened in her heart, made her shiver. Love, newly found by body and soul, made her burn. For a long, unmeasured moment her entire consciousness swung on the one bright mandrel of new, physical pleasure; the old defenses she had employed against Donnell to save her sanity snapped and then flared like dried leaves on an

Iona

autumn fire, and fierce joy broke free from its cold, dead chains.

She turned gladly to her husband and welcomed him into her heart and soul, ignoring as best she could the fey feeling that their time together might be very short. If their time together was to be so brief as to be numbered by hours, then she would give herself this gift and pray that it sustained her all the way to whatever end fate decreed.

She tugged Niall's head to her breast and arched as he suckled there. It was as it had been in her dreams. Her pulse thrummed and she relived the sensual lullaby's familiar night-fever.

Niall's loins pulsed beneath her hand and she cupped him gently. He was filled with life. When they joined, it would flow from him into her waiting belly and they would make a child.

Niall groaned at the pleasure of her soft touch, revelling in the feel of her hands upon his flesh. But the sensation was too strong to endure, the siren's call too alluring after the torment of his dreams. He shifted away in an act of self-defense before he disgraced himself. It was important that Lona share this moment with him.

His own long fingers found her heart, caressed, opened her as he prepared the way for their joining. His usually nimble fingers trembled as they sought their way.

Her skin is so fine! The fire painted golden light over the flush of sudden passion and made her glow with life. Her fine gray eyes were open wide and she smiled, unafraid.

With care, his hands encircled her knees, lifting her legs gently as he moved between them. The slight tremor he felt spoke of her own deep feeling, the heat of her body told him of her arousal. He thought that naked desire was the most beautiful thing that a woman could wear.

Lona looked up to see her reflection mirrored in his eyes. She looked wanton, her hair wild—and she did not care. With a soft moan, she pressed her body upwards. Covenanters said that kissing was shameful, but all she desired was that Niall's mouth should touch her own. That she might be overwhelmed with kisses and by the tidal passions surging within her. She looked from his face to his broad shoulders and powerful chest and was filled with unexplainable awe and longing.

The touch of hands on her fevered flesh drove her toward the loss of her senses—and she rejoiced in it. And then his weight bore down on her, sweet, heavy. She cried out as he finally came into her. He paused for one moment and choked out her name, asking.

"Yes! Niall—" she answered in a whisper.

Then he was there all the way. Inward, upward, their movements becoming one as the tide finally crashed over them bringing the little death that would create a new life.

Niall finally tore himself away from the bed. He threw back the sheet and, still naked, went quietly to the window. The tapestry was pulled an inch aside showing an oblong of lighter gray against the black. The moon had returned, full and bright after the storm's first brief shower, and was casting its cold, dead light upon the sea about Tiree, and all who sheltered on the island. It was an ill omen.

Lona rose up and came to stand beside him. His

warm arm came around her naked waist, holding the cold of night and fear temporarily at bay.

"They're safe away by now, lass." He spoke quietly into her hair. His voice was calm as if he had not seen the shadow made of night-black lurking beneath their window where it kept an unfriendly watch with its pallid, demon's face.

"Aye . . . but we are not." She turned her cheek into the warmth of his body and returned his light kiss as she whispered. "Did he see them away, do you think? Will he follow?"

"Stir up the fire, lass," he said at last, briskly turning away from the casement and letting the curtain fall along with his comforting embrace. He did not answer her question. "Let us have some heat and light while we make our preparations."

"There is something we may do?" she asked, following him to the dwindling fire to add more peat and stir the dying coals to life. "We . . . we cannot just leave here, can we? We would be followed by that—that crow!"

"There is always something to do. Cheer up, lass. I've been in tighter spots than this and always managed to wriggle free of them. The trick is to have a plot all laid. . . . Did I ever mention that I have a few magician's tricks that help me cheat at cards?"

Niall spoke quietly but with humor, as they built up the fire and began to dress. His confidence and planning dispelled many of the night fears that had built their sickly webs around her. Perhaps it was a great risk they ran, playing cat and mouse with the *Hoodie Craw*, but she and Niall were both gamblers at heart—and they had no other choice but to play out their game if the Iona MacLeans were to live in peace after they were gone.

Melanie Jackson

They talked for a while, but once all their plans were done, Niall sent Lona back to bed to get what rest she might. He then pulled a comfortable chair nearer to the fire and set his stockinged feet upon the tinder to keep them warm. From his cloak's inner pocket, he produced an old pipe and a pouch of tobacco. He smiled at her look of interest.

"One of my immoral vices," he said. Then: "Close your eyes, lass, and do not fear. All will be well for us. God is on our side for this battle."

Lona pulled up the covers and pretended to sleep. They were all settled in and prepared to keep the dark vigil before the dawn, but even with the comfort of the glowing hearth and the blankets upon the bed, Lona felt the fingers of cold plucking at her spine. Her nerves had taken a chill at the sight of the carrion crow perched outside their window, but they were still steady.

If the crow chose to confront them, then one of them would die. And in this instant Lona knew that she would not suffer from any hesitation when it came time to see that it was the crow who perished rather than the man she loved. She swore it on what was left of her soul.

Chapter Twelve

The dreaded knock upon their door came an hour before true dawn. It was not entirely unexpected for fate to have turned on them at the last moment, and Niall had been adamant that they prepare for this eventuality; but the rapping still caused waves of sickening alarm to wash through Lona's body as she pulled on her shoes. That was the only article of clothing not already upon her person, for Niall had insisted that they sleep fully clothed.

Her husband ran rough fingers through his hair and pulled at his shirt's lacings to complete the picture of a man just torn from his bed. He looked over once to see that she had her shoes fastened and then told her to climb back under the blankets and wait on events. He even managed a swift smile, and it was not simply to raise her flagging spirits. She saw in the low light how his eyes glowed. They sparkled with light of battle. And through those suddenly opened windows that overlooked his soul, she saw a battle lust burning, a passionate fire that kindled on the hunger to outwit—even kill—the enemy outside the door.

How could she have forgotten all the steel that was girded beneath his gentle smile and humorous words, she wondered with a flash of exasperation that chased off fear's first chill.

Then all in an instant, Niall assumed a new air, one of utter dissipation. His approving smile became a leer. By the slight change of posture and expression, he transformed himself into another being. He looked and behaved exactly like the carousing court-gallant of lax morals and licentious habits he claimed Flambard was.

It was a sorcery that would be envied by the finest thespians in the land, and Lona realized for the first time that she was in the presence of a master spy who knew how to gamble his life on the skill of his wits.

Their wooden panel was flung wide and Niall reeled into the doorway, effectively barring entry.

Waiting in the dimly lit hall beyond their door was the black carrion crow and one of the other Englishmen, who seemed much the worse for his bout with Iona's export as he reeled more than Niall.

No MacLeans were with them or stirring in the passage beyond, she was glad to see. That did not, of course, mean that the MacLeans were unaware of this pre-dawn call but she did not want to know which—if any—of her kin had betrayed them, and which, if any, would try to defend them.

"Henri Flambard," said the cold voice. "Did you

truly think that you would so easily escape your sins by hiding under this new name in the devil-ridden land?"

"*Eh*? You! Go away, man. Can you not see that it is Niall MacKay you are addressing? My wife and I wish to be alone a while longer." Niall swayed a little, just a tiny bit, but it was enough to suggest inebriation. And if they failed to see that obvious sign of weakness, there was no overlooking the satyr's leer on her husband's face as he jerked his head her way.

Lona turned her eyes from her actor husband and watched with morbid interest as the other Englishman—*Nelson?*—flushed crimson and glanced away from their bed. He dashed a hand across his perspiring brow. It was easy to see the stain of embarrassed color in his whitened cheeks even by the lantern's poor light.

He believes the act! she thought with sudden hope. At least one of the hounds had been pulled off the scent and was going astray.

The carrion crow reacted not at all except to deepen his sneer. He had nothing but contempt for frail men's Sins of Virtue, and Niall was apparently guilty of lust and sloth in abundance—and probably greed and gluttony as well. "Two men have disappeared," the crow went on, still cold and sneering.

Niall sighed extravagantly. "Only two? After last night's revels I am amazed that it's only two who've gone astray. Dinna worry yerself, man. Yer boys'll be sleepin' it off somewhere. *Now go away, do!*"

Niall made as if to close the door. The crow stepped quickly into the room and turned his head toward the bed where Lona lay with the covers pulled up tight to her chin in a feigned modesty that hid her clothed state.

Melanie Jackson

"And what of you, Madame? Are you not curious about the two men who have disappeared?" The voice did not dispense any favor toward her. Lona wondered which sins she was guilty of—or if she needed any greater sins to earn his contempt beyond being Scot and Jacobite and female.

"Niall?" she said in a quavering voice, playing the part of the silly coward by worrying her lower lip and blinking her eyes. "Who is this man?"

"Hudson Coldsmith is my name." The crow paused for her gasp of recognition, but Lona chose to coquette with disaster and disappointed him with a display of bovine ignorance.

"See here, ye daft looby!" Niall began to expostulate. "If yer after the devil, gae chase him in Dartmoor! He's there often these days."

"Nelson! Enter this chamber and draw your pistol," the crow ordered.

A reluctant Nelson entered the room on unsteady feet and slowly drew out a pistol. He surreptitiously wiped some more sweat from his brow on his left sleeve cuff. He was only barely resisting the whisky's pull at his virgin gut, and his weapon was aimed none too carefully at either of the Nialls that swam before him.

"Are ye daft, man?" Niall demanded, seeing the younger man's gut-sickness and nervousness. "To draw a weapon in the house of a MacLean? They'll use ye for an arrow butt do ye fire that pistol."

Nelson looked very unhappy to be pointing his pistol at anyone. This inferred total ignorance on his part, and that fact made Lona hope that Duncan might truly be ignorant of the crow's intentions.

"Perhaps," Nelson began, rolling a pleading eye in the crow's direction.

Iona

"You will do as you are ordered. It is your duty," Coldsmith told him. He turned back toward the bed. "Very well, Mistress MacLean—"

"MacKay," Niall interjected helpfully. "She is nae a MacLean any more."

"Since you are not curious about the missing men, I shall simply tell you who they are." The crow ignored Niall's words and Nelson's wavering gun. The Calvinist God was armor enough for him.

"Man, we dinna care who they are," Niall tried again. "The remaining tribes of Israel could be lost and I'd not care just now—*nor would my wife.*"

Lona noted that he sounded wonderfully lustful and yet completely forceless. She did wonder if *lustful* was the best role to be playing before this particular enemy; and then she decided it was. He would be distracted by his religious zeal and perhaps fooled long enough for them to lure him into a trap.

"They are a boatman of Tiree, one Gavin MacLean, and a crofter from Iona, called Callum Bethume." The crow was again waiting for some reaction. "They are both escaped Jacobites that have been harboring on Iona."

"Jacobite? Callum Bethume?" she repeated in a high, squeaky voice. Fear was not at all difficult to counterfeit with the *Hoodie Craw* standing over the bed.

"Go look under the table in the dining hall," Niall recommended, mighty calm for a man who was about to be accused of being an aider and abettor to escaped rebels. "Half the men on Tiree are snoring there."

"They're not there." Nelson spoke up unexpectedly. The young man was almost certain that he had been called out on a fool's errand by this unpleas-

271

ant, churchish spy, and wished only to return to his broken slumber before he fainted dead away or threw up on the floor. "I checked while searching for Garrison and Clive, but that doesn't mean—"

"Silence! I will tell you when to babble." Nelson subsided quickly under Coldsmith's reptilian eye, but his expression had turned resentful. Coldsmith was not his superior officer and he resented having to answer to the Puritan witch-hunter. "They are not on the isle. *I* have searched! And Gavin MacLean's boat is missing."

"So? Like as not, the idiot's gone to fish this morn," Niall yawned.

"He is fishing no doubt. He is out to net a rebel's treasure!" Coldsmith announced in a ringing voice that would likely raise the household.

Lona found it hard not to shush him. She did not want her kin involved in any sudden attempt to delay or detain the *Hoodie Craw*, for that would certainly lead them all to the gallows.

"What?" Niall allowed chagrin to appear in his face and tone. "Nay! It canna be. Naebody knows aboot the treasure!"

"I see that you don't mean to deny knowledge of this rebel hoard, Flambard."

"Nay. That I don't—Yer certain, man, that he's gone? 'Tis a large isle after all."

"Of course I am certain," Coldsmith answered, slightly taken aback by Niall's attitude. People were wont to cower in fear when he accused them of such heinous crimes. "The rebel knows that the island is deserted this night and it is the perfect time to steal the treasure. Had not this thought occurred to you, Flambard?"

It sickened Lona to listen to the crow be sly. He

Iona

thought to trap them into a confession by appealing to their greed, and to convict Niall as a Catholic by using the name Flambard again and again.

Niall cursed once, swung around unsteadily and approached the bed. He sat down beside Lona and reached out to pat her with a clumsy hand.

"Now, lass, I want ye to think hard. Where would this Callum be going?" The face that turned her way was calm and reassuring.

"I—I—" She let her eyes go round with astonishment. Niall was not the only one who could feign emotions.

"Speak up, woman!" Coldsmith barked. "You are in danger of being named for harboring a Jacobite—"

"Hush, man," Niall interrupted, "And lower yer tone. Ye'll get nothing by scaring the girl and I don't want the entire Clan MacLean upon us. They are in ignorance—and I'd prefer to leave them so. Come on now, Lona, lass. Think hard."

"But I don't know—" she began uncertainly, and chewed on her lip a bit more.

"She knows," Coldsmith said grimly. "She simply needs to be questioned in the proper manner."

Nelson just stared at his compatriot with confused eyes. He appeared near the point of collapse and was clearly uncomprehending of the import of this latest event except to be repelled. Lona spared a moment to wonder how much whisky he had actually consumed in the course of the evening, and was grateful that even with a bellyful of the water of life, he still resisted the idea of *questioning* a woman. A kind heart would make for a slower hand with the drawn pistol.

"Hush!" Niall said again. "If she had known anything, she'd have given it to my cousin. Why do you think Donnell and I were sent here?"

Melanie Jackson

"Sent here?" That gave Coldsmith a moment's pause.

"Aye. Now curb yer tongue and cease yammering about Flambards. An' dinna trouble yerself with any more thinking," Niall said unkindly. "The king will not thank ye for yer interference."

"How dare—"

"It is not needful that the left hand know what the right hand is doing. And there are many who serve in *humble* ways, Coldsmith." The tone was not at all humble.

Lona blinked. *Niall was claiming to be a spy for the English?* They hadn't discussed this strategy beforehand. Then she remembered some of the rumors about Flambard. The story fit them well enough and might work to fool Coldsmith for a time.

The tale, she reflected, *might even be true.*

"Now, lass. For the last time: Where would Callum go? Where did yer brother go when he was off alone?" Niall rubbed his face like one trying to wake up. His tone was mildly harassed.

"Hector?" she asked stupidly. The Scots had perfected the human bovine. It was a beast seen only when the Sasannachs were nearby to appreciate the performance. She had never had occasion to use it before, but she had watched Hector become slack-jawed often enough to counterfeit the expression now.

"Aye, Hector," he answered with obviously strained patience. "Ye must speak up truthfully. Yer brother took something that dinna belong to him. Now Mr. Coldsmith and I want it back. Think, lass. Was there a special place where no one else went? Perhaps somewhere Hector forbade ye to go . . ."

Mr. Coldsmith wisely kept his mouth shut but

hell was burning in his eye. Niall would have to watch his back, she thought uneasily, as she dutifully wrinkled her brow and tried to look like she was cogitating. It was only an exercise in deception. She had already guessed what Niall wanted her to say.

"There . . . There is a cave," she began.

"Aye?" Niall prompted.

"It is not too far from Callum's cottage," she said.

Niall's eyes gleamed with approval. His back was to the room so he could risk another small smile.

"That would be on the north side of the island?" he affirmed.

"Aye . . . But I am afeared to go there," she announced in a quavering voice.

"Can a boat be taken there?" Niall prompted, ignoring her plea. "Or will he go to the sound first?"

"To the sound. He keeps a boat there, but 'twould be suicide to take one to the north in darkness," she answered obediently, following his lead. "The ghosts would smash him on the rocks."

Niall patted her leg. There was real approval on his face and he didn't bother to hide his grin at her latest fabrication.

"Never mind about that foolishness, lass. Now get up and dress yerself in something warm."

"Dress?" she and Coldsmith said together.

"Of course, man. Use yer head. We'll need a guide. And I don't fancy leaving the wench here to spread the tale around tae her kin."

Lona thrust her lip out and tried to look sulky at the suggestion that she would talk to anyone. Niall just laughed at her.

"Now, lad," he addressed the swaying Nelson. "How many soldiers do ye have on the isle?"

"Just us four," Nelson again tried to speak. "And Garrison. But on Mull—"

"Silence, you fool! Don't tell him anything."

"Don't be a fool yerself, Coldsmith—we need tae know who we may count on to help shift the treasure."

The implication was that the hoard was so vast that the three of them could not move it alone. It was a brilliant move, she admitted. Already the drunken Englishmen's eyes had taken on the hue of green greed that matched his sick complexion.

"So there are these other two lads, Garrison and—"

"Clive, but he's out cold," Nelson supplied, casting a glance in Niall's direction that was eloquent in its cupidity.

"They are the ones who are sleeping 'neath the table?" Niall confirmed, making note of the young man's appetite for treasure.

"Yes." The answer was happy. Coldsmith's lips were compressed in furious disapproval of the loose talk and he was glaring direfully, but Nelson didn't notice. "Should we try and rouse them?"

"Nay. Why bring others to share the reward?" Niall answered, playing to the greed. "We'll find this hoard first and then brag of it to the world. . . . Well then! So it's three able-bodied lads to one auld man. I like the odds. Nae need to lengthen them or we'll lose the sport."

"Don't forget the traitor, Gavin." Coldsmith was not yet persuaded. "He is bound to be in this, too."

Niall waved a negligent hand. "He isn't likely to be involved—and even if Callum wanted to share the treasure, Gavin is just another auld fool. We'll do well enough."

Iona

Niall turned back to the bed.

"We'll step out into the hall while ye dress. But be quick about it, lass. I dinna wanna be approaching Iona when the tide is going down."

Niall, temporarily in control, ushered the two men into the hall. Lona knew that the situation wouldn't last. Once they were away from her kin, or Coldsmith found more soldiers to do his bidding, he would again take charge. The crow was only content because he wanted to recover the treasure quickly and he believed Niall to be drunk, unarmed and unwary.

Lona threw back her blankets. She had only a few minutes in which to prepare, but thanks to Niall's suspicious mind, all they needed was conveniently at hand. Niall's purse, his pistol and two knives—one for her—were quickly bundled into the pockets of her cloak. Her hair was braided and fastened securely so it would not blind her by whipping about in the winds on Iona.

She would give the weapons to Niall later, after the crow had relaxed his vigil. For now, he was too suspicious to allow Niall a knife or gun and they did not want him to raise a fuss until they were safely away from Tiree.

Lona took a last look around the nearly dark bedchamber where she had spent her wedding night. Through the opening of the drape she saw that the dawn was penciling its first line of light over the sea. It painted the low clouds with an evil green.

She said a brief prayer for strength and then walked calmly for the door where Niall was waiting with the enemy. She was grateful that the other two Englishmen were safely in the arms of Morpheus. Winning free of four men would have been difficult; but two? Two they could deal with right handily.

Melanie Jackson

She hoped that they would not have to harm Nelson; he seemed young and kind—and only a little greedy. With the right tale, he could be left alive on the isle to be rescued later. But the *Hoodie Craw?*

She knew Niall's thinking was much as her own about this subject. The crow believed in bloody persecutions and would hound the MacLeans forever if something wasn't done to silence him.

The easiest thing would be to feed him to the island's voracious sea. Lona resolved to be the one to do the deed, since it was for the benefit of her clan, and she already had blood on her soul. She did not want Niall to have this mortal sin on his conscience.

The tide was on its way out from the isle and it made for a difficult landing. Nelson had rowed for the majority of the distance, tiring himself nicely, with Niall only taking over the oars when they approached the sound.

He had a marker of sorts to aim for. There was a scraggly hedge at the edge of the cockle-shell beach that was being slowly tortured to death by the twice daily tides that lapped at its roots with a salty tongue. It showed dark against the cliffs and was plain to the sight.

It was also in their favor that the outgoing tide revealed to them a great deal more of the island's fangs than Niall had seen on his first trip through the sound, and that made obvious the many places to avoid putting his fragile, borrowed keel.

Still, the trip was hard enough on him, and Niall was very grateful that the worst of the rain had passed them by before he threaded the sea-going needle into the frothing bay. If the sea had not been

Iona

newly calmed, they would have all perished before gaining land.

None of the lethal scenery had been missed by the passengers, and they were all quite glad to pull themselves out of Callum's borrowed boat onto sharp, white sand and away from the carnivorous bay—especially since Lona had spent her time reciting impassioned prayers from the Mass for the Deliverance from Death. Neither Englishman was Catholic, but they easily recognized the Latin passage that began: *Salvum me fac, Deus* . . .

Coldsmith, in particular, had several times during their crossing looked like he was preparing to meet his God. More than anyone else, he had relied on the efficacy of prayer—but pessimistic Calvinist prayer, of course, and that was not very likely to propitiate the Pictish dead.

"Look!"

Nelson had woken during his vigorous exercise and was growing more alert by the moment. He pointed excitedly at the old hedge. They all turned to stare.

Tattered clouds left from the storm were dragged across the last of the moon; silvery, dead light and then deep gray dark moved over the beach in uneasy waves that confused the eyes as they tried to adjust to the dawn twilight that left the depths of the shore seeming as flat as a painting hung in the deepest shadows of the keep.

But they all knew what he was pointing at; the outline was quite clear against the dark foliage.

"The boat," Nelson said. "I can see it in the hedge!"

"Aye. It looks like Callum's boat," Niall agreed.

Melanie Jackson

Lona prayed that the moon stayed hidden for a while longer, or they would surely see that one side of the derelict had been stoved in and was now covered in a year's cobwebs.

"Let us hurry," Lona urged, shaking Niall's arm and carefully passing him a knife and his pistol through the slit his cloak. "It is not wise to be on the beach when the ghosts are walking."

"Ghosts?" Nelson asked and began to look about. He had been too drunk earlier to catch her references to Iona's hostile spirits.

"Silence!" came the predictable order.

Lona decided to take the initiative and guide the others up the trail. She did not carry a lantern; she needed both hands to safely lift her skirt and cloak. This would be an ill time to fall or to drop her weapon.

The path was treacherous and quite a likely place for a false step, but with the sand beneath she knew it might not prove a fatal plunge. Also Niall was bringing up the rear and quite likely to go down with the others should she push them.

The cliff walk where Donnell had fallen was the best place for an accident, she calculated with enforced calm. The ground was falling away bit by bit and the hard wind grabbed and growled like witches fleeing from the Sabbath. Just a small push, she encouraged herself, and it would all be over; Niall and the MacLeans would be safe.

They soon paused for breath. The deserted keep loomed above them, and Lona was aware for the first time of its incoherent design. Had her father truly thought that they would live here for always? If so, then why had he not paid more attention to the design? Painted in dawn light, it looked wattled,

Iona

scaly, a temporary hovel black with damp and mold that she could almost smell above the sea's rotting flotsam.

And it was abandoned. The wet stones and shuttered windows looked like they had been huddling around a cold hearth for a millennium. No vigil fires were burning. No one waited for her family's return. There were only ghosts.

Lona pushed the lonely thought away and started down the next path. She concentrated solely on keeping her footing while being buffeted by the wind and thought not about what she would soon do.

Boulders eventually hid them from the ocean's blustery breath and the sounds of the lapping waves. There was an abnormal stillness of atmosphere in the vale that might have been the result of the fabled calm after the storm, or the peculiar shelter offered by the tall stones. Lona was sure it was neither of those things, and it raised the hair on her arms and made her heart pound audibly.

Indistinct shapes swam out of the darkness as they approached the place where the ancient shades lived. Lona was glad, as she thrust her hands between the stones, that there were no snakes on Iona. Saint Columba's first miracle had been to drive them all out, along with the frogs and the monster in the loch.

But not the ghosts. Those had remained through the Gaelic and Norse invasions. Knowing that the thought was unnerving, she whispered it aloud. "The only terrifying things that walk on Iona are the ghosts of the Picts."

"M'dear, you look near enough to a ghost yerself in this light," Niall answered, as though trying to calm her. "Surely the spirits will nae harm their kin."

"They are pagan spirits and they killed Donnell," she insisted. Then added, so that Niall would understand that she was not truly hysterical: "They'll kill Callum, too, if he's gone into their cave. He'll be dragged into a cold cairn and seen no more."

"Och! Such an imagination!" Niall chided, but he could see that Lona's words had terrified the young soldier and had even the stolid, unimaginative Coldsmith looking about uneasily. He silently blessed the feminine perspicacity that had told her just what to say to aid in the enemy's distraction.

Not that much additional distraction was needed. The deep fractures in the lichened wall beside them looked like slitted eyes in a leprous face that followed their every step with an animate, malevolent gaze. These rocky excrescences with their dead, marbled orbs appeared with great regularity along their path and it was, as Niall had observed once before, easy to believe that the stones were sentient and that ghosts were walking abroad on the stony isle. Especially when they reached the north end of the island and the fey whispering began.

If he himself was unnerved by the sound, what must Nelson and Coldsmith—with his authentic belief in devils—be thinking?

Bad thoughts, Niall hoped. *Terrifying notions that will lead to mistakes.*

The lantern in Nelson's fingers began to tremble. The crow was somewhat steadier of fist, but he lifted the light about a great deal as he peered into the crevasses where the wind moaned and muttered in its alien tongue.

"Woman, if you have led us astray, I'll *personally* see that you suffer on the rack before we string you

Iona

up." The threat was muttered through Coldsmith's clenched teeth and only Niall heard it.

If his face had been sober before, it was now deadly grim. The first flush of pleasure at outwitting the English had worn off with the cold sea journey, and Niall was left with the earnest and deadly need to kill the enemy in the swiftest manner possible.

Then the cliff walk was before them. The sheltering stones fell away leaving a long drop clear to the stony sound. Niall did not wait for Lona to pause outside Callum's deserted croft. The crow had betrayed himself; the Ionans would not be spared. Niall could show no mercy or hesitation at carrying out this execution. It was not a duel; there were no seconds to judge the fair-play. He tucked up his ruffles as he walked the deceptive trail so they would not be a hindrance when the moment came.

Without warning, Niall swept out an arm made swift by fury. It caught at the crow's thick cloak and toppled Coldsmith over the crumbling edge. His woolen wings unfurled around him as they gathered wind but he did not fly; he screamed all the way down to the sea, still clutching the lantern in his hand.

Nelson spun about wildly and cried out in shock. His glass beacon swung wide and smashed against the rocks, leaving them only the light from the fading moon, occasional flashes of distant lightning and the first rays of the clouded dawn with which to see the narrow, crumbling path.

"The ghosts," Lona whispered. She sounded hysterical, but her actions belied her words. Niall watched as she rapidly backed away from the Englishman, giving him no chance to take her as a hostage if that was his intent. Her own dagger darted out and was instantly concealed in her skirt. Her voice was panicked, but her eyes were cold and her hands did not shake. Clearly, she was of a mind to finish Nelson did he not listen to Niall's appeal.

Niall was both pleased and appalled at the bloodcurdling show of courage, but did not take the time to comment on it.

Once she was safely away from the Englishman, Niall pulled out his pistol and pointed it at Nelson. The barrel glinted in the gray dawn light, cold and deadly, and as steady as stone.

"What are you doing?" Nelson demanded, quite shocked by Coldsmith's tumble and the sudden appearance of a pistol from a man who was previously genial, drunk and unarmed.

When Niall spoke to the younger man there were no frills or Lowland embroidery in his speech.

"If we were able to follow the wisdom of Solomon, perhaps we could cut the treasure in twain and take half of it with us and give the other half to you as a bribe to let us go. Alas! Other wisdom has prevailed and we can offer you no bribe."

"What are talking about? What are you going to do?" The young voice shook. His eyes were fixed upon Niall's pistol as he dared himself to try an attack.

"Don't do it." Niall's voice was a harsh command. His face was hard with truth. "Take some advice from one who is older and no longer finds intrigue and pointless battle to be amusing. Though I feel no enchantment with the idea of drawing English blood, I will shoot you where you stand if you try for that pistol in your belt."

Iona

"Don't do it, Nelson," Lona urged from behind him. "These stones are no place for capering and lunging. And the ghosts will smother you under the rocks if you harm us."

"The ghosts." Nelson swallowed and risked a quick glance around himself. The wind was up to its usual vocal tricks and the boy was credulous enough to believe Lona's hysterical talk.

Iona's habitual morning drizzle began to fall. Niall hoped that it was enough to cool any of the boy's remaining ardor for heroism that a pistol and the threat of ghostly revenge had not dimmed.

The third act is almost over. On to the close, he said to himself. *Your new life is waiting.*

"Be smart, lad, and you'll live to dandle your children on your knees."

"You ask me to throw away my honor and allegiance as if it were a trifle?" But the boy was thinking about it, Niall could see. The terrifying view from the cliff path was helping him make a decision as well.

"Nay. Keep your honor—and your life. What good would it do to throw it away on this ghostly isle? There's no shame in surrender to a superior force. How can you stand against the dead?"

A flash of lightning, much closer now, revealed momentarily the path to the causeway winding desolate and white between the stones where the sea thundered like a hundred cannons.

"Do you see that path?" He jerked his head toward the half-submerged causeway. The wind was picking up strength. It whipped Niall's locks about.

"Yes."

"My wife and I are going to leave now. You may tell George that I resign with regret, but I cannot

Melanie Jackson

allow him to torture and hang my new wife as Coldsmith had planned to do."

"You're leaving from down there?" Nelson was horrified. He protested, unthinking. "You'll perish for certain! And what of the treasure? How will you move it?"

"Very likely we *shall* perish. But all you need to decide is if you wish to die also." Niall stared hard at the boy. "Aye or no? . . . *No*. Then very slowly, draw out your pistol with your thumb and first finger, and drop it over the side. Do it very carefully, lad! Or you're dead on the instant."

Nelson thought for another moment and them complied. He had the full sum of it, and knew his position was untenable. They could not hear the pistol when hit the rocks over the renewed pounding of the sea. The tide was returning with the dawn and growing ever louder as it sought to regain its lost territory and to swallow its latest prize.

"Who lives may learn," Lona muttered, relaxing her hold on the *sgian dubh*.

"Now listen to me carefully, for I want you to pass on this message to the MacLeans." Niall had raised his voice and spoke concisely. "There is no treasure on this isle. Hector MacLean took it to France long ago. The two Jacobites you're after have no doubt fled there as well. There are no other rebels on this isle."

"But the boat—"

"It's a derelict. You'll see that when you return to the beach."

"When I return to the beach." Nelson sounded dazed. Up to that moment, he had not believed that he would actually be spared.

"If you are feeling brave, you can try and take the

Iona

boat back to Tiree. I would wait for the next low tide. Or to be rescued by one of the returning islanders. They'll be here soon, along with your sleeping friends. But it is your decision. I care not what you choose to do, for we shall be long gone by then."

"And what of you two?" Nelson asked bravely. "You say I should keep my allegiance. But how can I when she is wanted as well as the other rebels."

"Do you make war on women, lad? Is that what your parents taught you?" Niall demanded, and Nelson's eyes fell before the anger in his gaze. "We're going down there, my wife and I. There's another boat waiting. We're taking it to one of the other islands and getting passage from there. She'll never set foot in Scotland again. I swear it. Now, believe me or die."

"You're going to Mull?" Nelson asked, still trying to do his duty by discovering their path of flight.

Niall raised his pistol to point at Nelson's head. "Don't make me shoot you, lad. Just keep quiet and all will be well."

Nelson looked again at the causeway. The sea was foaming whitely and running quick. It was clearly a suicidal notion to think that an escape by sea was possible.

"You're mad," he muttered. "Better to hang than to drown in that ghastly sea."

"That's a matter of opinion. Turn around now and start walking," Niall instructed.

"Why?" he asked suspiciously.

"You'll go first because I don't want you pitching rocks down on our heads while we're climbing."

"Oh." He was obviously chagrined that the treacherous idea had not occurred to him. "Very well."

Niall waited until Nelson had turned and taken his first step, and then clubbed him over the head with one of those same rocks. It was a telling blow but not lethal.

Nelson fell hard and had to be dragged from the edge of cliff by swift hands.

"We aren't actually going all the way down the causeway are we?" Lona spoke for the first time in several minutes. She put up her knife and knelt long enough to tie the shawl that had held their weapons around the Englishman's forehead in a hasty bandage.

"Nay. Callum is waiting for us back at the beach. I saw him give a signal as he came ashore." Niall looked down at his wife as she rendered aid to the enemy who would have hanged her. It proved again that she was a compassionate soul. More compassionate than he, certainly. He would have left the boy to bleed.

"You did? But how did he know we were here?" Lona looked up and offered a weary smile.

"They've been keeping a watch. I wager Iain hied himself to LaCroix's ship in record time as soon as the crow came to fetch us. But even without him, I expect that Gavin and Callum would have seen the lanterns on our climb from the beach and assumed that the worst had happened. Shall we be going? The tide is getting worse every moment and I don't fancy testing Gavin's skill this morn."

Lona looked down at the unconscious Nelson.

"Will he be all right, do you think?"

"Aye. If he doesn't thrash about too much upon waking." Niall smiled with real pleasure as he realized that they were finally done with their drama, and it had not ended in tragedy for the MacLeans.

Iona

"Don't worry about the blood, lass. It looks horrid but scalp wounds always bleed like the devil."

She nodded in agreement and accepted Niall's offered hand. They paid no attention to the moaning from the caves behind them as they turned on the ledge and began to walk toward the beach. They had other problems of more immediate import than Iona's unhappy ghosts. The sky was weeping an oily rain that was steadily greasing the cracked path and undermining what little stability remained to the narrow cliff walk.

The time had come for them to flee Iona's crumbling ramparts or they would very shortly be joining her other, illustrious dead down in the hungry sea that waited below.

Chapter Thirteen

Their descent began. The island, ever fickle, seemed to be regretting its earlier decision to drive everyone away and therefore had decided on an old tactic of delay; mist. Mist was not unheard of in the morning hours on Iona. It was even the norm when they did not have rain in its place. But this thick fog that closed about them on the cliff trail was dense to the point of choking. The long ghostly tendrils followed the path of inhaled breath into the lungs, and stopped the normal flow of air with its soft white fingers as though trying to manacle them to the isle with the very air they breathed.

"Hurry, Niall!" He could barely hear Lona's soft gasp among the wind's moanings. If he had not had her right hand clasped in his, he would not have known from which direction the voice came. The

Iona

fog seemed to cause auditory confusion—perhaps even hallucinations.

He allowed Lona to take the lead and set the pace, trusting her not to lead them astray; for if anyone knew the isle's foibles and danger spots it was her. All the same, he kept a firm grip upon Lona's hand so that he was ready to pull her to safety should her heavy skirts trip her or the unstable path completely crumble away beneath her hurried feet.

"A little farther . . . The mist will thin below, I hope. Watch out for the path . . . It is tumbling down piece by piece."

"Aye." Niall could hear it as the stones cracked and fell away behind them. It was an added goad that spurred them on their way.

It seemed an eternity until they were again among the larger boulders which gave a solid barrier between them and the frothing sea. But they were still far from safe. The fog persisted in clinging to them, touching their noses and mouths with unpleasant salty digits, so Lona did not greatly slow their pace, even in shelter.

The ghostly babbling of the errant breeze was louder there among the stones, and Niall could actually see where the haunted breaths stirred the white fog to a turgid roil. Disturbing shapes loomed suddenly around them and disappeared again with like speed. . . . A superstitious man would soon be reduced to gibbering by the sights and voices. Niall was vindictive enough to hope that the isle's auditory tricks would be waiting for the British hounds when they finally invaded Iona that morn.

Niall knew that the sun was rising out at sea, but the dawn light was so diffused by the mist that he could not have said which way was east but for the pounding surf to the right of his shoulder. Lona was only a dark shadow floating beside him, where they trotted two abreast on the temporarily level trail.

He realized, as they passed a sharp curve decorated with a patch of rough gorse, that this was the same place where Lona had waylaid him two weeks before to demand an accounting of his and Callum's activities. He would not have guessed the location so precisely but for the one oddly shaped stone that had been cleft in twain, and bore along the length of its scar two patches of scabrous lichen in the shape of out-stretched hands. He had wondered before, with a sick, imaginative fancy, if when the unwary man or beast stepped between those leprous hands, did the fingers snap the stone shut, closing the victim into a rock tomb?

He hadn't tested his gruesome theory then by setting foot within, and rational man or no, nothing would prevail upon him to attempt such an act at the present moment—even had they time to test such wild theories, which he suspected they did not.

"How fare thee, m'love?" He forced himself to speak through the white cloud that stopped his mouth. He could almost feel its ghostly digits prying at his lips trying to get inside.

It annoyed his rational mind that such fantasies were birthed in his imagination, but they were there all the same and quite vivid in their haunting. He kept his teeth clenched against the white invasion, not wanting something so foreign and unhealthy invading his lungs whether they had been King Macbeth or Abbot MacKinnon in life or no.

"I am well, Niall Mackay . . . and thee?" Lona's jaw was also locked against the fog's intended possession.

Iona

"Also well," he said loudly, defiantly, into the churning mist.

He was answered by the isle with a vibrating shudder from the moaning stones. It shook the path beneath them like it had been smote with a hammer.

Lona stopped immediately.

"This way. Make haste!" She started up the hill toward the keep.

Niall did not waste time objecting as the path they had been following was suddenly nonexistent. He did not care to be scrambling up the wet, loose scree toward the keep that would likely fall down atop them if the island kept up its trembling, but he was not so churlish as to express doubt about their new course when no other path was available. He was glad that he had kept his silence when Lona had stopped at the keep's outside wall and pushed aside a stand of shrubbery that revealed a half-sized door of weathered planking. The incising on the worn wood suggested the work of the monk tombstone carvers.

The door opened silently. The tunnel beyond was dark and unappealing, but Lona plunged into it with the conviction of a rabbit bolting for its hole. Niall followed. In only a moment, he could smell the wind-whipped plants of the herber, and realized that he had found Cook's shortcut across the isle. He gave vent to some of his pent-up feelings by muttering an imprecation under his breath.

"Said I not so? Often?" she asked breathlessly. "But evil or not, the sneak-thief saved Callum and Gavin this night, and I am thankful."

Niall didn't argue; the cloying mist had encircled the wall and was rolling toward them at a deliberate pace.

Melanie Jackson

They did not enter the darkened keep, but merely skirted the kitchen and rejoined the familiar, fog-shrouded path that led to the beach. Niall did not ask why Lona had picked up their pace from a trot to a run. The rising crescendo of voices—that very probably were only sea birds who had come ashore and been lost in the mist—was becoming unbearable to the ears. The eldritch screaming encircled his head and assaulted him all sides in a confusing cacophony of shrill sounds.

"Is it the ghosts?" he asked aloud without thinking.

"I ken not," she answered quickly, tugging at his hand with frozen fingers. "Nor would I advise a halt to stop and ask. I mislike the trembling in these stones beneath our feet."

"Agreed . . . Wait!" Niall pulled her to a stop. They had reached the pitch where the trail forked. The left path went to the front of the shuddering keep. The other down to the sea.

"Why?" Lona demanded. She looked up once at the shifting silhouette of her home. It was a completely alien place now. A ruin totally impregnable, haunted. It seemed impossible that she and her family had ever lived within its stony chambers.

"Let me go first." Niall set her gently aside and walked two steps down the right fork. Lona was correct; the ground was trembling like all the isle's dead were hammering on their tombs with mailed fists.

She turned to stare at him as he set her aside. He could barely make out her features but guessed her unspoken question.

"If I should slip and fall from these heights, you would perish, too."

"The sand—"

Iona

"—is filled with hard rocks and dead hedge that is sharp as a Pict's spears . . . Be at ease, m'dear. I've climbed this bit often in the last few days—carrying whisky barrels more times than not. And as you've noted before, I have a nearly cloven hoof and Cook is not here to lay traps for me." Niall reluctantly let go of Lona's chilled hand. They would need both limbs free for climbing. "Stay with me, lass. Don't go straying after ghostly voices. I would be hard pressed to find you in this damned mist."

Lona laughed without amusement. Her sudden exhalation stirred the fog and cleared the mist from her face for a brief instant. Her visage was as cold and white as the fog around her. Fear and exhaustion had put clefts in a bracket about her pale mouth.

"Fear not. I shall not linger here another moment beyond what I must. I want well-away from this place of the cold and dead. I don't know how I've borne it all these years." Her voice was still slightly raised to be heard above the wind and screeching.

"You shall love the French colonies," he promised as the mist closed back over his ladylove's face and hid her again from his view. "They are warm and blessed with sun. The flowers are thick upon the ground and perfume the air. It is an excellent place to raise our children and live a long life."

Niall did not await an answer to his vow but began to climb down. The stones where he tucked his fingers were damp and had about them a greenish pallor as though they had been smeared with a slimy mold. The smell in the air was also rotten, as if the sea had disgorged dead things onto the beach or—*a horrible thought*—the shark carcasses from the flensing shed had risen and followed them down the hill in an animate parade of howling, slimy aquatic things long since deceased.

He helped Lona as much as he was able, but in the miasmatic salt fog and hampered by her skirts which whipped about like a dozen agitated cats, it was all but impossible to judge where she might have difficulties. An eternity passed while he waited for the isle to try some other malicious trick, but the shuddering stones did them no real harm.

At last the cockle-shelled beach was reached. Niall plucked Lona from her rock perch and urged her toward the noisome sea. The mist was still thick with the scent of salt but at least the horrid voices and the ghastly stench were gone from the air.

Lona would have hailed Callum, but as she drew her first clean breath Niall set a finger to her lips and shook his head.

Odd, she thought, that in a moment of stretched nerves and danger she should feel the heat of his hand that came like a flame from the open hearth, blazing bright against the cold white around them.

Could a living thing burn with such a heat—a warmth that could drive away the dark and fog with only a small touch? She had not thought so, and yet the cold receded from her frozen lips and body as the winter's night gives way to the warm dawn of spring.

A last bit of stray lightning crackled into brilliance showing them a sky boiling with green-gray clouds. Niall's was a face of total attention: a slash of cheekbones, taut lips, narrowed eyes. He reached for her quickly, pulling her into his arms.

Pressed close against him, the fires banked down within her flared. The pulse that fed it grew lush and deep with each stroke of her heart. Strength poured

Iona

into her tired limbs. Feelings, defensively frozen for the time that she had needed to commit another act of violence, stirred from their deep hibernation and reached blindly towards Niall's great heat.

Niall's mouth found her ear. He whispered softly with warming breath: "Quiet, m'love. We can't know that it is Callum waiting in the mist."

Lona shivered. His quiet words were at such odds with the heat rolling through her in wave after wave of desire and relief.

"We must wait for the sign. . . . " His lips brushed over her temple, leaving a light kiss there.

A sudden flare of light came through the fog as a large, ship's lantern was unveiled.

"The devil swallow ye sideways!" Came the sudden colorful curse. "MacKay, where in the seven pits are ye?"

Lona laughed silently into Niall's damp cape. Only Gavin cursed and blessed with such fervor.

"Here, Gavin!" Niall pulled them both toward the light. His arm was secure about her waist, feeding her struggle against exhaustion with its heat and strength.

"The other Sasannach devils are done for then?" Gavin asked, peering behind them into the deep gray as though he expected soldiers to appear. Dawn still had not penetrated the isle's thick atmosphere and it was impossible to identify any definite forms in the mist.

"Aye. The *Hoodie Craw* is in the sea—"

"May the devil weave his shroud and pin the seams together." Lona gasped at the double curse uttered daringly within the ghost's hearing, and then found herself fighting against the insane urge to giggle.

Melanie Jackson

"Guid morrow, Mistress." Gavin turned her way and tipped his head politely. He had no cap to doff but that did not mean that he had to overlook the courtesies. "May Jesus be at yer head and the Virgin at yer feet."

"Good morning, Gavin," she answered, equally polite. "And many happy returns of this newly blessed day to yourself, as well."

"The other boy is on the trail at the causeway. He'll wake later," Niall went on, not participating in the ritual blessings. "The other two Sasannach are still on Tiree—likely sleeping the sleep of Bacchus."

"And may the devil behead the Sasannach and make quick work of his—*Did ye say that he'll awake later?* Whyever, man?"

"Gavin," Lona explained before Niall could answer. "He was just a *gillie*—"

"Hang a thief when he's young and he'll not steal when he's old! The bloody Sasannachs have raised more devils than they can lay, b'God. Next time they choose tae dance in the dark it may be that they'll ken more closely what they take by the hand."

"Aye. And think on the next time!" Niall urged, as Gavin showed signs of wanting to climb the trail and finish Niall's work for him. "We need someone to tell the other Sasannachs that there is no treasure on the isle—and that Lona and I drowned in the deep sea of the causeway while making our escape from justice."

"And is the lad that daft tae believe such tales?"

"Aye and aboot ghosts as well," Lona told him, her accent equally broad.

"Never mind that now!" Gavin smiled grimly at her mimicry but interrupted the game with a harsh head-shake. "We must make haste from here.

Iona

LaCroix has seen a Sasannach ship from Mull in the waters tae the east. We lost her in this damnable mist, but if we dae not escape against this tide while the fog is holding, she'll be at our door in two shakes of the wee lamb's tail."

"Then let us be off."

"Aye . . . and may cripples and crooks . . . " The rest of his curses melted into the fog with Gavin and the lantern.

Suddenly, from at their feet there came a pitiful mewling.

"What the devil—"

Lona dropped to her knees in the gritty sand and scooped up the slightly bedraggled kitchen cat.

"Niall, it's the moggie! She's been waiting for us to come back."

The keep's resident feline, once dignified and aloof, had itself draped over Lona's shoulder and its claws tucked politely, but firmly into the folds of her cape. She would not give up her place without a fight, and Niall could tell that Lona was equally determined that they should not be parted again.

"Aye, so it is. Come, love." He didn't bother to expostulate with either of them, but reached out a hand and drew his weary love and her living fur wrapper to her feet.

"The tide's a-wastin', MacKay!" Gavin bellowed crossly. "Give us aid!"

Niall and Lona stumbled after Gavin. Their damp clothes and footwear were something of a hindrance as they dragged themselves through the soggy, shifting sand, and then into the white surf that completely surrounded Gavin's borrowed row boat.

"What the devil ails the moggie?" Gavin demanded.

Melanie Jackson

"Nothing," Lona said firmly.

Gavin snorted, but didn't argue as Lona stepped toward the boat.

The cat, who had hung complacently until they reached the churning tideline, began to stiffen and let out a questioning chuff. Lona laid a calming hand over her nape, prepared to subdue the cat if it proved necessary. Niall looked from the moggie to an incredulous Gavin.

"That is a very small craft," Niall commented without inflection. He was looking out at the bay filled with its full compliment of stone fangs and frothing eddies that testified to more stones beneath the waterline. A granite keel wouldn't be adequate protection against them if Gavin misguessed his position.

"That it is," Gavin agreed, with jaunty impudence as he helped his cat-laden mistress aboard the small craft. He was careful to avoid the cat's teeth, which were on prominent display. "And very dangerous it would be if a clumsy man was at the oars. But today is a day of great fortune—'May sin and loss be kept from us for the course o the day!'—for Gavin MacLean has laid his hands upon the wood and—" A loud crack sounded from the trail above and man-sized hunk of stone toppled onto the beach with a solid thud.

"Aye! Tell us about it later." Niall turned and shoved Gavin toward the rower's bench and clambered aboard the tiny vessel. "I've no wish to end this cold day by swinging at the end of a Sasannach rope or crushed to death by falling stones. Let us be gone from this cursed isle whilst we still may."

"Aye. May the Sasannach rot in the pauper's plot for coming tae our isle!"

Iona

But that was the last curse that Niall and Lona were permitted to hear for the next several minutes. Gavin needed his breath to do battle with the waters that had turned and were rushing back into the sound with vengeful force that rammed their tiny boat with divine fury. The unhappy feline was also vocal with her displeasure at the conditions on the far-from-calm sea.

As they neared the mouth of the small bay and the greater turbulence of the ocean, Lona looked back at the island for a final time to wish it a less-than-fond farewell.

"Niall!" She gasped and pointed.

He and Gavin turned to look. A tongue of copper red was licking at the fog shroud at the top of the island's rounded hill.

"The devil has at last escaped frae hell," Gavin whispered.

The flesh on Lona's arms began to tighten as she watched the monstrous flames tongue the wet keep. They did seem like a breath from Hell that burned high and then low with each inhalation and expulsion of ghostly breath from the keep's maw.

"How can stone burn?" she asked, shivering with renewed dread. The cat moaned sympathetically.

"With tallow and a store of peat," Niall answered calmly. "And the odd table and chair. That's not the devil's fire. I'll wager that young Nelson has woken up and worked his way to the keep—marching at double time, too, if the path was falling from under his feet."

"By Gannies!" Gavin exclaimed. "May the cat bury him with its clap! The girning whelp had set the keep afire! And after ye spared his miserable life."

"Aye," Niall agreed. "But I don't think this is maliciously intended."

"Nay? Then what?" Lona asked. "Burning a person's home is usually considered to be a less that friendly act—even in the southern lands."

"I suspect that he means the fire as a signal torch . . . but that it may be somewhat out of control."

"A signal! But did he need to destroy the entire keep?" she demanded.

"Well," Niall placated. "I expect that young Nelson is in a wee bit of a panic just now. After all, he is alone on a haunted isle with the ghosts that you assured him could drag him underground and pile stones upon him. And he can't know that the ship from Mull is nearby. He thinks he needs something that will be seen on Tiree. I imagine that it may be seen at that. Gavin, the fog is beginning to lift. I suggest that we hurry."

"Och! A ween o blethers! The curse of the goose that lost the quill that wrote the Ten Commandments upon him! They'll not see it in Tiree but that grice'll have the Sasannach ship down upon us in a trice!"

Gavin applied himself to the oars with new enthusiasm and he began to hum a lively, repetitive tune in time with his rapid strokes.

Lona recognized the song and chanted the child's riddle that went with the simple melody:

I had a wee sister—They ca'd her Peep-peep;
She waded the black waters so deep, deep, deep;
She climbed o'er the mountains so hie, hie, hie;
But the puir wee thing, she still had but one eye.

Niall managed a smile for his ladylove as she

Iona

wrestled with the growling moggie who was apparently not a music aficionado.

"There'll be plenty of stars this evening for your *wee sister* to accompany. France rarely has fog on the coast this time of year."

"France." Lona sighed and looked out at the horizon. The fog was indeed lifting and Iona was rapidly falling away. In the distance she could make out the outline of Capitaine La Croix's ship. It was a low dark bulk barely lit by sun that edged into the sky.

"Are you greatly saddened, lass?" Niall asked softly as he put a comforting arm around her. He also kept his distance from the moggie's fangs, lest she forget her manners and try to vent her frustrations on his hide.

"A wee bit," she answered, leaning gratefully into his warmth. The cat also was inclined to lean, but Niall was tolerant of the claws on his cape. He had never much cared for that particular cloak anyway. "I have just come to realize that I didn't get a chance to say good-bye to anyone—and now they'll wonder if we have indeed drowned on the causeway."

"Nay." Niall's breath feathered her temple with the lightest of kisses. "Iain will tell them differently—at least he'll tell those who matter. . . . And in time the damn Sasannach will grow tired of the isles and loosen their hold. Then you'll be able to write to your kin."

"Aye . . ."

"And once we're settled in the colonies, you can even ask Iain and Cook to come to us. They're old, I know, but tough as sheep gut—especially that evil, old woman."

Lona chuckled. "The Lord will spare you from Cook. She hates sailing. A trip to Tiree is the limit of her sea range. She'll never come to the colonies, not even to plague us with her tongue."

"Ah, well! God's will be done." Niall didn't try to hide his cheer at her words. Cook was fun to tease and occasionally brangle with, but he had no wish to see her sour face daily unless it brought his wife great joy.

"But, Iain," Lona said thoughtfully. "He's another matter all together."

"Aye—and I'd be glad to have him. My ship can always use another skilled seaman. And there is always the plantation to see to, if he's of a mind to keep farming instead of roving the sea."

"Your *ship*? Your *plantation*?"

"Aye. I mentioned the ship before, I think."

"So you did . . . and it is not mythical?"

"Nay, lass. I am hurt by your lack of faith!" But his arm did not push her away; it pulled her closer to his side. He did not look hurt; he looked smug.

"Why then are we not using your ship to escape the Sasannach?" she demanded, turning her head up to study his grinning face.

"It's too big and too well known—and only just returning to France from a visit to the colonies."

"And what was it doing in the colonies?"

"Why, it was bringing some marble and glass to my home in New Orleans! It should be done by now. A mere score of rooms and a garden or two. I know that it is not quite as grand as a haunted keep, Mistress Doubtful, but—"

"Your home in new Orleans has a score of rooms. . . . "

"Aye . . . You didn't truly imagine that I was going to drag you into the wilderness without a roof over your head, did you, lass?"

"You know very well that that is *exactly* what I

Iona

thought," she scolded, pulling his collar aside and nipping him on the neck with sharp teeth.

The moggie chuffed her approval.

"Ow! You little devil!" he exclaimed, setting a hand to his injured throat. But his eyes were shining with amusement at her indignation.

"It serves you justly for teasing me so!"

"If we weren't at sea I'd—"

"What, Niall MacKay? You promised not to thrash me," she pointed out. Now she was smug. "You said that you would never, *never*—"

"I believe that I said *probably never*—and I did promise other retaliation if you tried any female tricks," he muttered, cupping a hand beneath her chin and setting his lips against hers.

They both forgot that Gavin and the sea-sick moggie were with them. The cat moaned a complaint at their behavior, but the boatman waited politely to interrupt until they were within hailing distance of the *Belle Ange*. Then he cleared his throat in an apologetic manner calling them back to their wet surroundings with a quiet cough.

"I'm not done with you, Mistress," Niall warned softly as he turned to take hold of the rope ladder that a crewman had dropped over the side of the sloop. He plucked the groaning cat off Lona's shoulder, tucked it about his own neck and started up the side.

Lona smiled at his broad back. She was not finished with him, either.

"*Bon jour, mes amis! Mon chat*," came a deep voice as Lona scrambled nimbly up the swaying ladder. After fleeing the falling scree of Iona, the scaling of a ship was as nothing to her. "Welcome aboard. We can be off to friendlier climes now, *oui*? I find always that the English are so indigestible."

"Bon jour, mon ami," Niall answered, helping Lona over the rail and then turning to clasp the captain's outstretched hand. The cat growled affectingly and Niall obligingly released her to seek shelter on her own. "I see that you need no long explanation. We are indeed anxious to rid ourselves of our present and unexpected company."

Ever polite, Capitaine LaCroix bowed in Lona's direction—a neat feat given the pitching of the deck beneath their feet—and swept off his three-corner hat in the manner of one still at court.

Gavin also was up and over the rail, the rowboat's lines clasped in his hand. Some of the crew rushed forward to help secure the small craft.

"I am all comprehension, *Madame. M'sieur.*" The tricorn was shoved back onto the captain's head nearly to the bridge of his prominent nose. He turned back to Niall. "Perhaps Madame would care to go use my cabin—and you as well. I am of course spellbound by your courage, but this brave wickedness truly takes the breath. I am myself of much meeker temperament and prefer not to provoke the fools who believe themselves in charge of this blockade by having you adorning my prow with your so-noticeable face."

"Are they coming then?"

"With such a large bonfire to guide them?" Lestan's tone was incredulous. "But of course the inquisitive bloodsuckers shall come!"

"Succinctly put," Lona murmured with a shiver. The sea's morning breeze was brisk on the raised deck.

Niall smiled reassurance at his bride and offered her his warmer hand.

Iona

"The capitaine is a clever man and the ship is fast. This fox shall return to his earth, never fear," he assured her softly. Then aloud: "Capitaine LaCroix, we shall leave ourselves in your capable hands."

"Then all shall be well."

The captain's cabin was shadowed, but there was enough light for Lona to take stock of her surroundings. The furnishings were fine and numerous. Obviously, LaCroix was not of a Puritan faith.

"Well, that is one tragedy averted. Tell me true, love. Will you pine for your isle?" Niall threw aside his dripping cloak and sat on a bench to remove his leathers.

"Nay. The people yes, but for the isle, this is an unfond farewell." Lona snatched the wet wool from off of the bench and hung it on a likely peg. Niall smiled as she turned about and he reached for the tangled ties of her own damp cloak.

"And perhaps you are fonder of your husband than you supposed you would be?" he suggested playfully. The exhilaration of triumph still coursed in his blood. He was prepared to enjoy the warrior's recreation.

Lona surprised them both with a sudden yawn.

"Your pardon!"

Niall chuckled. "I see that you are not so haunted by our ordeal that you will be unable to rest."

"I slept but fitfully last night," Lona reminded him, a smile creeping into her eyes. "If I am exhausted, 'tis all your doing."

"And I have not had a night's peace since coming to your isle."

"Nay? Poor laddie."

"You should sympathize. 'Tis all your fault," he

complained, tugging on the sea-wet cord at her throat.

"Mine? How so?"

"I was afeared that you would refuse to become my wife. And that I would be forced to coerce you to my bed." The stubborn strings at last came loose and Niall pushed her cloak to the floor.

Lona clucked and knelt to retrieve it. Niall followed her and knelt beside her on the boards.

"I also feared that you would insist on staying with Cook here in the isles. That you would not care for adventuring in a new land."

"There are limits to my altruism." She leaned forward impulsively and brushed her lips across Niall's damp cheek. He tasted of salt. "Alack! You have been deceived in me. I am not made for the sober life. I think I shall greatly enjoy adventuring in a new land."

"So, we are off a-roving again—but this is the end of sea travel, I swear it." Niall clasped her about the waist as the boat rolled sharply and then steadied again. "We'll find adventure aplenty on dry ground in the Americas. . . . Love?"

"Hmm?"

Niall's fingers were questing at the edge on her skirts. He stroked her ankle and then her calf.

"This woolen is quite wet. Perhaps you should disrobe," he suggested. Lona glanced at the door. Roughened voices could be heard on the other side of the partition. "They'll leave us be. And we are hours from land. Don't deny me," he pleaded wistfully.

"I had not thought to," she replied, and earned a brilliant smile. Niall caught her hand and turned it upward, planting a fevered kiss into her palm.

Iona

The string at her breast was quickly loosened. Then one at her waist, and the damp skirt was pushed aside. Lona did not fuss this time about leaving wet clothes on the floor, not even when Niall's fine linen shirt joined the sodden woolen pile.

Niall's touch was as respectful as urgency would allow, and Lona permitted her own fingers to touch at will; first hair, then nape, then shoulders broad. He was smooth and warm except for a scar at his ribs, which she had somehow overlooked the night before.

"Niall?" she asked, her fingers gentle as they explored the roughened skin.

"Musket graze," he muttered, stretching out under her caresses. "Pay it no mind. I've the odd nick on my legs as well."

"You are much like a cat. So warm and graceful. Shall I scratch behind your ears and see if you begin to purr like a moggie."

Niall groaned into her hair and pulled her to her feet, holding her securely as the world rode up and then down. Lona leaned comfortably into his warmth and strength and nuzzled contentedly.

"Enough, sweet witch, or I'll forget myself. That could be dangerous on a ship in rough seas."

"Yes," she agreed as her lips explored the soft fur on his chest. "Forget yourself."

Niall moaned again and staggered to the velveted bedstead. He fell backward toppling Lona down after him.

"You may have your wicked way with me another time," he promised, rolling atop her. "At this moment, my own need is too great for such teasing."

A bite on his shoulder was all she answered, but it was goad enough. Niall returned the nips with teeth and lips, finding the will to slow himself long enough to be sure that his lady wife had pleasure of him.

He need not have worried. Where he led, Lona followed. Passion burned in the dim room, Niall pouring himself into Lona and breathing in her passion in return. Lust consumed him; love renewed him. And he knew that Lona was likewise consumed in the fire, for his soul found its mate in a place as close to heaven as mortal man can be.

"Niall, my love . . . " she murmured, rocking gently now that the ship had escaped Iona's rough seas and was heading for more southern waters. "Ye've stolen my heart."

"Aye, and I'll treasure it always. Now close your fair eyes for a moment, lass," he urged, kissing her tenderly on lids that were bruised blue with a lack of sleep. He tucked the velvet coverlet up around her and smoothed her tangled locks. "Ye've been bonnie and brave enough for ten men in the last year and more. Rest now."

"But do ye love me, Niall?" The question was barely audible above the shushing waves.

"What a daft question! Of course I love ye!"

Lona managed a smile at his chiding tone. A humorous look came into his eyes. "I'll love ye, even if ye snore like an auld sheep and steal the blankets."

"I do not snore." She did not make any promises about the bedcover.

"You relieve me, m'dear. You know, I think I shall greatly enjoy having a wife to corrupt."

"Corrupt how?" she inquired with sleepy curiosity.

"Numerous ways. I might, for instance, take snuff from your wrist or . . . " His fingers trailed over her collar bone.

Iona

"Nay. That you shall not." Niall's brow flew upward and Lona explained apologetically: "I do not care for the scent of snuff."

"Then I shall have to content myself with showering you in other riches—like red silk chemises and some blue velvet gowns."

She chuckled sleepily. "And too think that I nearly summoned the will to refuse you."

"You would have married me regardless of any such willful folly."

"You would have taken me by force, then?"

"By any means necessary, love," he said lightly, but with truth. "You are my final reward for becoming a pattern-card of virtue."

"A pattern-card?" She slitted one eye.

"Are you not glowing with approbation at my miraculous transformation?"

"I fear I am too weary to glow." But her sweet lips smiled.

From outside the cabin door, a rough voice was raised in sudden prayer.

"Our fader who be-est in Heavin, hallowed be Thy name—" The voice intoned loudly.

"This sounds like one prayer that the Almighty may be forced to hear," Niall observed, as the deep voice rolled onward with its ritualized plea.

"—And lead us not unto temptation. But free us from evil. And keep the ship's gunpowder dry and near hand. Amen!"

Niall laughed aloud. "Do you think that he would—for a suitable fee—remain outside our door and entertain us with sonnets and verse?"

"Heaven forbid it! I'm so glad I've married a romantic man but just now I prefer to sleep," she meant to say, but the words trailed off unvoiced.

311

Melanie Jackson

"Sleep then, lass," Niall urged quietly. "There'll be time aplenty for poetry later."

In the space of a breath Lona slipped into the world of dreams. It was the now familiar image of New Orleans that filled her head with the rich smells of raw earth and wildflowers that she had never seen or heard named, but that she knew were waiting for her on the shores of their new home. Warm sun kissed her cheeks, and a darkly tanned Niall walked at her side with a a dark-haired babe in his arms.

And for the first time in years, there were no ghosts to whisper warnings in her sleep. Niall, her true love, had laid them all to rest.

Sandra August
Chasing Alfie

The little girl sitting next to her on the train isn't supposed to talk to strangers, and L.V. "Alfie" Foster knows better herself. But the handsome man across the car is eager to introduce himself, and the feisty reporter feels powerfully drawn to him. Brian Reed is certainly charming, but then he starts talking about his job. He is a private eye, and he is going to Glitter Creek, Colorado, to investigate the same murders as she. Worse, even though it is 1872, the silly man still believes in ghosts! A human being killed those miners, and L.V. plans to get the scoop for *The Denver Empire*. But in this investigation she senses something deeper than just a human-interest story. With a moonlit kiss and the help of the little girl from the train, L.V. pledges to unlock the secrets of a small town—and the heart of a hero.

___4566-4 $4.99 US/$5.99 CAN

Dorchester Publishing Co., Inc.
P.O. Box 6640
Wayne, PA 19087-8640

Please add $1.75 for shipping and handling for the first book and $.50 for each book thereafter. NY, NYC, and PA residents, please add appropriate sales tax. No cash, stamps, or C.O.D.s. All orders shipped within 6 weeks via postal service book rate.
Canadian orders require $2.00 extra postage and must be paid in U.S. dollars through a U.S. banking facility.

Name_____
Address_____
City_____State_____Zip_____
I have enclosed $_____ in payment for the checked book(s).
Payment <u>must</u> accompany all orders. ❑ Please send a free catalog.
CHECK OUT OUR WEBSITE! www.dorchesterpub.com

LOVE FOREVERMORE

MADELINE BAKER

The West–it has been Loralee's dream for as long as she could remember, and Indians are the most fascinating part of the wildly beautiful frontier she imagines. But when Loralee arrives at Fort Apache as the new schoolmarm, she has some hard realities to learn...and a harsh taskmaster to teach her. Shad Zuniga is fiercely proud, aloof, a renegade Apache who wants no part of the white man's world, not even its women. Yet Loralee is driven to seek him out, compelled to join him in a forbidden union, forced to become an outcast for one slim chance at love forevermore.

___4267-3 $5.99 US/$6.99 CAN

Dorchester Publishing Co., Inc.
P.O. Box 6640
Wayne, PA 19087-8640

Please add $1.75 for shipping and handling for the first book and $.50 for each book thereafter. NY, NYC, and PA residents, please add appropriate sales tax. No cash, stamps, or C.O.D.s. All orders shipped within 6 weeks via postal service book rate. Canadian orders require $2.00 extra postage and must be paid in U.S. dollars through a U.S. banking facility.

Name_____
Address_____
City_____ State_____ Zip_____
I have enclosed $_____ in payment for the checked book(s).
Payment <u>must</u> accompany all orders. ❏ Please send a free catalog.

Fairest of Them All
Josette Browning

A true stoic and a gentleman, Daniel Canty has worked furiously to achieve the high esteem of the English nobility. Therefore, it is more his reputation than the promise of wealth that compels him to accept the ninth earl of Hawkenge's challenge to turn an orphan wild child into a lady. But the girl who's been raised by animals in the African interior is hardly an orphan—and his wildly beautiful charge is hardly a child. Truly, Talitha is a woman—and the most compelling Daniel has ever seen. But the mute firebrand also poses the greatest threat he has ever faced. In the girl's soft kiss is the jeopardy which Daniel has fought all his life to avoid: the danger of losing his heart.

___4513-3 $5.50 US/$6.50 CAN

Dorchester Publishing Co., Inc.
P.O. Box 6640
Wayne, PA 19087-8640

Please add $1.75 for shipping and handling for the first book and $.50 for each book thereafter. NY, NYC, and PA residents, please add appropriate sales tax. No cash, stamps, or C.O.D.s. All orders shipped within 6 weeks via postal service book rate. Canadian orders require $2.00 extra postage and must be paid in U.S. dollars through a U.S. banking facility.

Name_____
Address_____
City_____ State_____ Zip_____
I have enclosed $_____ in payment for the checked book(s).
Payment <u>must</u> accompany all orders. ❏ Please send a free catalog.
CHECK OUT OUR WEBSITE! www.dorchesterpub.com

Flames of Rapture
LARK EDEN

"Great reading!"—*Romantic Times*

When Lyric Solei flees the bustling city for her summer retreat in Salem, Massachusetts, it is a chance for the lovely young psychic to escape the pain so often associated with her special sight. Investigating a mysterious seaside house whose ancient secrets have long beckoned to her, Lyric stumbles upon David Langston, the house's virile new owner, whose strong arms offer her an irresistible temptation. And it is there that Lyric discovers a dusty red coat, which from the time she first lays her gifted hands on it unravels to her its tragic history—and lets her relive the timeless passion that brought it into being.

_52078-8 $4.99 US/$6.99 CAN

Dorchester Publishing Co., Inc.
P.O. Box 6640
Wayne, PA 19087-8640

Please add $1.75 for shipping and handling for the first book and $.50 for each book thereafter. NY, NYC, and PA residents, please add appropriate sales tax. No cash, stamps, or C.O.D.s. All orders shipped within 6 weeks via postal service book rate. Canadian orders require $2.00 extra postage and must be paid in U.S. dollars through a U.S. banking facility.

Name_____
Address_____
City_____ State_____ Zip_____
I have enclosed $_____ in payment for the checked book(s).
Payment <u>must</u> accompany all orders. ❏ Please send a free catalog.

By Any Other Name

Lori Handeland

From birth, Julia Colton's father taught her that the Jayhawkers of Kansas were the enemy—especially the Murphys, who took the Colton's rightful land. But when Ryan Murphy saves her from a group of Jayhawkers, she begins to question her alliances. For when he steps in like a hero from a fairy tale, Julia sees a tenderness in his blue eyes she has never seen in any man. Soon the star-crossed lovers will forsake their families and risk all they have ever known for a love stronger than bullets and deeper than blood, a love that is just as true by any other name.

___52252-7 $5.50 US/$6.50 CAN

Dorchester Publishing Co., Inc.
P.O. Box 6640
Wayne, PA 19087-8640

Please add $1.75 for shipping and handling for the first book and $.50 for each book thereafter. NY, NYC, and PA residents, please add appropriate sales tax. No cash, stamps, or C.O.D.s. All orders shipped within 6 weeks via postal service book rate. Canadian orders require $2.00 extra postage and must be paid in U.S. dollars through a U.S. banking facility.

Name_____
Address_____
City_____State_____Zip_____
I have enclosed $_____ in payment for the checked book(s).
Payment <u>must</u> accompany all orders. ❏ Please send a free catalog.

Jackie & The Giant

LindaJones

It isn't a castle, but Cloudmont is close: The enormous estate houses everything Jacqueline Beresford needs to quit her life of crime. But climbing up to the window, Jackie gets a shock. The gorgeous giant of an owner is awake—and he is a greater treasure than she ever imagined. It hardly surprises Rory Donovan that the beautiful burglar is not what she claims, but capturing the feisty felon offers an excellent opportunity. He was searching for a governess for his son, and against all logic, he feels Jackie is perfect for the role—and for many others. But he knows that she broke into his home to rob him of his wealth—for what reason did she steal his heart?

___52333-7 $5.99 US/$6.99 CAN

Dorchester Publishing Co., Inc.
P.O. Box 6640
Wayne, PA 19087-8640

Please add $1.75 for shipping and handling for the first book and $.50 for each book thereafter. NY, NYC, and PA residents, please add appropriate sales tax. No cash, stamps, or C.O.D.s. All orders shipped within 6 weeks via postal service book rate. Canadian orders require $2.00 extra postage and must be paid in U.S. dollars through a U.S. banking facility.

Name_____
Address_____
City_____State_____Zip_____
I have enclosed $_____ in payment for the checked book(s).
Payment <u>must</u> accompany all orders. ❏ Please send a free catalog.
CHECK OUT OUR WEBSITE! www.dorchesterpub.com

ENCANTADORA

GAIL LINK

"Gail Link was born to write romance!"
—Jayne Ann Krentz

"Husband needed. Must be in good health, strong. No older than forty. Fee paid." Independent and proud, Victoria reads the outlandish advertisement with horror. When she refuses to choose a husband from among the cowboys and ranchers of San Antonio, she never dreams that her father will go out and buy her a man. And what a man he is! Tall, dark, and far too handsome for Tory's peace of mind, Rhys makes it clear he is going to be much more than a hired stud. With consummate skill he woos his reluctant bride until she is as eager as he to share the enchantment of love.

_4181-2 $5.99 US/$6.99 CAN

Dorchester Publishing Co., Inc.
P.O. Box 6640
Wayne, PA 19087-8640

Please add $1.75 for shipping and handling for the first book and $.50 for each book thereafter. NY, NYC, and PA residents, please add appropriate sales tax. No cash, stamps, or C.O.D.s. All orders shipped within 6 weeks via postal service book rate. Canadian orders require $2.00 extra postage and must be paid in U.S. dollars through a U.S. banking facility.

Name_____
Address_____
City_____State_____Zip_____
I have enclosed $_____ in payment for the checked book(s).
Payment <u>must</u> accompany all orders. ❑ Please send a free catalog.

ATTENTION ROMANCE CUSTOMERS!

SPECIAL TOLL-FREE NUMBER
1-800-481-9191

*Call Monday through Friday
10 a.m. to 9 p.m.
Eastern Time
Get a free catalogue,
join the Romance Book Club,
and order books using your
Visa, MasterCard,
or Discover®*

Leisure Books

Love Spell

GO ONLINE WITH US AT DORCHESTERPUB.COM